SPACE

CATHERYNNE M. VALENTE

OPERA

SAGA PRESS

LONDON SYDNEY **NEW YORK** TORONTO NEW DELHI

AN IMPRINT OF SIMON & SCHUSTER, INC.

1230 AVENUE OF THE AMERICAS, NEW YORK, NEW YORK 10020

SAGA PRESS and colophon are trademarks of Simon & Schuster, Inc.

For information about special discounts for bulk purchases, please contact Simon & Schuster Special Sales at 1-866-506-1949 or business@simonandschuster.com.

The Simon & Schuster Speakers Bureau can bring authors to your live event. For more information or to book an event, contact the Simon & Schuster Speakers Bureau at 1-866-248-3049 or visit our website at www.simonspeakers.com.

Book design by Greg Stadnyk

The text for this book was set in Caecilia LT Std.

Manufactured in the United States of America

4 6 8 10 9 7 5 3

Library of Congress Cataloging-in-Publication Data

Names: Valente, Catherynne M., 1979– author.

Title: Space opera / Catherynne M. Valente.

Description: First edition. | London ; New York : Saga Press, [2018]

Identifiers: LCCN 2017028788 | ISBN 9781481497497 (hardcover) | ISBN 9781481497510 (eBook)

Subjects: | BISAC: FICTION / Science Fiction / Space Opera. | FICTION / Science Fiction / General. | GSAFD: Science fiction.

Classification: LCC PS3622.A4258 S63 2018 | DDC 813/.6—dc23

LC record available at https://lccn.loc.gov/2017028788

For Heath,

Intergalactic glamrock ambassador to Earth

Earth

It's the Arockalypse
Now bare your soul.
—"Hard Rock Hallelujah," Lordi

1.

Boom Bang-a-Bang

Once upon a time on a small, watery, excitable planet called Earth, in a small, watery, excitable country called Italy, a soft-spoken, rather nice-looking gentleman by the name of Enrico Fermi was born into a family so overprotective that he felt compelled to invent the atomic bomb. Somewhere in between discovering various heretofore cripplingly socially anxious particles and transuranic elements and digging through plutonium to find the treat at the bottom of the nuclear box, he found the time to consider what would come to be known as the Fermi Paradox. If you've never heard this catchy little jingle before, here's how it goes: given that there are billions of stars in the galaxy quite similar to our good old familiar standby sun, *and* that many of them are quite a bit further on in years than the big yellow lady, *and* the probability that some of these stars will have planets quite similar to our good old familiar knockabout Earth, *and* that such planets, if they *can* support life, have a high likelihood of getting around to it sooner or later, *then* someone out there should have sorted out interstellar travel by now, and *therefore*, even at the absurdly primitive crawl of early-1940s propulsion, the entire Milky Way could be colonized in only a few million years.

So where is everybody?

Many solutions have been proposed to soothe Mr. Fermi's plaintive cry of transgalactic loneliness. One of the most popular is the Rare Earth Hypothesis, which whispers kindly: *There, there, Enrico. Organic life is so complex that even the simplest algae require a vast array of extremely specific and unforgiving conditions to form up into the most basic recipe for primordial soup. It's not all down to old stars and the rocks that love them. You've gotta get yourself a magnetosphere, a moon (but not too many), some gas giants to hold down the gravitational fort, a couple of Van Allen belts, a fat helping of meteors and glaciers and plate tectonics—and that's without scraping up an atmosphere or nitrogenated soil or an ocean or three. It's highly unlikely that each and every one of the million billion events that led to life here could ever occur again anywhere else. It's all just happy coincidence, darling. Call it fate, if you're feeling romantic. Call it luck. Call it God. Enjoy the coffee in Italy, the sausage in Chicago, and the day-old ham sandwiches at Los Alamos National Laboratory, because this is as good as high-end luxury multicellular living gets.*

The Rare Earth Hypothesis means well, but it's colossally, spectacularly, *gloriously* wrong.

Life isn't difficult, it isn't picky, it isn't unique, and fate doesn't enter into the thing. Kick-starting the gas-guzzling subcompact go-cart of organic sentience is as easy as shoving it down a hill and watching the whole thing spontaneously explode. Life *wants* to happen. It can't stand *not* happening. Evolution is ready to go at a moment's notice, hopping from one foot to another like a kid waiting in line for a roller coaster, so excited to get on with the colored lights and the loud music and the upside-down parts, it practically pees itself before it even pays the ticket price. And that ticket price is low, low, low. U-Pick-Em inhabitable planets, a dollar a bag! Buy-one-get-one specials on attractive and/or menacing flora and fauna! Oxygen! Carbon! Water! Nitrogen! Cheap! Cheap! Cheap! And, of course, all the intelligent species you can eat. They spin up overnight, hit the midway of industrial civilization, and ride the Giant Dipper Ultra-Cyclone till they puke themselves to death or achieve escape velocity and sail their little painted plastic bobsleds out into the fathomless deep.

Lather, rinse, repeat.

Yes, life is the opposite of rare and precious. It's everywhere; it's wet and sticky; it has all the restraint of a toddler left too long at day care without a juice box. And life, in all its infinite and tender intergalactic variety, would have gravely disappointed poor gentle-eyed Enrico Fermi had he lived only a little longer, for it is deeply, profoundly, execrably stupid.

It wouldn't be so bad if biology and sentience and evolution were merely endearing idiots, enthusiastic tinkerers with subpar tools and an aesthetic that could be called, at best, cluttered and, at worst, a hallucinogenic biohazard-filled circus-cannon to the face. But, like the slender, balding father of the atomic age, they've all gotten far too much positive feedback over the years. They really *believe* in themselves, no matter how much evidence against piles up rotting in the corners of the universe. Life is the ultimate narcissist, and it loves nothing more than showing off. Give it the jankiest glob of fungus on the tiniest flake of dried comet-vomit wheeling drunkenly around the most underachieving star in the middle of the most depressing urban blight the cosmos has to offer, and in a few billion years, give or take, you'll have a teeming society of telekinetic mushroom people worshipping the Great Chanterelle and zipping around their local points of interest in the tastiest of lightly browned rocket ships. Dredge up a hostile, sulfurous silicate lava sink slaloming between two phlegmy suns well into their shuffleboard years, a miserable wad

of hell-spit, free-range acid clouds, and the gravitational equivalent of untreated diabetes, a stellar expletive that should never be
forced to cope with something as toxic and flammable as a civilization, and before you can say *no, stop, don't, why?* the place will
be crawling with postcapitalist glass balloons filled with sentient
gases all called Ursula.

Yes, the universe is absolutely riddled with fast-acting, pustulant, full-blown life.

So where is everybody?

Well, just at the moment when Enrico Fermi was walking to
lunch with his friends Eddie and Herbert at Los Alamos National
Laboratory, chatting about the recent rash of stolen city trash bins
and how those "aliens" the blind-drunk hayseeds over in Roswell
kept flapping their jaws about had probably gone joyriding and
swiped them like a bunch of dropouts knocking over mailboxes
with baseball bats, just then, when the desert sun was so hot and
close overhead that for once Enrico was glad he'd gone bald so
young, just then, when he looked up into the blue sky blistering
with emptiness and wondered why it should be *quite* as empty as
all that, just at that moment, and, in fact, up until fairly recently,
everybody was terribly distracted by the seemingly inevitable,
white-hot existential, intellectual, and actual obliteration of total
galactic war.

Life is beautiful and life is stupid. This is, in fact, widely regarded
as a universal rule not less inviolable than the Second Law of
Thermodynamics, the Uncertainty Principle, and No Post on
Sundays. As long as you keep that in mind, and never give more
weight to one than the other, the history of the galaxy is a simple
tune with lyrics flashed on-screen and a helpful, friendly bouncing disco ball of all-annihilating flames to help you follow along.

This book is that disco ball.
Cue the music. Cue the lights.

Here's what you have to understand about intergalactic civil wars: they're functionally identical to the knockdown, door-slamming, plate-smashing, wall-penetrating, shriek-sobbing drama of any high-strung couple you've ever met. The whole business matters a great deal to those involved and far, far less than the pressing issue of what to have for lunch to anyone outside their blast radius. No one can agree on how it started or whose fault it was, no one cares about the neighbors trying to bloody well sleep while it's banging on, and not one thing in heaven or on Earth matters half as much as getting the last word in the end. Oh, it was all innocence and discovery and heart-shaped nights on the sofa at first! But then someone didn't do the laundry for two weeks, and now it's nothing but tears and red faces and imprecations against one person or the other's slovenly upbringing and laser cannons and singularity-bombs and ultimatums and hollering, *I never want to see you again, I really mean it this time* or *You're really just like your mother* or *What do you mean you vapor-mined the Alunizar homeworld—that's a war crime, you monster*, until suddenly everyone's standing in the pile of smoking rubble that has become their lives wondering how they'll ever get their security deposit back. It's what comes of cramming too much personality into too little space.

And there is always too little space.

But in the end, all wars are more or less the same. If you dig down through the layers of caramel corn and peanuts and choking, burning death, you'll find the prize at the bottom and the prize is a question and the question is this: *Which of us are people and which of us are meat?*

Of course *we* are people, don't be ridiculous. But *thee?* We just can't be sure.

On Enrico Fermi's small, watery planet, it could be generally agreed upon, for example, that a chicken was not people, but a physicist was. Ditto for sheep, pigs, mosquitoes, brine shrimp, squirrels, seagulls, and so on and so forth on the one hand, and plumbers, housewives, musicians, congressional aides, and lighting designers on the other. This was a fairly easy call (for the physicists, anyway), as brine shrimp were not overly talkative, squirrels failed to make significant headway in the fields of technology and mathematics, and seagulls were clearly unburdened by reason, feeling, or remorse. Dolphins, gorillas, and pharmaceutical sales representatives were considered borderline cases. In the final tally, *Homo sapiens sapiens* made the cut, and no one else could get served in the higher-end sentience establishments. Except that certain members of the clade felt that a human with very curly hair or an outsize nose or too many gods or not enough or who enjoyed somewhat spicier food or was female or just happened to occupy a particularly nice bit of shady grass by a river was no different at all than a wild pig, even if she had one head and two arms and two legs and no wings and was a prize-winning mathematician who very, very rarely rolled around in mud. Therefore, it was perfectly all right to use, ignore, or even slaughter *those* sorts like any other meat.

No one weeps for meat, after all.

If that one blue idiot ball had such trouble solving the meat/people equation when presented with, say, a German and a person not from Germany, imagine the consternation of the Alunizar Empire upon discovering all those Ursulas floating about on their cut-rate lavadump, or the Inaki, a species of tiny, nearly invisible parasitic fireflies capable of developing a sophisticated group consciousness, provided enough of them were safely snuggled into the warm chartreuse flesh of a Lensari pachyderm. Imagine the profound existential annoyance of those telekinetic sea squirts who ruled half the galaxy when their deep-space pioneers encountered the Sziv, a race of massively intelligent pink algae who fast-forwarded their evolutionary rise up the pop charts with spore-based nanocomputers, whose language consisted of long, luminous screams that could last up to fourteen hours and instantly curdle any nearby dairy products. And how could anyone be expected to deal with the Hrodos with a straight face when the whole species seemed to be nothing more than a very angry sort of twilit psychic hurricane occurring on one measly gas giant a thousand light-years from a decent dry cleaner?

None of them, not to mention the Voorpret or the Meleg or the 321 or any of the rest of the nonsense that wave after wave of intrepid explorers found wedged between the couch cushions of the galaxy, could *possibly* be people. They looked nothing like people. Nothing like the Aluzinar, those soft, undulating tubes of molten Venetian glass sailing through the darkness in their elegant tuftships. Not a bit like the majestic stone citizens of the Utorak Formation or the glittering secretive microparticulate of the Yüz, and *certainly* nothing remotely resembling the furry-faced, plush-tailed, time-traveling drunkards of the Keshet Effulgence, who looked improbably similar to the creatures humans called red pandas (which were neither red nor pandas, but there's language for you), nor any of the other species of the Right Sort. These new, upstart mobs from the outlying systems were most *definitely* meat. They were fleas and muck and some kind of weird bear, in the case of the Meleg, and in the case of the Voorpret, pestilent, rotting viruses that spoke in cheerful puns through the decomposing mouths of their hosts. Even the 321, a society of

profanity-prone artificial intelligences accidentally invented by
the Ursulas, unleashed, reviled, and subsequently exiled to the
satellite graveyards of the Udu Cluster, were meat, if somewhat
harder to digest, being mainly made of tough, stringy math. Not
that the globby lumps of the Alunizar were any less repulsive to
the Sziv, nor did the hulking, plodding Utorak seem any less dan-
gerously stupid to the 321.

Honestly, the only real question contemplated by either side
was whether to eat, enslave, shun, keep them as pets, or cleanly
and quietly exterminate them all. After all, they had no real intelligence. No transcendence. No soul. Only the ability to consume,
respirate, excrete, cause ruckuses, reproduce, and inspire an
instinctual, gamete-deep revulsion in the great civilizations that
turned the galaxy around themselves like a particularly hairy
thread around a particularly wobbly spindle.

Yet this meat had ships. Yet they had planets. Yet, when you
pricked them, they rained down ultraviolet apocalyptic hellfire on
all your nice, tidy moons. Yet this meat thought that it was people
and that the great and ancient societies of the Milky Way were
nothing but a plate of ground chuck. It made no *sense*.

Thus began the Sentience Wars, which engulfed a hundred
thousand worlds in a domestic dispute over whether or not the
dog should be allowed to eat at the dinner table just because he
can do algebra and mourn his dead and write sonnets about the
quadruple sunset over a magenta sea of Sziv that would make
Shakespeare give up and go back to making gloves like his father
always wanted. It did not end until about . . . wait just a moment . . .
exactly one hundred years ago the Saturday after next.

When it was all done and said and shot and ignited and
vaporized and swept up and put away and both sincerely and
insincerely apologized for, everyone left standing knew that the

galaxy could not bear a second go at this sort of thing. Something had to be done. Something mad and real and bright. Something that would bring all the shattered worlds together as one civilization. Something significant. Something elevating. Something grand. Something beautiful and stupid. Something terribly, gloriously, brilliantly, undeniably *people*.

Now, follow the bouncing disco ball. It's time for the chorus.

2.

Rise Like a Phoenix

Once upon a time on a small, watery, excitable planet called Earth, in a small, watery country called England (which was bound and determined never to get *too* excited about anything), a leggy psychedelic ambidextrous omnisexual gendersplat glitterpunk financially punch-drunk ethnically ambitious glamrock messiah by the name of Danesh Jalo was born to a family so large and benignly neglectful that they only noticed he'd stopped coming home on weekends when his grandmother was nearly run over with all her groceries in front of the Piccadilly Square tube station, stunned into slack-jawed immobility by the sight of her Danesh, twenty feet high, in a frock the color of her customary afternoon sip of Pernod, filling up every centimeter of a gargantuan billboard. His black-lit tinsel-contoured face stared right back at her from behind the words: DECIBEL JONES AND THE ABSOLUTE ZEROS LIVE AT THE HIPPODROME: SOLD OUT! Somewhere in between popping out of his nineteenth-century literature course at Cambridge for cigarettes and never coming back and digging through the £1 bin at London's shabbier thrift shops hunting for every last rhinestone, sequin, or lurid eye shadow duo, he had found the time to invent the entire electro-funk glamgrind genre from scratch and become the biggest rock star in the world.

For about half a minute, give or take.

It's a song as old as recorded sound, and you already know how it goes: given that there are billions of people on the planet, *and* that a really quite unsettling number of them are musicians, *and* the suicide-inducing low probability of paying even one electric bill via the frugal application of three chords and a clever lyric, *and* that such musicians, if they can produce anything good, have a high likelihood of getting around to it sooner or later, *and* the breakneck speed at which a digitally entangled global population fueled by faster-than-instantaneous gratification consumes units of culture, *then* being the biggest rock star in the world is highly likely to be a short-lived gig with no snacks served at intermission, and even at the absurdly primitive crawl of Earth's collective attention span, any successful front man is guaranteed, sooner or later, to wake up on the floor of his flat with a sucking black hole of a hangover and a *geologically* terrible haircut asking: *Where is everybody?*

Many solutions to this conundrum of mid-list musical misery have been tried: a comeback solo album, a reunion tour, licensing one's former incandescent hits for mid-priced car commercials, a solid redemption arc on a reality television program, a shocking memoir, giving up on dignity and taking a run at Eurovision, a quieter but steady career in children's film sound tracks, focusing on one's family, charity work, a crippling heroin addiction, acting, a sex scandal, public alcoholism, producing, or sudden violent death.

Decibel Jones left the planet.

Life as an ethereal glamtrash satyr had never been simple. It hadn't been restful. It hadn't been recommended as part of a healthy and complete breakfast. But Decibel Jones was made for the thing. Kick-starting the whole lunar-powered pyrotechnic stained-glass orgasm of his career had been as easy as going home from a dodgy pop-up nightclub in Shoreditch with a girl who could sing like a novelty motion-activated Halloween witch and a boy with neon lavender hair.

Rock *wants* to happen. It can't stand *not* happening.

Decibel Jones was ready to go again at a moment's notice with no refractory period at all, rolling back and forth between the soon-to-be Absolute Zeros—drummer, serial keyboard assaulter, and "girlfraud" Mira Wonderful Star and instantaneously gratifying man-of-all-instruments "boyfrack" Oort St. Ultraviolet—like the future could wait forever. Of course, they never made a real go of it much beyond that first night. Oort was mostly straight and hardworking, Mira was mostly monogamous and militantly cynical, and Decibel was mostly none of those things, except when he thought they'd look good with a paisley coat. But they agreed to keep up the pretenses of an android-alien-demigod orgiastic musical-erotic triad for the studio label.

By the time their double-platinum album *Spacecrumpet* came out, they were living the electric sheep dream. You could tune any radio to any station and hear Decibel and Mira shouting out their hit "Raggedy Dandy" while Oort thundered through the verses on guitar, accordion, cello, electric hurdy-gurdy, theremin, and Moog—all of which, plus the tuba, he eventually combined into the iconic Oortophone. The ticket prices were high, high, high. U-Pick-Em neon-lit hotel rooms, a dollar a bag! Buy-one-get-one specials on attractive and/or menacing opening acts! Booze! Drugs! Costumes! Stagecraft! Quiz shows! Christmas album! Hot! Hot! Hot! And, of course, all the groupies you can eat. They spun up overnight, hit the charts, and rode the Laser-Comet Demolition Derby Glamasaurus Rex till the gas ran dry and the flames went dark and the colored lights guttered out like old birthday candles.

Lather, rinse, but probably never to repeat.

Yes, music is the food of love, but the industry chews up the rare and precious and horks it up off the side of the balcony to make room for more. It's a predictable story. It's cold and depressing. It has all the cheeky imagination of a man standing alone at a bus stop watching the rain soak through a paper bag in the road, but it is, unfortunately, the story of Decibel Jones up until a certain Thursday in April, and its explicitly foreshadowed and rather obvious end would have gravely disappointed his poor grandmother and her bags of lemons and butter and seitan dropped all over Piccadilly Square if only she paid a bit more attention to the music industry.

Yet, for a while, Decibel Jones and the Absolute Zeros loved nothing more than showing off. Give them the soggiest cast-off thigh-high stocking's worth of a tune and the most obnoxiously Campari-drunk open-mic-night-reject half-sucked raspberry lolly of a lyric, and in one night, Dess and Mira and Oort would turn around a glamgrind anthem perfectly crystallizing the despair of the young enslaved by the London real estate market crossbred with the desperate futuro-cosmic hope of murdering a Martian catwalk in a satin slip while guzzling a rubbish bin full of cheap ruby port, as sung by the comet-pummeled ghost of Oscar Wilde snorting stars like meth. Give them a hostile, empty stage with a lighting rig left over from a lesser-known BBC period drama, a putrefying zombie of a soundboard, and a room with more cigarette butts than people, and before you could say *no, stop, don't, why?* the place would be a new planet crawling with gorgeous post-postmodern broke-down fashion-wraiths filled with the unfaceable existential horror of all unpaid interns, the pent-up sexuality of unwalloped piñatas, and cheap, quasi-infinite lager.

It wouldn't have been so bad if Decibel and Mira and Oort were merely the endearing dandies they pretended to be, enthusiastic tinkerers with tradesman skills to fall back on and a near-matrimonial commitment to an aesthetic that could, at best, be called, and was, by the *Guardian*, "a continuously detonating carnival-cum-Bollywood-dream-sequence in which you may, at any moment, be knocked sideways by a piece of dismembered French clown or tenderly made love to by a prize Neptunian show-horse behind the lyrical equivalent of the fairy floss cart" and, at worst, by NME, "an incomprehensible and humiliating radioactive bukkake show of genres, styles, and vocals akin to a peacock vomiting forever into the howling void without one single note of merit, true innovation, or even a nodding acquaintance with the concept of depth in art—but you can dance to it. If you hate yourself."

It wouldn't have been so bad if *Spacecrumpet* had been just *slightly* less of a rocket ship to everywhere they'd ever wanted to go. If Mira hadn't made a reverberating hypersonic beeline straight for heroin junction and total dysfunction. If Decibel hadn't tried to act. If Oort had known a little more about studio accounting. If their tireless manager, good old brilliant bloody Lila Poole, hadn't been quite so good at fulfilling their every need in every city at every hour, tucking their chemical diversions of choice into their suitcases like a mum packing her babies' school lunches without saying a word about where she'd gotten the dodgy ham for Mira's sandwich. If their follow-up to *Spacecrumpet*, that cautionary tale dressed as a concept album titled *The Vibro-Tragical Adventures of Ultraponce*, hadn't been called "muddled" (the *Guardian* again), "punishable by law" (*Spin*), "unfit to be used as potpourri in Bowie's least-frequented sock drawer" (*Mojo*), and "so seemingly perplexed by the fact of its existence as to recoil in mincing horror from its own reflection in a hallway mirror and repeatedly punch itself in the face while calling itself a series of unprintable nineteenth-century slurs" (the *New Yorker*). If Oort hadn't gotten that nice hotel manager pregnant. If the world hadn't gotten so grim and serious that it didn't want to hear any more from a gang of dandies rolled in glitter and ganache.

If, one awful night in Edinburgh after a half-empty festival show, Mira Wonderful Star hadn't suggested they get married for tax purposes, and Decibel Jones hadn't laughed.

If Mira's uncle hadn't spent her whole childhood taking her on long country drives when she was upset at the usual plot twists of the full surround-sound teenage theatrical experience, driving and driving through soft hills and stone walls and dumb-faced sheep that probably never got rejected or failed a test or got sent home for uniform violations just because none of the recognized Catholic saints ever had pink hair, driving until heated seats and potholes passing by underneath her like drumbeats had gotten her so calm and comfortable that she forgot what awful thing had happened in the first place, so that in the face of any subsequent trauma, Mira bolted for the nearest car and unlit road.

If Lila Poole hadn't left the keys to her rented van on top of the cut-rate minibar.

If a certain suburban badger hadn't had a vicious tussle with his cubs and wandered out onto the highway to Stirling complaining to himself about the slovenly habits and terrible taste of young badgers today who had no respect for the rights and privileges of their elders.

If Mira hadn't had so much respect for the rights and privileges of all living creatures that she swerved hard rather than add to the tally of furry roadside suffering in the United Kingdom, and smashed windshield-first into a completely horrified Scottish moor.

If a reporter hadn't asked when they were going to get a new drummer less than a month afterward. If Decibel hadn't broken the guy's nose and cheekbone. If that reporter hadn't been employed by a rag with enough bored lawyers on retainer to choke a humpback whale.

But, like the slender, silver bombs of the postatomic age, Decibel Jones and the Absolute Zeros blew up far too hot and wide and fast. All those "ifs" became "whens," one by one by one, and there was no detour *around* them that joined up again to a reasonable facsimile of happiness but *through*. Neither Decibel nor Oort nor poor dead Mira ever imagined the power of the ordinary to gum up the works of the epic. They never bothered checking the studio's numbers. They always agreed that tomorrow was the day they'd stop acting like kids at a beach arcade where you never ran out of coins and get organized, drink responsibly, start doing this thing right and rocking like adults. They thought that the only battle was making it, and after that, nothing would ever really be hard again. They never calculated the unforgiving algebra of three as opposed to the simple arithmetic of two or one. They never counted on the depravity of young highland badgers and the depth of their hostility toward their long-suffering fathers.

Worst of all, they really believed that the magic they made together could keep them safe from the predatory world, no matter how much evidence against piled up dustily in the corners of secondhand vinyl shops. But through every if and when, Decibel Jones remained a cosmic constant. He could hardly help it. He could no more put on a gray flannel suit and hide from the utter core of his being than he could go back in time and take Mira seriously, take her in his arms, and take her home.

Life is beautiful. And life is stupid.

Yes, Decibel Jones was absolutely riddled with unrepentant, self-igniting, full-blown, arena-filling *glam*. Even as the friendly, bouncing disco ball of this story finds him, fifteen years and three failed solo albums down the track, snoring through a recurring dream of stained-glass sex scorpions, infinitely filled arenas, and rental vans made entirely out of marshmallows, down pillows, and the stuff of airline black boxes on the tea-and-biohazard-stained floor of an unfurnished, utilities-not-included, shared-bathroom garret in Croydon, glam poured out of him in rivers of glitter-jammed tears, over-rouged sweat, and drool that could get up and play an F chord all by itself.

So where was everybody?

Well, just then, just at the moment when Decibel Jones was waking after a long night of pretending he was still twenty years old again, chatting with middle-aged respectables who used to love him when they were in school, discussing the recent rash of sullen young pop stars and how those "aliens" the blind-drunk farmers over in Cornwall kept flapping their jaws about had probably only come to England looking for a better life that didn't include regular aerial bombardment by foreign powers, just then, when the morning sun was so obnoxiously bright and ignorant of the whole concept of personal space that for once Decibel was glad that these days he could only afford a flat with one window that faced the side of a greeting card company's head offices, just then, when he opened his eyes onto a midlife blistering with emptiness and wondered why it should be *quite* as empty as all that, just at that moment, and, in fact, up until the events of that afternoon, everybody was terribly distracted by the seemingly unending, white-hot, existential, logistical, mostly mundane troubles of their own day-to-day lives.

Shall we stop? Is the lesson clear?

The story of the galaxy is the story of a single person in it. A cover version, overproduced, remastered, with the volume cranked up way past eleven and into the infinite.

Or at least it's the story of Decibel Jones and the Sudden and Conspicuous Conquest of Earth by Space Flamingos.

3.

Take Me to Your Heaven

Decibel Jones was lying passed out on the floor of his flat in a vintage bronze-black McQueen bodysuit surrounded by kebab wrappers, four hundred copies of his last solo album, *Auto-Erotic Transubstantiation*, bought back from the studio for pennies on the pound, and half-empty bottles of rosé when the aliens invaded.

Somehow, he always thought it would be different—and Decibel had thought about it rather a lot. His family had lived above a video rental shop in Blackpool during those delicate prepubescent years when any idle passing moonbeam, pigeon, or discarded air hockey puck can swell and shine with meaning on its way toward becoming a lifelong fetish. For his part, little Danesh inhaled a heady, unleavened diet of science fiction films, despite his grandmother's insistence that they were neither halal nor anywhere near as good as *Mr. Looney of the Tunes*, as she called her favorite American program. He had spent many afternoons, surrounded by siblings slaloming through the furniture, trying to convince his *nani*, the very one who would drop her lemons in Piccadilly Square years later, that *Alien* was far, far better than Elmer Fudd and Bugs Bunny, far more serious and meaningful than a goofy, dumb cartoon, only to be hushed by a wave of her hand and a brief lecture on her personal philosophy of pop culture criticism.

"*Jee haan*, but they are the same! One hunts, one runs; one chews the carrot, one chews the Sir John Hurt. One makes eggs that go BANG! One makes Acme traps that go BANG! See? Sameful. Only *Mr. Looney of the Tunes* is more actual, on account of how aliens live in your big Danesh-head and bunny rabbits live in Coventry. Also, mine is bright and happy and makes a colorful noise, so I put it on top of yours that is droopy and leaky and makes a noise like the dishwasher. Double also, if aliens *were* real like bunny rabbits and talkbacking grandsons, they would never be so ugly, because God would not allow such a one to get to the stars when beautiful people are being stuck on Blackpool. I am right, I win, point to Nani."

Danesh had never won an argument with his grandmother. Somehow, Nani-logic acted on Dani-logic like base on acid, leaving him to ponder the nature of xenomorphs and lagomorphs without his usual astringent sizzle.

And then there had been that first, perfect night with Mira and Oort, well past any witch's hour, when the bells in Greenwich struck Truth O'Clock. She'd leaned over his chest to light her cigarette on a votive candle of St. Jude and said:

"It's perfectly absurd to think we're alone in the universe. But if they ever do come, Danesh—it is Danesh, isn't it? Well, Danny Boy, if they ever *do* come, it won't be anything like *The Thing* or *Predator* or any of that *Doctor X-Files* rot. They'll be better than the best of us. They'll have art and poetry and music." Then she'd remembered she was supposed to be a punk, and her voice changed. "The Thing don't curl up in a rainstorm and listen to the *White Album* of Thing-World because Thing-World don't do nuffink but Thing about, all twenty-four/seven slaughterparties and exploding blood and shit like that." She'd blown out her smoke and put the end between Oort's lovely lips, still smeared with violet lipstick, and Decibel had nodded along amiably like he always did, taking whatever Mira and Oort thought up and giving it a boost into the ionosphere:

"Think about it, mate: How could a species like that develop the massive technology you need to achieve faster-than-light interstellar travel, yeah? All they do is hunt and eat. They're just stupid murderlumps or killbots supreme with a side of zombie-mayonnaise. Where's the nerdy shy Predator scientist who figured out how to build a spaceship while all the big jock Predators were down the pub ripping one another's spines out, eh? Nowhere, because she don't exist. You don't see great white sharks fiddling with nuclear fusion or whatever. Scorpions don't go to the moon. We got nothing to worry about down here."

And Mira Wonderful Star had nuzzled down cozily between them like a big lanky cat, content for probably the last time in her life, and sighed out: "When the aliens come, there'll be one queue to fight them and one queue to fuck them, and the second one'll be longer by light-years."

Dess had stroked her long hair, mesmerizingly dyed all the colors of an oil slick. He was still working at Mr. Five Star in those days, a howling void-in-the-wall chip shop that seemed determined to deep-fry his soul and serve it with tomato sauce. Her petroleum-hair smelled like smoke and the artificial strawberry scent of cheap shampoo. His fingers smelled like potatoes and oil. Like Blackpool and the boardwalk and his greasepaper past becoming a greasepaper future at the horrifyingly breakneck speed of one second per second. He hated it. No matter who he wanted to be, that smell under his fingernails told the world the truth.

"Maybe," he'd murmured as the sky turned ultramarine outside a narrow window Dess would've cleaned if that wouldn't mean admitting he actually lived here. "Maybe it'll be like that part in the old cartoon where the coyote's been hunting and chasing and starving and working his machines so hard that he doesn't even notice when he's already run off the road, over the cliff, and out into the open air. When he just looks at the camera with helpless doggy fear on his crooked old face before gravity kicks in and he loses everything, which, really, if he was paying any kind of attention, he must've known he would all along."

"All right, Eeyore," Oort had said, grabbing one of Decibel's shirts off the floor instead of his own. "There's only one thing for dismal donkeys, and that's ice cream for breakfast."

"Come on, up you get," Mira had said, laughing, groping for her bra under his crappy bed. "Let's get that tail nailed back on, Mr. Thing of Thing-World."

She hadn't *known* the effect her phraseology would have on him, she'd just said the perfect words without trying. She was just perfect, without trying.

They'd only been able to find gelato at that hour, but one pistachio, one coconut, and one mango madness turned them from hungover kids into a cozy nation with a population of three, their Magna Carta signed in sugar and dairy under the improbably auspicious half-burned-out electric sign of Mackimmie's Remarkable Gelato, which, due to Mrs. Mackimmie's reluctance to throw out anything that still worked by the vaguest of definitions, read only: ACME ARKABLE GELATO.

A decade and a half later, ten pounds (pounds that he rather needed, really) lighter, with "Moon Scorpion Mega Disco" having had its day on the *Spacecrumpet* B-side and the encore of "Alien Sexqueue" improbably blowing out the sound system in the Royal Albert Hall that Christmas Eve, Decibel Jones still thought any happily annihilated itself rather than let the big blue bird in their lounge rooms come to the slightest harm.

"Please do not be distressed," continued the creature in a somewhat less resonant voice. "I can readily speak in whatever manner results in the most manageable level of ontological crisis for you. Some crisis is to be expected, given the circumstances. I chose a dialect you associate with warmth and safety, but I have obviously overshot my mark. I will fish inside the wetlands of your memory for another." The anglerfish-flamingo's deep, lovely eyes filmed over with a reptilian translucent eyelid. It seemed very troubled by the quality of the fish in Decibel's swampy head. Finally, the eyelid retracted. The alien opened its dark beak and bonged out five loud, psyche-rattling, but tremendously familiar musical notes into the sad, empty flat.

"What the blithering *hell* did you do to yourself last night, Dess?" mumbled the former greatest rock star in the world as he came out of his awestruck daze to find his forehead stuck prayerfully to the filthy floor. If he'd have known company was coming round, he would've tidied up.

The alien trumpeted out the same five notes again. It seemed to be enjoying itself.

"Got to call Dr. Collins," Decibel coughed out. "Got to tell her there's a blue flamingo in my flat quoting my nan and *Close Encounters of the Third Kind*. She'll have a pill for that. Always does, old girl. She's a good egg. She's no Lila, but her egg, it is *emphatically* good."

The alien's endless eyes filmed over again. The light dangling over its thick, curved beak dimmed and brightened fitfully. Finally, it began to sing, skipping back and forth between voices, voices Dess knew like his own, voices speckled with static from the pocket radio he'd saved up for when he was eight:

interstellar contact would look just like his beloved flickies. The business would proceed, given the bent of governments everywhere, more or less instantaneously from first contact to all-out war, Do Not Pass Diplomacy, all stern gray manly ships and even manlier military mustering and one-piece identical futuro-communist uniforms and ray guns that meant business and stoic, long-faced generals facing off against stoic worm-farm-faced extraterrestrials like it was bloody laser-light-show Waterloo, and all of it just waiting for one sexy, sexy human hero to sort it all out for them.

But when it finally did happen, the alien invasion turned out to be much more like Mr. Looney of the Tunes than Mr. Ridley of the Scott.

Point to Nani.

They landed, if it could be called a landing, in everyone's lounge rooms at once at two in the afternoon on a Thursday in late April. One minute the entire planet was planet-ing along, making the best of things, frying eggs or watching *Countdown* or playing repetitive endorphin-slurping games or whatnot on various devices, and the next there was a seven-foot-tall ultramarine half-flamingo, half-anglerfish *thing* standing awkwardly on the good rug. Crystal-crusted bones showed through its feathery chest, and a wet, gelatinous jade flower wobbled on its head like an old woman headed off to church. It stared at every person in the world, intimately and individually, out of big, dark, fringed eyes sparkling with points of pale light, eyes as full of unnameable yearning and vulnerability as any Disney princess's. Those not in possession of lounge rooms encountered the newcomer in whatever places were most familiar and intimate to them. Any-one at work had quite a surprise waiting in the break room. Some, absorbed in accounts payable or receivable, absentmindedly hung their suit jackets up on its towering hat rack of a head; its long greenish-ivory neck flushed pink with embarrassment. A slender, glassy proboscis arced up from the center of its avian skull until the weight of the round luminous lamp at its tip bent the whole thing down quail-style between those trusting eyes, where it flick-ered nervously, its fragile-looking legs poised like a ballet dancer about to give the *Giselle* of her life. But every *Homo sapiens sapiens* in the biosphere, at that moment, came face-to-face with the feathered beyond.

Decibel Jones groaned.

He tried to open his eyes. Unfortunately, he hadn't washed his face before collapsing into a bitter heap of despair, and the maquil-lage from last night's gig at some top-shelf forty-something's birthday to-do had solidified between his eyelashes into a cement composed entirely of shame and fuchsia glitter. Nothing for it. Eyes will do what eyes will do. Back to bed, that was the thing. Or back to floor. Floor had always been a good friend. Yet Dess had that primitive mammalian sense that he was being *watched*, some-how, and not in the way he liked to be. Not by adoring crowds of thousands, but by one singularly focused creature in the shadows beyond the watering hole, a creature not like himself, a creature much faster, stronger, and hungrier than he had ever been in all his days of running down nothing more wily than a Korean-fusion food truck. He clawed the smears of last night's sparkles from his eyelashes and sat up, upsetting several bottles of cream sherry and rosé and one of those shiny metallic pet rocks with brand reboots and limited edition colors that were all the moronic rage at the moment. His looked something like a guava from the future.

Oort always said he drank like a pensioner.

"The later the worm the farther from the bird," sai[d] seven-foot-tall alien lantern-fish-flamingo softly. Its voi[ce] toed around the attic room. "According to me, you will spen[d] whole Danesh-life sleeping not peeping. You see, while you[were] in Snoozepool, I was making a rhyme about your nature be[cause] you are lazyful and I am not. Most Efficient Nani makes pr[opos_]als and tea both at the same time and wins gold for Englan[d]."

Decibel Jones began to cry.

It wasn't that his head felt like someone had smashe[d it] with a cricket bat wrapped in raw rancid bacon, though it [ ] wasn't that the alien was speaking in his grandmother's [voice,] though it was, a gesture Dess would later decide showe[d] effort. It had nothing to do with the words. Everyone cried [when] the creature first spoke to them. No, not cried. They *wept[.* They] wept like the cavemen of Lascaux suddenly transported in[to the] Sistine Chapel just in time for a live performance of *Pha[ntom of] the Opera* as sung by Tolkien's elves. Their senses simply we[re] built for this, weren't meant to come anywhere near thi[s kind] of velvet-barreled sensory shotgun, loaded for bear. Hu[mans] wept in baffled, unspeakable, religious *awe*. They fell o[n their] faces; they forgot to breathe. The sound of the alien's vo[ice hit] their ears like every ecstatic moment, every compass[ionate] instinct, and every profound sorrow all wrapped up in a [song] about protecting the beautiful and innocent and fragile [in a] darkness full of teeth. To each of seven billion humans, [it was] as though they were hearing, not an alien greet their s[pecies] for the first time, but their favorite children and their aili[ng par-]ents singing a duet about how much and how desperate[ly they] needed them.

In that first moment of the new age, humanity woul[d]

"Dearly beloved, we are gathered here today to travel the world and the seven seas everyone's looking for London calling from outer space I just walked in to find you here with that sad look upon your face now all the young dudes carry the news red gold and green gunpowder and gelatin dynamite with a laser beam two thousand zero zero party over, oops, out of time you can watch the humans trying to run to all tomorrow's parties but there is nothing more than this starman waiting in the sky he'd love to come and meet us but tonight Mr. Kite is topping the biiiiilllll . . ." The interstellar flamingo trailed off, lifting its long beak like a wolf howling. Then it added quietly: "And the colored birds go doo doo doo doo doo doo doo doo doo . . ." It paused. "Is this timbre and syntactical style acceptable, Mr. Jones? Do you feel secure and at ease and fully able to process what is happening to you? The remaining representations of extraspecies contact in your psyche are . . . much more aggressive, but I can try if that is what you need to relax. However, I should warn you that I do not feel comfortable with them, as I do not personally identify as a predator. I eat plankton."

"If you could turn down the fortissimo just a tick, that would be grand." Decibel tried to get up and abandoned that idea right away. "Hand me that water, will you? There's a love. There's a good figment of my imagination. Here, Figgy, Figgy, Figgy."

The ultramarine being's gaze flicked over toward a plastic bottle with an inch or two of water still going stale in it. It shifted its weight awkwardly on those long, long reedy legs, legs that looked totally incapable of supporting its weight, and cleared its long throat. The Jell-O flower fascinator on the side of its head drooped. The bioluminescent lantern hanging down from its proboscis flickered with watery light. The light seemed to *swell* at the tip of the bulb, like a raindrop about to fall. The glow swirled, pregnant, a thousand and one shades of blue. The creature shifted its

weight from one impossibly slender blown-glass leg to the other.
Its clawed foot left something in the thin, cheap carpet, something alive, a fuzz of silver spores, spreading out from its footprint
in an unsettling imitation of henna patterns. A flurry of loose
fibers stuck to the dark talons like dandelion seeds.

And Danesh could smell it.

He could hear it breathing and feel an incredible heat pouring
off of it, and he could *smell* it. A sopping, salt-green-sweet smell,
like sugar and seaweed baking in an oven.

"Come on, up you get, time to get your tail nailed on," that
Thing of Thing-World said in the raspy-soft cigarettes-and-
cynicism alto of Mira Wonderful Star.

"Mushy, mushy, Wonderful," Jones said automatically, before
he could stop himself. Greeting Mira like he always had, because
he'd been so delighted with the way she answered the phone, as
delighted as if she had invented it herself and no one else in the
world had ever said *moshi moshi* instead of "hello" before.

"Mushy, mushy, Dess."

Mira's lovely platinum-plated voice hung in garlands around
his flat like they were still kids with toy ambitions and nothing
bad had happened to any of them yet, and that, finally, was more
than Jones could take.

"What the *fuck*?" he screamed, scrambling away from the
impossibility of what was happening to him until his back came
up against the wall with a hard thud. "What is going *on*?"

The outer space abomination gave up and snapped irrita-
bly: "I'm afraid we really must be moving along. The situation has
already been successfully explained to 64.1 percent of your population, whereas you and I are making very little progress. I am not
angry, only disappointed. All our precontact simulations catego-
rized you as a Down-to-Clown Unflappable Guy Who Can Handle

This Sort of Thing No Problem with a high probability of Being Actually into It All the Way."

Dess rubbed his eyes and popped his knuckles against his temple while the big blue bird did its trick with the eye-film again. "Listen, I'm just . . . I'm just having a bit of a rough go of it today, what with the preponderance of gin that happened to me last night and being a useless lump and serving no further purpose to anyone anywhere and being visited by the Flamingo of Christmas Future *way* before the bell strikes normalcy. *I need a minute.* I'll be into anything you want after breakfast and a coffee and serious medication, okay?"

The beautiful beast took a deep breath of Croydon air. When it spoke again, it sounded exactly like a waitress Decibel had met a thousand years ago, on the star-spangled leg of the Glampire Planet Tour. His first contact with an American in her native habitat. Cleveland, midnight, the Blue Lite Diner. The alleged food should've been reported to The Hague, but the waitress had been pretty in a dairy country sort of way: red hair, pink lip gloss, a lot going on up top. RUBY, her name tag had read, and Ruby'd been the most aggressively, positively *militantly* friendly person he'd ever met. She'd touched their shoulders affectionately while she took their order, called Dess "honey," "sweetheart," and worse, and most horrid of all, she seemed to genuinely care how he was getting along with his jet lag. Afterward, he'd felt as though he'd been run over by a semitruck full of high-fructose corn syrup, giggles, and goodwill toward one's fellow man. It had all been deeply off-putting. And though they toured there for three months straight, his first impression of the colonies was never proven wrong: Americans all acted like they were trying to pretend they hadn't just chased a fistful of ecstasy with a noseful of coke to save themselves from a police officer only they could see.

And now the big blue bird was trying Ruby's voice on like a dress six sizes too small.

"Hello there, cutie! My name is Altonaut Who Runs Faster Than Wisdom Along the Milk Road, fourteenth Lyric of the Aaba Verse, and I'll be your galactic liaison this afternoon! Can I tell you about our specials? As our appetizer tonight, we've got a totally *scrumptious* annihilation of everything you ever thought was true served on a bed of mashed anthropocentrism! My species' name is so rich and thick and ooey-gooey, you couldn't possibly get your adorable little noisehole around it, so just call us the Esca and we'll get along just fine! Fresh off the griddle and drenched in a delicate diplomatic glaze, the Esca have shipped in all the way from Bataqliq, a yummy little world of semiaquatic goodness served alongside a medium-rare red giant star in the constellation you call Cetus. Now, sweetie, I know trying new things is scary, but you just gotta give us a try! And for dessert, we've prepared a positively decadent transgalactic civilization while you were spending happy hour chowing down on a deep-fried sampler platter of total and complete ignorance. Well, sorry, darling, but happy hour is over and the drinks are all full-menu price. Luckily, you've got a tall glass of me to put a little courage in ya. And, as I come with a free slice of information vital to the survival of your species, you pretty much can't afford not to clean your plate." The leggy blue monster lifted its beak and trumpeted cheerfully. "Congratulations! You are the sentient galaxy's ten thousandth customer!"

"Road Runner," mumbled the ultimate glamgrind messiah of the late 2010s, still not entirely amenable to having this conversation that would not stop having him.

"I'm sorry, but I need more grammatical context to understand your statement," the creature's voice said, abruptly abandoning its waitress's uniform. It blossomed all over again into cosmic grief at the ultimate impossibility of communication between two living beings.

"Your name, what you just said." Dess spoke more clearly this time, forcing back the vomit that wanted so badly to add itself to the other stains on his floor. "Altonaut Who Runs Faster Than . . . Faster Than . . . urk."

"Faster Than Wisdom Along the Milk Road, yes indeedy, quick 'n' speedy!" Ruby the American Waitress and Emissary of the Great Galactic Empires was back. "It's a family name, honeybuns. Don't make fun, now. It's not nice."

"You're the Road Runner. Meep, meep." He began to laugh harder than he'd wept. "Point to Nani," he choked out between bouts of laughter. Finally, he opened his eyes wide and spread his fingers into a jazzy shimmy. If only he had an amusing sign to hold up as gravity kicked in and he fell off the cliff that hadn't been under his feet for quite some time now.

YIKES.

HELP.

GOING DOWN.

"Meep, meep, Nani! Meep, meep, *boom*."

Then, with great conviction, Decibel Jones threw up.

4.

Sing Little Birdie

Interestingly, a remarkably high percentage of the *Homo sapiens* population opted for a fondly remembered waitress or bartender when that tall drink of otherworldly water offered them their choice from a nostalgic buffet of comforting, familiar voices. Perhaps this is because humans are accustomed to receiving information from girls with notepads and name tags without getting their pride bruised by a girl with a notepad and a name tag knowing more than them about anything at all. Perhaps because, no matter their luck in life, they knew in their bones that at least they were better than the kid who brought them their steak medium, not medium-rare, and so could cling to the idea that humans were still the ones being served with a smile, the ones who were always right, the ones with a place at the table, not a place at the dishwasher, for a few precious minutes longer. Perhaps it was just because, when the paradigm shifts directly into a brick wall, all anybody really wants is a stiff drink.

Even more interestingly, almost everyone else chose the voice of their favorite children's television show host to spell it all out for them.

Those with access to neither restaurants nor quality children's television had to content themselves with hearing the news from an enormous mutant bird-fish that sounded uncannily like their parents.

Thus, with minor alterations accounting for personality, nationality, sheer gibbering terror, and surprisingly frequent attempts to pick up the Esca representative like it really was a poor bartender just trying to do her job and get through the night, roughly the same conversation took place over the next ninety minutes or so in every lounge room on the planet.

This is that conversation.

"You're an alien," said a stay-at-home mum in Inverness.

You betcha!

"From another planet, is that the general idea?" asked the Queen of Denmark, Margaret II.

Got it in one! What a clever little Mags you are! Who gets a gold star? HER MAJESTY DOES!

"Is it a good planet? Do you like it there? Does it have peppermints and toys that light up?" asked an eight-year-old boy in Ghana.

I'm so glad you asked! Bataqliq is a real tasty cup of soup: small, hot, watery, thickened with valuable exotic muds and tender chunks of nutrient-dense holoplankton! As homeworlds go, the old BQ is just enough to whet your appetite and leave you wanting more out of the universe. But it's home, and home is where you hang your haplogroup! You know, I betcha you'd just love the larva of the porla urchin—tastes a lot like peppermint! Well, peppermint that's been locked up in a tower to go mad for years and years. And yes, honey, all my toys light up.

"What's that 'fourteenth Lyric of the Aaba Verse' thing all

about? What's a verse?" asked the arthritic owner of a fish thali cart in Goa.

Now, kids, new words don't scare us, do they? Of course not! Learning is FUN! "Verse" is just about the closest word I can find in your language for what we call ourselves. Today's lesson is all about the supercool stratified sociology of the Esca! A breeding pair and their offspring are a Verse, the kidlets are Lyrics, the ruling classes are the Chorus, the proletariat are the Key, and the mercantiles are the Bridge. All Esca together, on any planet, we call the Choir. Can you remember all that? I knew you could! But enough about li'l old me! What's the collective noun for you folks at home? We are very interested in your culture, if you have one to share with the class.

"How do you know how to speak Portuguese?" asked a Brazilian petrol station owner who dreamed of writing mystery novels. "You read my mind? Always figured aliens would read minds. Dirty trick if you ask me."

Oh, no, no, no, we're not that kind of joint, darling. The Esca aren't telepathic—we leave that to the finer establishments! But, and the good Lord knows I don't mean to brag, we are what you might call mnemopathic. I can't tuck a napkin under my chin and go to town on your thoughts in real time, but I can have a wee nibble on a sampler platter of your strongest memories. Think of it like a big, steaming bowl of stew. No, you can't taste every little onion or bay leaf that went into it. But you can sure as hellfire get a mouthful of meat. So, this, that, and the butter in the roux: you remember speaking Portuguese, so I remember it too.

"Why did I cry when you first spoke? I never cry. Why do I feel like I want to take care of you and protect you when we've only just met and you're a bird-fish-man?" asked an old man who had swept the chantry in Notre Dame Cathedral every day for forty years.

Oh, you poor thing! What a clumsy cow I am. We'll get you cleaned right up. The thing of it is, evolution is such a cutthroat industry! Even a hole-in-the-wall like primeval Bataqliq was just slammed with super-competitive potentially sentient species. If we wanted to climb to the top of the local scene, we had to get up very early in the morning, I'll tell you what! We found our niche in the end. Here's a friendly tip: if you want to protect yourselves from predators, you don't always have to order up scary teeth and poison sacs. I can heartily recommend trying out disproportionately large eyes, slender, snappable legs, and an invitingly soft and vulnerable neck, all elegantly arranged to arouse feelings of protectiveness, compassion, and love, especially in mammals. Same reason puppies and kittens and babies are so cute—to trick you into taking care of them! Don't feel bad, it's not your fault. You literally can't help it and neither can we. Plus, our famous neoteny is paired with an exquisite auditory capability. The Esca don't make noise using just plain, store-bought diaphragms and larynxes, but by locally sourced air passing over and through the holes in our rib cages. See? That's our house-made crystal-cartilage alloy there. Totally unique in the universe. Our specialized anatomy serves up a mouthwatering range of infrasounds, but they can be a bit too spicy for some discerning xenotypes, provoking a profound involuntary emotional response! I'm basically a giant vibrating nonconsensual feelings-flute. Isn't that something? Humans do seem particularly allergic. I'll turn the music down, no problem. But no need to tell you lot all that! You've built so many infrasound amplifiers over the centuries, such as the one you are currently sterilizing with your mop and broom. You just gotta know how it works! Makes you feel like God's sitting right there next to ya, stealin' your frites. Only it's not God. We're a bit low on God today. It's just resonance.

"Why *me*? Shouldn't you be talking to the President or the UN or someone important? Why am I special?" asked a grocery clerk in Chagrin Falls, Ohio.

Aw, that's so precious! Don't worry, sweetheart, you're not special at all! I'm talking to every human entity on this biosphere simultaneously. The Esca are a single Verse of sentient beings, one unified planet at peace with itself that speaks, to outsiders at least, with one voice. You are . . . not. This seemed like the best way to make sure everyone gets their share of supper. I'm not even here, strictly speaking. I am physically present in only one location on this world. No, I'm not gonna tell you where, you naughty thing! That would be cheating! I have projected a dynamic inter-active holointrusion of myself into everyone else's sensorium. These first contact gigs sort of run on rails, anyway. Like chatting with a waitress before she takes your order! It might seem personal and intimate, on account of how going out on the town is a real rare, memorable treat for you, but she lives on the town. She's done this a hundred times and the girl's on autopilot. Besides, the information I've got waiting under the heat-lamp for you is too important. I can't wait for your monarchs to decide to hide it, lose control of the narrative, deny the evidence, call me a weather balloon, confess and resign, and finally leak a half-redacted version of what I tried to say to a newspaper friendly to one faction or another. Who has the time? This way, nothing can be hidden from any member of your . . . crowd, I am told, is the correct word, though it is very ugly compared to Verse. You should change it to something with a grander scope. Also, this way, I don't have to repeat myself seven billion times.

"How many of you are there?" asked the Prime Minister of Ukraine.

Our ship is docked on the dark side of your moon. Does it ever make you sad to have only one moon? It would make me sad. We are a small ambassadorial vessel, nothing fancy-pants. We watched your television for a long time and got the feeling you would overreact to an adult-size fleet. Ship's complement is one hundred fifty-four. However, contextually, I'm pretty sure you mean either how many are here on your planet or how many intelligent nonhumans are there in the galaxy? The answers *are, respectively: just me down here and quintillions up there. Septillions. More. And yet, we are many fewer out there than once we were. The dinner rush ain't what it used to be.*

"That's a lot of Big Birds," remarked an ambitious young oxycodone dealer in Connecticut.

Oh, no, I did not mean to say there are quintillions of Esca. We are a modest species. It's not considered good table manners to tick off your species' exact numbers in mixed company, any more than you discuss the locks and alarms you have installed in your house with strangers. It's not . . . safe.

"You're not alone?" asked a wealthy actor in his New York penthouse apartment.

Not even a little! It's so nice of you to be concerned, though. The Esca were chosen from among the minor races to contact you by the Great Octave, comprised of the Alunizar Empire, the Utorak Formation, the Keshet Effulgence, the Linearity of Smaragdi, the Trillion Kingdoms of Yüz, the Sziv, the Voorpret, and the 321. The Esca were chosen because, obviously, unspoiled species respond positively to us, given the whole nonconsensual feelings-flute thing. We are also the most recent species to be accepted into the arms of the Warm Fuzzy Galactic Family. You will be given a comment card at the conclusion of our conversation. Your feedback is appreciated.

"Are you going to kill us all?" asked the Chancellor of Germany's husband.

Possibly. Probably? Not me, personally, *of course. All signs point to . . . maybe? Very suspenseful, isn't it? Exciting!*

"If you're going to slaughter us like dogs anyway, why bother stopping in for a chitchat first? Just nuke us from orbit, why not?" asked a retired accountant on a fixed income in Costa Rica.

There is a process, señorita! Veggies before dessert! The Keshet picked up radio broadcasts sloshing around this area ages ago. You're

very loud! Table for seven billion, chop-chop! We all found what we heard
a bit disturbing, but at least you could dance to it. Here's the catch, kitten:
whenever evidence of a new species with significant potential for expansion is discovered, we all get very nervous. Sometimes, the new kids
are clearly on the up-and-up, bright-scaled and bushy-tailed sensitive
sweeties who really have their shit together. But not everyone cleans up
nice for company. Not everyone can be trusted to play nicely with all the
other children. Sometimes, a species gins up the technology necessary to
well and truly muck things up for the rest of us before they develop anything like self-awareness or complex reasoning or radical empathic per-
spective, before their philosophical digestive tract can handle something
spicier than malice aforethought or semibenign neglect. These borderline cases must be . . . tested to see if they possess true sentience. You
wouldn't enroll a wolf in a preschool for the gifted and advanced just
because it learned how to sit and speak and shake a paw, now, would
you? That's obvious. It would be a slaughterhouse. With juice boxes. We
have a responsibility to those who were here already when that chap
with fangs and fur turned up pretending to be civilized.

"Of course we're sentient!" protested the newly minted CEO
of Sumitomo Mitsui Trust Holdings in Tokyo. "Look around!
We've done so much! We've had . . . Kant! And Einstein! And
Descartes! And . . . and Kurosawa and the Internet and Nekobasu
and Mr. Rogers and game shows where you don't even win anything except happiness! We've been to the moon! We saved the
California condor. You and I are talking, back and forth! You can't
do that with a turtle or a jellyfish or a washing machine. How can
you doubt we're sentient? I donate to charity, you know."

Please don't make a scene, sir. It's not personal. You've got to order
off the kiddie menu until you can sit still in your big-boy chair. The galaxy nearly roasted itself to ashes over the question of which species were
and were not sentient. The ruins still smoke. The widows still weep. And

quite frankly, Mr. Rogers notwithstanding, you're a mess. I mean, honestly. You just made the argument for the survival of your species and you didn't even mention a single female, except, presumably, half the condors. I don't know why you would even bring up the Internet. The xeno-intelligence officer responsible for evaluating your digital communication required invasive emergency therapy after an hour's exposure. One glance at that thing is the strongest argument possible against the sentience of humanity. I wouldn't draw attention to it, if I were you. We know very well that you've been to the moon. You're starting to consider mining your asteroid belt as well. You're just shy of figuring out how to shuffle your horde of hormone-curdled control-obsessed malignant narcissists offworld. In short, you were about to become our problem. But now there is no problem! Now there is a process.

"I really don't know what you're talking about," said the Speaker of the United States House of Representatives. "We're doing great. Turn on any news channel, they'll tell you. Taxes are low, business is booming, crime is down, the Patriots win the Super Bowl every year, and we're finally getting our country back. I'll admit, it used to be a real nightmare around here. If you'd have shown up five years ago, I'd agree with you. So many filthy, ungrateful protestors, clogging up traffic, breaking windows, whining about every little thing that didn't go their way. But that's all in the past! Look around! Clean streets. Quiet streets. Empty streets ready for commerce. Everyone I know is happy."

Everyone you know is a monster, sweetie. We've watched a lot of your media, you know. It's an excellent way to evaluate societal sentience. You seem to be very concerned with monsters. Monsters from above, monsters from below, monsters among you, monsters from the sea, radioactive monsters, machine monsters, magical monsters, serial monsters who can only be stopped by monsters with badges. It's a whole thing with you people. We got terrifically bored after a while. After all, you always win against the monsters, even though you're the ones slowly cooking your planet because you can't be bothered not to, butchering one another for fun and profit, making up elaborate stories that start with being calm and treating everyone with kindness and equality but somehow always end with somebody getting enslaved, absolutely obliterating the other species with whom you share a world so you can take a photograph with their corpses or gobble up their best features in hopes of achieving a more satisfying erection, and being generally willing to sell the fleeting, unique, fragile lives of everyone you've ever met if it means you can consume a slightly larger share of resources than they can. You can't even agree on whether or not a sick child should get a tissue without having to really work for it. None of you seem to be able to stand one another. How will you treat us, if you are allowed to swarm across the galaxy? Which of us have horns or tusks or claws we feel quite attached to that might arouse your sluggish organs? Yes, of course, you've done some clever things with your time. No one is denying that rhythmic gymnastics are really just terrific. But in a clinch, you lot would rather watch someone suffer untold horrors than watch them enjoy so much as a cool drink if you don't have two of your own, and yours have cherries in them as well as more ice and little paper umbrellas, and even then most of you would still prefer to take theirs and have three. This is not the behavior of a sentient race. It is the behavior of wild animals. Even your babies view anyone who doesn't look just exactly like their parents with seething suspicion. It's baked in to you. I'll put this in words you can understand: humans are hideous, pain-guzzling, pollution-spouting space monsters who might threaten our way of life. Now, how does that usually pan out in the movies, kitten? At least we let you try to convince us we're wrong. I doubt you asked the dodo birds what they thought about it before you blasted the last one in the face with a blunderbuss. But lucky you—we're better than that. We are not monsters. We have our process. The process works. We do not deviate from the process. Perhaps you could think of it as instructions from corporate. Not to be disobeyed, if you don't want to be sacked.

"So what is it?" asked a green-haired barista in Melbourne who was considering going back to art school. "The process, I mean. And we're not all like that, by the way. I'm vegan. I run a dog rescue."

Cheer up, humanity! You've got reservations at the hottest nightspot in the galaxy! You will send a representative to beautiful Litost, where all the fashionable species have gathered for the Metagalactic Grand Prix. There, you will compete with the Alunizar, the Keshet, the Yüz, the Esca, and all the rest of us, except, of course, the vast Naranca Empire, as they don't play well with others. They don't really grasp the idea of a contest that isn't mostly entirely about them or an aesthetic that isn't up to its epaulets in military tat, and anyway, their current emperor is a slowly rotting mango on a plastic lawn chair, so their own sentience status is a bit up in the air at the moment. (You will also be judged against other aspiring species rounded up from the corners of what we like to call the "developing multiverse." It's nicer than "crapslums" or "under the astronomical bed.") All of us together will take part in a glorious contest requiring all the strength, intellect, and art of our various kinds. Prove to us that you are more than the sum of your most unpleasant parts. Prove that you've learned literally anything from your embarrassing history. Prove that, if we teach you how to plant corn, you won't give us a repeat performance of Manifest Destiny's Greatest Hits. Prove you're better now. You don't even have to win! As long as you don't come in dead last, your species will rise and join the party in the sky already in progress. But if you can't even defeat one measly tone-deaf head-on-backward galactic civilization, I'm afraid all memory of your collective existence will be lovingly collated and archived, your planetary resources tenderly extracted, and your species totally annihilated. Your organic material will be seamlessly reincorporated into your biosphere and your planet left in peace to try again with dolphins or something in another billion years or so. FUN!

"Never," proclaimed the President of the United States. "We will not lie down and let you destroy our way of life for your entertainment. We will stand. We will fight. We will never give up. You may frighten others with your little speech, but you're messing with humanity now. We are capable of so much more than you can imagine. So much more than your barbaric ritual sacrifice. We will rise up and defend this planet, and in the end, our spirit, our courage, and our nuclear stockpiles will prevail."

Look at you! Who's the cutest? YOU'RE THE CUTEST. And what a sense of humor! Your mummy must be so proud. Don't be stupid, we would obliterate you. My clumsiest offspring play with more powerful weapons than your most psychotic defense contractors dream of on Christmas Eve. We know what you're packing, and we don't care. I have fashion accessories more technologically advanced than the business end of your cutting edge. No. This is how it works. This is all we have found that works. You will send your best to Litost and you will compete. Or you will die now—86'd right off the board. And while I've enjoyed our time together, I'm really not fussed either way. Though I must say that leaping directly to declaring war on us does not make much of an argument for human sentience. That is the response of an ant colony. Do better. As for barbaric, there must be a test, mustn't there? One must separate the sublime from the merely anatomical. Unless you think we should invite your koalas or subway rats to the galactic table? Because I don't see you setting up diversity programs so that elephants can apply to university, and many of them are a far sight cleverer than your average President. You forget we've watched your history live in Technicolor. I'd say you've got your trousers on backward if you think thermonuclear war is less barbaric than a little artistic competition among friends.

"What . . . what's the contest?" asked a fisherman in Papua New Guinea as he sat down on a long flat rock to weep. "What do we have to do?"

Don't cry, baby. It's not so bad, I promise. All you have to do is sing.

"But that's easy!" spluttered a record executive in Los Angeles. "That's *fine*! We accept! No problem! Humans are fucking *amazing* at music, you'll see. Christ, you had me worried for a minute! But this is gonna be spectacular. This is gonna be *iconic*. Say hello to your new champion, Big Bird, because mankind shakes its groove thing like nothing you've ever seen. We got this one in the bag."

No.

"What do you mean, no?" asked the program director for BBC4.

N! O! Spells NO! The importantest word you can make out of teensy tiny N and weensy old O—that's NO! The biggest little word I know, know, know! I mean no. Humans are not particularly good at music. Oh, you're all right, I suppose. You have some deeply basic understanding of rhythm and melody, but so do dolphins, darling. I hate to break it to you, but, just as an example, without thinking too much about it, the Vulna of Jadro Nebula use their entire homeworld as an instrument. You blow into the northern magnetic pole, as I understand it. Anyway, it's not just about a good beat, it's what you do with it. Showmanship. Theater. Flash. The Trillion Kingdoms of Yüz won three cycles ago with an upbeat little earworm called "Love Means Forgiving the Sins of Our Colonial Expansion Phase," and when the bass dropped, their entire proletariat became a comet. So, you see, coming in second-to-last may be too much to hope for a planet that still uses Auto-Tune. While a guitar and a primate in leather pants are nice and all . . . oh, how to explain so even our live studio audience can understand? You know how, when a baby's crying and wailing, you put it on your shoulder and pat its back—pat, pat, pat-a-pat-pat? And it sicks up some milk and spit and tummy juices all over Mumsy's nice jumper and then looks just TERRIFICALLY pleased with itself? THAT'S what human music is like! Compared to the rest of the galaxy, of course; I'm sure it's just fine for you.

"That seems . . . rather rigged in favor of the hegemony," said an anthropology professor in Zurich. "Has any 'borderline case' ever actually pulled that off? Or is this an elaborate sacrifice ritual?"

Gosh! What you must think of us! Of course the new kids in town come through sometimes! It'd be pretty damn horrible, otherwise. I said, we're not monsters.

"Uh-huh. When's the last time a newbie won?" asked a professional gamer in Seoul.

Won? Never. Successfully avoided obliteration? Here's lookin' at me, kid. The last newly added species to triumph on the biggest stage in the universe was us. Me, in fact. In my pre-interstellar diplomacy life, I was the lead singer of the brinefunk underwater big band combo Bird's Eye Blue. So you see, I sympathize with you, I really do. I get it, all the way. This is all so overwhelming and not at all how you want to spend a Thursday afternoon. The Esca used to be a really nasty piece of work, I don't mind telling you. Selfish, temperamental, clinically depressed— seriously, a doctor on Pallulle diagnosed our whole species. Someone killed my grandfather for being under eight feet tall. Half our planet had been turned into broiling salt flats by the Üürgama Conglomerate's experiments. We just couldn't see past how much the other Esca pissed us off. Plus, we had a real problem with libertarians. But we pulled it out in the end. I don't know, I guess something about the radical upending of our perception by the sudden invasion of a vast, technologically superior galactic civilization really brought us together. Bird's Eye Blue dazzled the crowds with our interstellar hit "Please Don't Incinerate Us, We'll Be Good from Now On, We Promise." We came in tenth. It was a sensation, nearly a scandal—no new fauna on the block had ever placed so high. The royalties still fund our entire defense industry.

"And how long ago was that?" asked the President of Mozambique.

A mere thirty-four years ago, by your commemorative word-of-the-

day calendar. Last year, by the Tunicate Calendar of Aluno Secundus.
Time is a constant annoyance in the great beyond.

"How many have lost?" asked a science fiction writer in Lublin, Poland. "How many species have you destroyed?"

Six. Well, seven technically, but the Andvari barely count, as they launched a preemptive strike before curtain call. Oh, sorry, eight. I forgot Flus. Before my time. And hardly controversial or even very interesting. Borderline cases only come up every once in a while. And not all of them completely fail to prove their worth.

"So you're saying we'll lose. There's no hope. It's . . . it's over," said a lonely marine biologist on assignment in Antarctica. "Probably for the best. Used to be a lot more ice around here, you know."

There, there, poppet. Let's turn that frown upside down! That's not what I'm saying at all! We have prepared a list of human musicians we think might do reasonably well, given current trends in popular music throughout the civilized galaxy and the relative advantages and disadvantages of your psycho-audio-anatomical makeup.

"This has to be a joke," said a theater critic in Chicago, staring at the names glowing on the slice of crystal the Esca held up helpfully at her eye level. "Yoko Ono?"

Oh, yes! My friend Öö is really, really hoping she's available! He's become quite the fan. He knows all the words to "Don't Worry Kyoko" and asked me to check while I am here and see that Kyoko is all right. Öö is very concerned. We know she must be just horribly busy, world tours and masses of fans and the like, but it is fairly important. Do you think she'd be interested?

"Well, she's dead, so, no," said a leather-clad teen punkster in Toronto. "And so is Kraftwerk, Ryuichi Sakamoto, Tangerine Dream, Brian Slade, the freaking *Spice Girls*, are you kidding me? Ugh, okay, Insane Clown Posse got themselves paralyzed from the neck down screwing around with magnets, Björk lost her voice in an accident with a narwhal and a spinning wheel years ago, and just go fuck yourself, no, Skrillex is not going to go down as the savior of humanity. It's just not happening. I'd rather die in a sea of nuclear fire."

How embarrassing! It seems our research is somewhat out-of-date. I will speak to Öö. The Keshet are time travelers and excellent at cultural reconnaissance—but not very organized. They eat all the stationery supplies. I've tried to give Öö a day planner so many times, you'd never believe it! He just buries it for the winter and expects an orderly workspace to come up in the spring. But there are many more possibilities! We were very thorough.

"What's . . . what's *wrong* with you? Why do you like this stuff?" asked a middle-aged graphic designer in Berlin. "Grace Jones, I get. Brian Eno, I suppose, if you must. Even RuPaul, I can *almost* understand. But Jefferson Starship? Nicki Minaj? Hüsker Dü? *Courtney Love?* I mean, *really?* And Donna Summer just seems wildly out of place with all the rest of them. There's no aesthetic unity here at *all.*"

I love "MacArthur Park."

"Right. Okay. Cool. No, sorry, it's not cool, that's awful. Good Lord." A Liverpudlian nightclub owner crossed her arms over her chest. "A moment ago I was nearly pissing myself in terror, but now I'm just . . . well, I'm just a bit offended, frankly. We've got a *lot* better than this, you know. And nearly everyone on this stupid list is dead or old as the sands of sodding *time*. Didn't you find Beyoncé while you were flipping through the oldies section? Bowie? Led Zeppelin? The Beatles?"

Oh, certainly! The Beatles? Sure did! Fat lot of rubbish if you ask me, except for "Revolution 9." Yes, well, if they're willing to stick to that sort of thing, maybe we could come around to the idea eventually.

"I don't even know what to say," said a psychologist in Perth,

Western Australia. "This is just embarrassing for everyone involved. 'Whoever wrote the theme songs for the television programs *He-Man* and *She-Ra*'? 'Apple II'? *Those* made your list?"

There has to be someone we can all agree on. Someone still alive and reasonably healthy whom we can bear to listen to for more than thirty seconds without severe nausea or instantaneous narcolepsy. Come on, you can do it! Let's all put on our thinking caps and work together!

"I seriously doubt it," sighed out a Mongolian yak herder.

"Not if those are the only options," snapped a Hungarian actuary.

"Truly, we are not amused," said the Queen of England, Charlotte I.

But in a drafty, unfurnished, utilities-not-included flat on the far, far, *far* outskirts of London, a single, furious voice rose above them all.

"What the bloody goddamned rabbit-fucking hell is my name doing at the bottom of that list?" shouted Decibel Jones.

5.

We Wear Spring Clothes in the Wintertime

The first Absolute Zeros show was held on the hot, vast, dark second floor of the Hope & Ruin pub in Brighton, home of pound-a-pint Tuesdays; the toughest pub quiz in the Anglosphere, which featured questions chosen by anyone who could prove to the MC that they were tits-deep in a doctoral dissertation; an open mic night that bashed up the conceptual boundaries of the terms "open," "microphone," and, indeed, "night," with reckless abandon; and Archibald Arthur Gormley, owner, operator, and the oldest functioning alcoholic in the Eurozone. Gormley was ancient already when the Kinks had the grand idea of a well-respected bowl haircut. He was yelling at punters to get off his stool in those fat and rosy days when the place was just called Hope and the bit about Ruin was but a twinkle in the Commonwealth's economic eye. In his smug middle age, he saw Bowie come in for a pint when he was still a slip of a thing called Davie, playing weddings in a three-piece suit, and in the spotty, nervous face of the future grand duke of glam, Archibald Arthur Gormley yawned.

As the band's designated Organized Person, Oort St. Ultraviolet had chosen the Hope & Ruin for their debut because, despite their mind-smearingly cool sound, actual London venues had proven

mystifyingly indifferent toward smashing rookie acts of unadul-
terated musical genius, as they were toward all bright-eyed, irre-
sponsibly coiffed kids fresh off the home-editing software suite,
and really, anybody whose drinks they might have to comp for
the night, if they could possibly pull it off without offending any
particular glowering council housing castaway who might, by
some horrible accident, turn out to be the future of rock-'n'-roll.
As Musad Atallah, the talent manager for Robot Custard, the hottest indie stage in South London, told his interns: gatekeeping is
a noble calling, much more delicate than fannish enthusiasm or
hipster disdain. An uncurated open mic was as good as a neon
sign blinking out: I AM A HELPLESS FUZZY DUCKLING WANNABE
TASTEMAKER WITH NO TASTE TO SPEAK OF AND UNGUARDED TAPS,
PLEASE ASSAULT MY EARS AND ABUSE MY GENEROUS NATURE AT YOUR
EARLIEST CONVENIENCE. But velvet ropes that never opened would
have to be replaced by video poker machines and a secondhand
snooker table within the year.

Oort had to go all the way to Brighton to find an open mic that
didn't have a positively gladiatorial audition process and a waiting list as long as the M1.

This careful velvet aloofness of any scene accessible via
London public transport was the third most significant factor in
the meteoric rise and awkward, plummeting face-plant of Decibel
Jones and the Absolute Zeros. They were all the cooler and more
seemingly exclusive for being hard to find, hard to see, and easy to
talk about to everyone you met. The second factor was a woman
wearing a crochet dress and a mushroom-bob haircut while trying to chat up Archibald Arthur Gormley when Oort, Mira, and
Dess started to tune up for their first real set at two p.m. on a
Wednesday—a set that consisted of two songs they'd written on a
series of increasingly moist Acme Arkable Gelato napkins and an

upbeat champagne-bubble cover of "War Pigs" by Black Sabbath. The first was that, against all laws of interpersonal and artistic probability, the Absolute Zeros, once upon a time, were incredibly, irresistibly, downright irritatingly *good*.

If you'd looked up that afternoon from your admittedly absorbing IPA toward the stage of the Hope & Ruin, you wouldn't have seen anyone you'd recognize as Decibel Jones. Not from those rickety singleton tables as ringed with pint-glass condensation as an Ent's arse, not from Archibald Arthur Gormley's cracked leather stool as he cringed away from the aggressively jolly Yorkshire bird hovering at him with her ginger 1970s mushroom-bob hair, so disturbingly *un*chic that it came around to being almost, if not quite, punk. Not even from the back of the joint, for whom standing room only was but a distant dream. There was no vintage McQueen then, no style consultants to tell them no. Mira Wonderful Star had cut and stitched and remixed the contents of their local Oxfam's damaged/as-is bin like a garage mash-up track. In a deconstructed ballroom gown whacked up out of a spandex "Slutty C-3PO" costume, a silver brocade Christmas tree skirt, and a gauzy black shower curtain with metallic blue appliqué roses all over it, Mira Wonderful Star sat at a drum set the quality of which wavered between obnoxious child's toy and legitimate rubbish, with a retrotrash white 1984 Casio mini keyboard propped up to her left on an empty Boddingtons keg. Her uncle Takumi had given the drums to her for Christmas when she was thirteen, purely to fulfill what he saw as a solemn duty to embody the Archetype of the Cool Uncle as depicted in the twentieth-century domestic comedies he lovingly annotated and catalogued the way some people catalogue exotic butterflies, his efforts having been made somewhat more difficult by the fact that Cool Uncle Takumi had raised his beloved embodiment of the Rebellious

Niece from the age of four. Oort St. Ultraviolet, not yet the man of a thousand instruments, fiddled with a crappy plastic capo and his grandmother's begrudgingly lent hundred-year-old concertina, in an alleged outfit consisting of a dismembered ladies' red sequin blazer, low-slung, mercilessly tight trousers that had been a wine-stained wedding gown only a few hours before, and a cricket jumper with the name GEORGE embroidered lovingly on the hem in purple thread with a jaunty bat on either side.

Decibel Jones stood at the mic stand shirtless, petrified, in his own set of what Mira firmly believed was the only correct type of trousers for a rock star, treating hip bones on a boy like cleavage on a girl and choking off blood supply like a pre-suffrage corset. Dess's pair had pretty clearly been someone's mum's idea of a formal St. Patrick's Day frock in its previous life, all green satin paisley and vintage '80s gold accent chains. Over it all, but under the black plastic bat wings, he wore the one thing you'd recognize from the *Spacecrumpet* album art, the one article of clothing that survived the transition from coming home smelling of potatoes and rancid oil to smelling of cigarettes and his own cologne brand and barely coming home at all, from Danesh Jalo to Decibel Jones: a long, flared, faux-fur-lined, lightly distressed rose-and-cream aristo-coat from a local community theater production of *Les Liaisons Dangereuses*. Mira had unstrung a heap of dollar-store fake colored pearls to edge the collar, sleeves, and hem, doused the fur with her corner chemist Apocalyptic Oil Spill #4 hair dye, and after that night, Dess never washed that Technicolor dreamcoat once.

He named it Robert.

Unfortunately, pearls and sequins and metallic appliqué roses reflected almost none of the already miserly light from the Hope & Ruin's deeply basic rig. Shadows loitered where no experienced stage manager would let them. An unkind white spotlight washed out those three terribly young and hungry faces, dappled by the corpses of a couple of spiders that'd gotten stuck between the gel and the lamp around the time when disco was cool. The air outside shimmered with muggy afternoon heat. The stage was wholly, utterly, indescribably black, crisscrossed with the stellar cartography of a thousand hopeful handsome smolderers all made of the same needy stuff, scraping their bootheels, dragging their guitar stands, and dumping their hearts into a sound system more suited to calling bingo than calling London. It was, to be perfectly honest, a depressingly bleak sight, far bleaker than a lifetime spent working in air-conditioned cubicles or watching a kebab slowly revolve in front of a space heater like a sweaty meat planet or ringing up an eternity of cough suppressants in your dad's tiny one-location drugstore after he finally gives up the till, far bleaker than a mere total absence of anything to look forward to. They were a study in absurdity, a near-psychotic commitment to an aesthetic no one had had a chance to laugh at yet.

Decibel Jones wrapped his fingers around the shaft of the mic and opened his mauve-and-glitter-painted mouth.

"Er. Hiya. How's everyone doing tonight? Er. This afternoon?"

The bartender blew his nose on the tail of his shirt. Six other open mic'ers sat in the front with six soda waters slowly decarbonating before them, all dressed in earnest, sincere, salt-of-the-stage flannel and jeans, an on-trend uniform of off-the-rack authenticity tailored perfectly to the current white-knuckle zeitgeist of homespun artisanal emotions strung on banjos of working-class vulnerability, all trying their hardest to look as though they'd have come even if they weren't on the roster. A cashier from Ladbrokes chomped down a curry on his lunch break with one eye on his phone. Three or four unemployed twenty-somethings pranged darts into the wall without looking over or lowering their voices. Cool Uncle Takumi looked up from editing his new article on the quest for the divine in John Candy's oeuvre and clapped with football-mum supportiveness from a respectful distance, in case a legion of front-row fans miraculously appeared, fashionably late.

"Yer holdin' back on yer old Gormer," a truly Stygian horror-drone buzzed out of Archibald Arthur Gormley's tracheotomy valve, which his wife had called his "smoke hole" before she left him for that chap who ran all those marathons in his seventies. "Whaddoaye come 'ere for if ye won't gimme a full legal pour?"

"We're doing *splendidly*, darling," called the lady with the ginger mushroom-bob, a music critic done in by the death of print journalism whose name was Lila Poole. "You all look a *treat*!"

"Right. Yeah. So . . . we are . . ."

Decibel Jones coughed, not himself yet, not twenty feet tall in Piccadilly, not praised to death by the *Guardian*, not flirting with Ruby the American waitress, nobody's messiah, not anyone at all, not even properly Decibel Jones yet—last night, they'd been the Möbius Hips, this morning they'd definitely decided on the Things, and then Mira had chucked that one between, she said, a scotch to steel her nerves and a Midori to light her up insides. And suddenly, he couldn't think of what they'd come up with instead, couldn't think of the lyrics to "Raggedy Dandy," still so new that they ached, couldn't think of what train they were meant to take home or what time he had to be at the shop tomorrow, couldn't think of anything but the unlovely mating honks of those twenty-something dartheads battering his cochlear well-being, honks that, if he was down a dark street or on a playground, usually meant he was about to get the shit kicked out of him for being a mincing little ponce or whatever vivid racial slur they had in stock that week. Words and phrases bobbed to the surface of their monotonous posturing pubstep drone: *arsenal, piss-up, I know a bloke, it's your round, it's not mine, I don't care what she says, fucking West Ham, mate.*

Dess froze, and his whole life nearly threw an axle and tipped itself into a ditch full of Mr. Five Star's fryer oil. He felt ridiculous. In these ugly green paisley trousers and stupid glitter bat wings and half a discontinued makeup rack. Not Robert, of course. Robert was fine. Robert was grand. Robert was right. But all he had up Robert's perfect sleeve was two rubbishy songs that were more gimmick than the white-hot fire of real *music*, the sort of music people would play over and over in their bedrooms at night, the sort that scrambled up your senses so wonderfully that you laughed and cried into your pillow at the same time, the sort of music that felt like you'd always known it even though you'd never heard it before, the songs you'd put on a mixtape and press into someone else's hand saying, *This, this says how I feel better than I ever could.*

Additionally, standing up there in mascara and platform heels with plastic goldfish in the soles was no way to *not* get the shit kicked out of you for being a mincing little ponce. In his mind, he'd thought of them playing the witching hour at Robot Custard under magenta and ultramarine lights to a crowded dance floor full of yearnful students, not hipsters but tricksters, grooving on the wub-wub bassline of the whole throbbing universe, sucking MDMA and hope out of locally sourced glow sticks. What was magical at two in the morning was tawdry and cheap and dangerous to your general health at two in the afternoon. They were supposed to look like those acoustic-hearted flanneleers at the front tables, with their carefully stubbled jawlines, sipping their responsible preset soda waters, mentally calculating whether to soulfully close their eyes at the key change or at the big note so it really, *really* looked like they believed in love after layoffs at a mill they'd never known as anything but high-end lofts for lease. That was what was hot right now. That was what record labels wanted to hear. Those nice white boys with their pre-distressed jeans and pre-distressed hearts mumble-crooning artificial grit. Nobody understood what the Absolute Zeros believed so hard, they couldn't even wedge it into their lyrics yet: The world had gotten gritty enough. The only thing left to do in all that dirt was to *shine*.

But Dess wasn't shining. He was just a dumb tart in someone else's frock staring down failure like you could ever make *failure* blink. Failure was here before you and she'll be here after you and she won't even notice you go.

Fucking hell, what was he *doing*? He was going to fail, right now, in front of Mira and Oort, the only people in his life who'd never seen him behind a counter, only like this, the way he wanted to always be, his Arkable Gelato nation, his Acme Brand Instant Tunnel to the Future. He was going to be little Dani forever, seven years old, wearing all Nani's silk scarves at the same time, his face covered so proudly in lilac-lipstick doodles he'd drawn himself, standing in the middle of the lounge room singing along with Marvin the Martian like it was straight-up Wagner, so eager to please Nani, so thrilled to show her he really could sing like the people on TV, dying to be the utter focus of her attention.

And they'd all ignored him.

That old Blackpool flat was a dingy mirror of this Brighton pub. No one said anything. His sisters had snickered and whispered and texted furtively, most likely telling everyone they knew what fuckery was going down before their very eyes. His oldest brother had kicked a soccer ball expertly into the side of his big Danesh-head. The younger boys had wrestled obliviously in the kitchen.

And in the end, Nani had looked up from some murder book or other, groped in the side table for her hearing aid, and said:

"Eh? Did you say a thing, my handsomest? Nani did not have her magic ear in. Why have you dressed like Creature from the Scarf Lagoon? What is happening to your face?"

She'd squinted at him, because her reading glasses turned the non–murder book world into a watercolor smear. Dani knew even at age seven and three quarters that she hadn't meant the next bit to be cruel, that the poor old thing had only been startled out of the butler staving the mistress's head in with a pipe by her grandson becoming Decibel Jones before her very eyes and who could ever be prepared for that, but Nani had *laughed* at him, and it was the end of his childhood. Nani had called out to his brothers and sisters, erasing any possibility that they hadn't seen, that plausible deniability was maintained, and that none of this was really happening, and she'd announced to the capacity crowd at the Royal Jalo Hallway: "Look who has done an art on himself, our wee Mr. Tate of the Modern!"

He'd frozen. Just like now. Just like then. He was standing on that worn red rug and he was going to sing Wagner the Martian in a hundred scarves that smelled like home and love and safety and everyone was going to laugh in his face or, worse, ignore him like a stain on the ceiling, like he wasn't even there, like he'd never existed in the first place.

Mira saved him. The first time of many times. She banged out a riff on her kiddie drums behind him, leaned into her mic, and yelled like they were already playing a sold-out arena, loud enough to blow a dart from 20 to 1, loud enough to stun your old Gormer sober:

"WE ARE DECIBEL JONES AND THE ABSOLUTE ZEROS!"

Oort St. Ultraviolet opened up the throttle on his gran's concertina, and for the first time, in front of God and the dartboard and shrimp-flavored crisps and everyone, Decibel Jones began to sing.

No one ignored him. But Archibald Arthur Gormley did laugh. He laughed and laughed in total silence while bright-eyed, ambitious Lila Poole patted his shoulder and tears streamed out from under his glasses, down his booze-blooming cheeks, and into the soft darkness of his smoke hole, seeping toward the last part of him that remembered what it was like when he was young and everything in the world sounded just like that.

He wept into his single pint.

6.

There Must Be Another Way

These are the rules, guidelines, regulations of the Metagalactic Grand Prix as agreed to by everybody left standing after the Battle of Vlimeux:

1. *The Grand Prix shall occur once per Standard Alunizar Year, which is hereby defined by how long it takes Aluno Secundus to drag its business around its morbidly obese star, get tired, have a nap, wake up cranky, yell at everyone for existing, turn around, go back around the other way, get lost, start crying, feel sorry for itself and give up on the whole business, and finally try to finish the rest of its orbit all in one go the night before it's due, which is to say, far longer than a year by almost anyone else's annoyed wristwatch.*

2. *All species currently accepted as sentient must compete.*

3. *All species applying for recognition as intelligent, self-aware (not a huge barrel of dicks), and generally worth the time it takes to get to their shitty planet, wherever that may be, must compete.*

4. One song per species.

5. Special effects and stagecraft of all kinds are encouraged;
   however, no harm must come to the audience, the audience's families, or the linear timelines of any active spec-
   tators.

6. Please dress accordingly—that is, in the traditional costume
   of your people. But make it cool, all right? Give it a little
   showmanship. Make an effort. If you do not comply, your
   representatives will be sentenced to not less than six years
   of hard labor. We're not trying to run the trains on time in
   Drabtown here.

7. Please provide a written translation of your lyrics to the
   umpire. And no trying to show off by singing in Alunzish!
   Stay in your linguistic lane. Your accent will always be terrible.

8. New compositions only! No sloppy seconds.

9. Judging will be conducted in two phases: by audience
   acclamation, and a considered vote by a panel consisting
   of the representatives of the Great Octave, the new applicant's chaperone species, and an old computer from Kogu
   the Belligerent's house on Planet Yoomp.

10. At no time may anyone cast a vote for their own species,
    as this is selfish and boring and ruins it for everyone—
    looking at you, Alunizar.

11. *Offensive verses must confine bloodshed to the staging area.*

12. *In the event that an applicant species comes in last, their solar system shall be unobtrusively quarantined for a period of not less than 50,000 years, their cultures summarily and wholly Binned, their homeworld mined responsibly for resources, and after a careful genetic reseeding of the biosphere, their civilization precision-incinerated from orbit so we can all sleep at night. Every effort will be made to spare unoffending flora and fauna. The planet's biological processes will be allowed to start over without interference, older, wiser, more experienced, and able to learn from its mistakes. Any new species arising from said ecological matrix may reapply in the future without prejudice.*

13. *In the event that an applicant planet defeats at least one species of proven sentience and achieves some rank other than miserably dead last (so to speak), they shall be welcomed with open arms, spores, antennae, tentacles, wings, or other preferred appendages into the Untidy Lounge Room of the Extended Galactic Family.*

14. *In the event that a sentient species finishes in last place, they shall all go home and have a hard think about where they've gone wrong in life and promise never to do it again.*

15. *The final scoreboard shall determine the proportional distribution of all communally held Galactic Resources for the next cycle. (See attached documents for a full explication of*

said resources.) As this is kind of a big deal and has been, historically, the source of every war other than this one, see Rules 10, 17, and 18.

16. The undersigned, all their descendants, and any subsequently discovered civilizations we decide we can stand to talk to at parties, unto the heat-death of the universe or the next bout of belligerent stupidity makes all this maximally moot, whichever comes first, solemnly swear to play fair, listen with open minds, vote their feelings, not their ambitions, and not stack the roster with too many rookies all at once, so that everybody gets a really solid chance at not being vaporized if they don't deserve to be.

17. Any violators of Rule 16 shall be subject to the gentle ministrations of Rule 12.

18. The winner shall compel their government to pick up everyone else's drink tab, as well as put us all up and pay for the catering when we do this whole thing over again next year, no take-backsies, no changing mobile numbers, no pleading planetary austerity—take out a loan from the Intergalactic Happy Friendship Bank like everyone else, you skinflint.

19. Try your best and have fun!

After the Corking Incident at the thirtieth Grand Prix on the Utorak homeworld of Otozh, the subsequent trial, surprise exoneration, and politico-musical ascendency of the perpetrators—Igneous Lagom Opt, Aukafall Avatar 0, and the Entity Known as

Monad—a twentieth rule was added. At the time, the change was so controversial that protesters threatened to blow the thirty-first Grand Prix out of the sky if the Octave adopted it. However, with the launch of the Keshet Holistic Live Total Timeline Broadcast, the effects of Rule 20 proved so unreasonably, voyeuristically, nail-bitingly *fun* to watch from home that the protesters got completely addicted to viewing parties, and it became the galaxy's favorite guilty pleasure and fundamentally changed the way the game was played, spectated, and won.

> 20. *If a performer fails to show up on the night, they shall be automatically disqualified, ranked last, and their share of communal Galactic Resources forfeited for the year. Do try not to actually kill anyone. It's a dreadful bother to clean up the mess.*

7

Miracles Are Happening from Time to Time

The watery drop of light that had been busy swelling at the tip of the Esca's proboscis reached critical mass. It plopped onto the filthy floor of Decibel Jones's flat. It splashed as it hit the carpet, and the splashing light formed itself into an image, a projection, alive with *intention*. As he watched, an army of musical notes and scales and flats and sharps danced and whirled over a photo-topographical neon watercolor of the Bataqliq sonic swamps and the Occasional Mountains of Caj that were valleys in winter and Himalaya-crushing peaks at the height of summer.

Decibel Jones knew those notes. He'd know them anywhere. They were "Raggedy Dandy," which was, just maybe, the only *really* good song he'd ever written.

The conversation between Decibel Jones and the roadrunner bore almost no resemblance to the global template. It was mostly sung rather than spoken word, for one thing, and involved an extended dance sequence and a bit with a cat.

"Is that really it?" Dess interrupted halfway through. "We just sing better than one other beastie and we get to live?"

"Yes. Does it seem barbaric to you? Sixty-seven percent of your population used that word."

"No, it makes sense to me. It's perfect."

"Why?"

Decibel shrugged. "Life is stupid and beautiful that way."

The Esca smiled; for the Esca can and do smile. All its feathers flushed an excited shade of cobalt. He had said something good, then. Somehow, the world's luckiest fuckup had done something right for once, though God and all his angels knew what. He'd only said what he meant, which was, when you thought about it, a minor superpower, because so few people ever did. The blue creature danced coquettishly toward him on those impossible, dumb legs that couldn't hold up a plastic garden flamingo, let alone this living, breathing version.

"Three hundred light-years from here, there is a small world called Bataqliq flying through the black, as blue as this world, and as dear. It is my world. It is where the antique Esca first opened their eyes and looked up into a sky filled with the mutation-nurturing warmth of a single white star, burning as if for us alone, looked out beyond the bracelet of our twenty mountainous moons, into the all-possible cosmos, and first pondered whether to save some seeds and berries against the possibility of a lean and hungry winter rather than devour them all at once. Do you know what your people call that sun that gives my people life?"

"No," said Jones.

"You call it Mira Wonderful Star."

"I knew somebody called that once."

"I am aware, Mr. Jones."

"Sure you're not after her? I'll warn you, she's tough to get ahold of these days." Decibel stared out his grimy window. "She could have done your job, no problem. Save the world with a song? Just give her a minute to tune up. I'm just . . . Mr. Elmer of the Fudd. Not even that."

The roadrunner crossed the little garret room, leaving wet, mandala-moldering footprints on the scuffed carpet. It bent its enormous head and brushed the tip of its lantern against Dess's forehead.

It felt like a kiss.

It felt like every kiss anyone had ever laid on anyone else, the good, the bad, the all-time great, the let's just be friends. All those kisses, all those mouths, all those feelings, electrified and painted blue.

Dess didn't know why he did it, or even, honestly, how. It had been years since this sort of thing had been a prominent water feature in the courtyard of his life. It had been years since it was how he made friends and self-medicated and got inspired and entertained himself and borrowed a cup of confidence from friendly neighbors. It had been years since he'd felt himself enough to try. He put a hand on the roadrunner's thin, jeweled, holey rib cage, and the hand was welcome there.

"I'm not sure I know this song," he whispered. "How does it go?"

By the time the rest of the world was finishing its exposition, an exhausted Decibel Jones had agreed to it all, to go to the stars and sing for his species, to follow that wascally wabbit, confessed his sins, called out for breakfast, and become, entirely unbeknownst to him, resoundingly and inexplicably, though not by any human definition, pregnant.

Point to Dani.

Water

The house is full of children, the relatives have come.
I am going to put on my green dress.
—"Party for Everybody," Buranovskiye Babushki

8.

White and Black Blues

Decibel Jones was already well on his way, but not to the Metagalactic Grand Prix.

To Whitehall.

The instant the hungriest unpaid intern shadowing the lowest-ranking secretary to the most unremarkable Member of Parliament saw that the only living name on the alien's pop chart was a British subject, a nondescript black car carrying two nondescript men in black suits and black sunglasses spontaneously materialized out of a zebra crossing halfway to Croydon.

Unfortunately, that trod-upon intern was merely quick, not alone.

Thus, just as Dess and the roadrunner were arguing the merits of Richard Harris's version of "MacArthur Park" vis-à-vis Donna Summer's, a veritable unkindness of nondescript black cars descended furiously onto the pavement outside. A flock of fists pummeled the door and rang the buzzer, a gaggle of angry men's voices squawked out, "Danesh Jalo, Danesh Jalo, this is Insert Steely-Eyed Organization Here! It is imperative that we speak with you immediately!" A murder of identically loafered feet kicked the door down and marched up the rickety staircase, and by the time Decibel Jones thought to wonder where the Esca had gone all of a sudden, he was crowdsurfing back down the walk-up staircase on a chattering brood of government shoulders.

But the flight of the G-men broke apart when they hit their wall of parked cars. One after the other, square-jawed men born with surnames like Brown, Davies, Evans, Taylor, and Price and given names like Mister, Officer, Agent, Leftenant, and Specialist pecked and flapped at him. They took turns grabbing Decibel's McQueen-sheathed elbow with extravagantly aggressive masculinity and attempting to assert their dominance using only biceps, baritones, and a genetic inability to remove their sunglasses.

"Watch the Swarovskis, boys," Dess protested. "Damage this little number and I'll drop a whole fucking tax bracket."

"Mr. Jalo, I'm with MI5, and you'll need to come with me at once."

"MI6, Mr. Jalo, and this is my jurisdiction, Evans, so fuck off. Overseas intelligence. Very, *very* overseas, I should say."

"The intelligence may be foreign, but Danesh here is quite domestic, Taylor, which is MI5's territory, so it's you who'll be fucking off, I'm afraid. Better luck next invasion."

"Now, Danny, my lad, don't let these two confuse you. Metropolitan Police Antiterrorism Squad, at your service. Get in the car, there's a good fellow."

"Stand down, Davies, you're relieved. You can all stand down. Downing Street calling, Mr. Jalo. The Prime Minister wants you."

"Well, I can't say I haven't given it the occasional thought—the PM's a bit of all right," Dess managed to quip. If he lost everything else, pride, priapism, and producer credit, Decibel Jones would never, never give up his swagger.

"That's enough of that, sir. Now, I'm to bring you to COBRA to meet with the emergency committee, of which the Prime Minister is chair, so there must be some manner of mix-up, but it'll all sort out at Whitehall."

"Son, I'm your liaison to the United Nations, it's imperative that I take you into protective custody. This *clearly* isn't a UK op, you asshats. Go have a cup of tea or whatever it is you all do while the big boys are talking."

"The Foreign and Commonwealth Office kindly invites you to eat a shit, Yank. He's ours and you know it. We'll let you know if anybody descends from the heavens asking for Taylor Swift, won't we, lads?"

The caws of the authoritarian brood started coming thicker and faster, until Decibel felt vomit rising again. He knew better than to struggle when in the grip of bureaucracy, but he couldn't breathe. The smell of dry-cleaned blazers and recently-signed-in-triplicate forms was overpowering. Where was a bloody damned giant space flamingo when you needed one?

"SAS, Jalo, on your feet, look lively, fall in."

"Home Office, Danesh, come along now."

"UKSA, sir, you'll want to follow me."

"GCHQ, Mr. J, on you get."

"OAA, Dan, let's get a move on, shall we?"

"Wait, what the hell's an OAA?" yelled the Prime Minister's secretary from the back of the rookery.

"Office of Alien Affairs. We're new." The OAA agent checked his watch. "In . . . two and a half minutes, it'll be the ninety-minute anniversary of our founding."

"*Daily Mail*, Dess, let's get you away from these jolly jackboots and down to the newsroom on the double-quick. The people have a right to know what kind of person is going to represent them! Now, be honest, mate, don't you think the first UK ambassador to another world ought to be a bit more, I don't know, *English*?"

Decibel yanked his overmistered arm out of the reporter's skinny talons. "Oh, go eat an *entire* bucket of co—"

"Beg pardon, Mr. Jones—I'm a great fan of your work, by the way, really, I've set my employer's ringtone to 'Terms of Service' for years. I've been charged by the Queen to convey you directly to Her Majesty's Audience Room. I believe you'll find that Head of State trumps these earnest chaps any way you look at it. Right this way, sir."

Decibel Jones sighed and shook his head. Today was fired. Today was well and truly sacked. Today could, in point of fact, fuck all the way off. "Well, 'Terms of Service' is just about the only song on that album I didn't write, so what a fantastic job you've done with your sucking up. Full marks."

There were too many of them. Decibel pinballed through the parliament of men in black, from manful grip to manful grip, until he just toppled into a car the way he used to when his manager had to beat off a gauntlet of handsy fans to get him to his next gig. They were screeching down a side road in reverse before he even figured out what car had got him in the end.

———➤———

The glitterpunk glamrock messiah peered across the shadowy expanse of the official vehicle of Decibel Jones's Grand Tour of Government Agencies. It was a kind of munted limousine, with a cavernous rear arranged so that the two passenger benches faced each other. Four oversize, oddly insectoid sunglass lenses reflected the sunlight flitting through tinted windows.

"Afternoon, gents," Dess said, and hoped to Christ his voice wasn't actually shaking as much as it felt like it was.

Silence. Cool, unfeeling, taxpayer-funded silence.

"That arse from the *Daily Mail* had a point, Mr. Price," one of the mystery men said finally.

"Indeed he did, Mr. Brown," the other said with a nod. "It's quite a little bit of egg on the face of the Commonwealth. Of the three of them, he's the only one actually *born* here, and he's what . . . Pakistani-Nigerian on his dad's side and Welsh-Swedish on the matrilineal? How does that even get past the first date? The girl was some sort of Japanese/Franco-Jewish muddle from Dublin by way of sodding Warsaw, but I gather she's out of the picture, and the other chap is a God-and-all-the-angels-save us refugee *Turk*. Of course, it's unclear whether they actually *want* his backing band, but I can't imagine they crossed the void of space on the strength of his solo album. Why our new friends couldn't have opted for a nice English band instead of this porridge of regrettably issued work visas, I'll never know."

"We *are* English, you tit," Decibel said with a sigh, glancing at his fingernails, which were much in need of a filing. He was used to this sort of thing. He was used to this sort of thing by the time he was twelve. He'd always had the kind of face that made people squint and try to think of a polite way to say, *Just what exactly are you, kid?* As though he might legitimately answer *rhinoceros* or *sea-cow* or *Aldebaran*. And that bit of genetic luck had saved him more than once. If they couldn't tell, they couldn't bring themselves to do anything about it. Usually. "So was my nan, if you want to have a squabble about it. Not that that stopped you lot. Some might say we were a pretty nice spread of humanity between the three of us. Two, now, but still covering a lot of territory. Rather ideal, if you ask me."

His escorts continued to ignore him. He was used to that, too. Ten million teenagers once screaming your name never meant one piddly thing to the authorities when you dressed like he did.

"It's certainly not a good look on us. Is he gay as well? Good Lord."

"I'm sitting right here," Decibel sighed.

Mr. Brown flipped through a folder on the seat next to him and continued on as though Decibel Jones were no more than a cupholder. "It's a bit unclear, but that's the youth for you these days. There's been the odd paternity suit, but none paid out. The three of them were always a bit suspect, if you ask me. All musicians are. Jones did say he was an 'equal-opportunity bisexual' in an interview right after *Spacecrumpet* hit, but his female fans got their feathers ruffled—or, rather, their parents did—at which point he said he was omnisexual, whatever that means, and then he seems to have made up a lot of words that give me a right headache. What in blazes is a 'boyfrack' other than an insult to the language?"

"Oort St. Ultraviolet shook loose all my combustibles," Dess answered with the gentle smile of having lost something wonderful. He picked at a loose stitch in the leather of the door handle. "And every time we touched, it was an endless earthquake in a faultless land."

Mr. Price gave him a disgusted look, which was impressive, given that his eyes were still invisible behind dark glasses. Correctly deployed, a curled lip can communicate entire essays on the effects of moral turpitude. "At least Mr. Çalışkan is married to someone the name of Justine in Cardiff with two kids."

"I don't see where you get off fretting about whether or not the end of the world is family-friendly. Do you really think the giant singing space aliens *care*? Every minute you spend sniffing around bedrooms past is a minute I'm not writing the song that saves the species, you know." The words went all sour in Dess's mouth, and for the first time in his life, he started to feel the black adrenaline of stage fright coming on. It was an old arrogance, one that still fit him around the shoulders, but was far too tight in the middle. He hadn't written a new song in four or five years, at least, and it hadn't been a good one then. This was a joke, a very unfunny joke, and whether he was the setup or the punch line, he'd no idea.

Humanity was doomed.

At last, the men in black deigned to speak directly to him.

"Obviously, we have a team of the best songwriters working round-the-clock to create a winning track for you, so don't worry about that."

Dess stared resentfully out the window at the passing lamp-posts. "Oh, I'm sorry, I thought they wanted *us*," he grumbled.

"Can't leave this sort of thing to the people who thought *Ultraponce* would be a smash, can we? You'll also be outfitted with the latest in audiovisual recording equipment. The emergency committee will run down the most important data to acquire, particularly in terms of propulsion, ship design, weaponry, cultural intel in terms of what that might tell us about their tactical predilections, once you arrive at Litost—which is, what, Price, sixty-five-hundred-odd light-years away? In the Eagle Nebula, we think. Now, unfortunately, we don't actually have any way of transmitting information at that distance, so unless you can sort out how *they* do it, it'll all be recorded and retrieved when you return."

"That is entirely unnecessary," said a new voice. Decibel Jones turned his head toward it, and his mind was genuinely delighted to see the roadrunner, or at least its projection, suddenly sitting calmly next to him in the back of the car. His body, however, reverted instantly to the primeval instinct to escape predators by jumping out of a closed shatterproof window into traffic. He bounced off of it and back into his seat, trying, halfway through, to look cool doing it and failing profoundly. The Esca's proboscis-lantern was cramped by the low roof. It did not seem bothered.

The alien spoke in the voice of Her Majesty Queen Charlotte I, having skimmed the mind of Mr. Brown and Mr. Price and found there an abject longing to have lived at a time when being in service to a monarch granted a great deal more leeway in the pummeling-of-peasants department.

"The Grand Prix is the most-watched event in the galaxy, more popular even than *Live from Aluno It's an Exceedingly Censored Comedy Night* and *The Yurtmak Present: Super Murderderby 9000*. It will be broadcast throughout the galaxy from the moment the human hopefuls land on Litost."

The agents glanced at each other, which was the only expression of shock and horror at the sudden appearance of an alien in their car that their training allowed.

"Ma'am," Mr. Brown began automatically, though the Queen was quite clearly not present. "I really don't see why we don't get a say in all this. Mightn't we have an audition process of some sort? Or at least present you with a more contemporary list of our own favorites? I quite like the new Parental Guidance album. Have you heard them? Real spit-and-shine boys. British boys. We could be proud to have those lads stand up for England . . . er. For the planet. Really, how *are* we meant to put 'gendersplat' on a personnel intake form?"

The Esca turned its oceanic gaze on Decibel Jones. "We presumed it meant he was like us. The Esca possess four genders: male, female, fugue, and clef. The male inseminates the eggs of the female, the fugue then ingests the eggs and provides nutrients over the period of gestation, and the clef prepares the birthing grotto by producing a genetic bath of virile fluid, song, and information-rich light generated by its *kuma*." The creature raised those large, gentle eyes to the lantern hanging from its head by a ribbon of glassy flesh. "At which point the infant offspring explode rather forcefully from the flutecage of the fugue and complete their development immersed in the aforementioned multisensory broth. It's all rather beautiful, even if the fugue does not generally survive. I myself am clef and took 'gendersplat' to mean Mr. Jones was also. Is that not correct, Mr. Jones?"

"Close enough, darling," Dess replied, shrugging, unable to beat back a deeply inappropriate bout of laughter. "What's the pronoun on that?"

"You do not have the embouchure to pronounce it, more's the pity. You may use 'she' for your convenience, as it contains both your limited binary terms. It is inaccurate, but English leaves us few options, as 'it' implies an inanimate object, which we are not, though you may be—that is, of course, the question at hand. Regardless, your input is neither needed, wanted, valued, nor at all welcome, gentlemen," the Queen's voice said out of the beak of a blue lantern-bird. "You may not believe it, but we are *helping* you. You are terribly lucky; another chaperone species might have actually let you audition your own performers. But the Esca are sensitive to the needs of lesser worlds, having only recently earned our place among the great ones. We have chosen. We have given you an advantage you may not deserve. Our ship awaits. Impatiently."

"Wait," Decibel Jones said with a sudden frantic horror. "Parental Guidance isn't so bad, really. At least they churn out albums every year. At least they're dependable. I'm . . ." He looked pleadingly into the eyes of the weird blue future, and even he had no idea whether he was pleading to be excused or to be told he was everything the world had ever needed. His voice dropped to a whisper. "You have to know I'm a has-been, if I'm even that. A barely-was, really. I'm . . . I'm the coyote. I make the most magnificent contraptions, and I always think this time, this time everyone will see how good I really am, but they only ever burn me up and leave me starving to death."

The roadrunner nodded kindly. "Mr. Jones, would it help if I told you that somewhere out there, so far away that, if you left today, your great-great-grandchildren would die before they ever got to try the sandwiches at the first available fuel depot, on a world of lava and oceans of acid orbiting a double star, there is a crystal balloon filled with intelligent gas named Ursula who knows all the words to 'Raggedy Dandy'?"

Decibel Jones's matinee eyes went soft and round. He grinned. "It does, actually."

"I am gratified," said the Esca.

Mr. Price and Mr. Brown were not finished. "This is rank madness, ma'am. Begging your pardon. You say we've got to sing better than some lizard-person from Planet X or we'll be destroyed. Fine. You say we've got no choice. Fine. But we're all human beings. We all stand to get blown to bits if this . . . this boy doesn't pull it off!"

"I . . . I need my band, though," Decibel said softly. He put his hand on the roadrunner's spindly knee. His fingers slipped through the projection and onto the black leather seat beneath. He stared at that for a bit, feeling strongly as though he'd had his fill of oddity for the moment and knowing there was only more to come in the pudding. "What's left of it, anyway. It's no good without Oort. And Robert. Fuck, I left Robert! Everything happened so fast. You've got to get him back for me or the whole thing's off."

"We would never book Decibel Jones without the Zeros. As I've said, we aren't monsters," the roadrunner assured him. "I am afraid, however, that forgetting your coat does not constitute an emergency. Every world has coats. You will survive."

"We are representatives of Her Majesty's government and the office of the Prime Minister and *Homo sapiens sapiens*, goddammit," spluttered the agents, half out of their seats though the car was still hurtling along. "We should be allowed to choose our own representatives. Our own warriors!"

"I am sorry, dear boys. But this is not a war. It is not about you, nor are you a part of it. Every child in the galaxy learns the truth about politics at their mother's proboscis. For lo, does not Goguenar's Third Unkillable Fact tell us: 'Though any species on any dumb gobworld may develop sentience (the poor bastards), no government ever does'? Think on it, Mr. Brown. Mr. Price."

Only meters from the Whitehall car park, Decibel Jones and the roadrunner dissolved into a very pretty swirl of magenta steam that smelled largely of fish and disdain.

9.

Diamond of Night

The first Metagalactic Grand Prix was held on the hot, vast, dark planet of Sagrada, homeworld of the Elakhon, the oldest function-ing civilization in the galaxy. They were ancient already when the first Alunizar had the grand idea of opposable nubs. They were yelling at gravity to get off their lawn when the Keshet were noth-ing but a twinkle in the space-time continuum's eye. In their smug middle age, they saw the fall of the great Empire of the Itrij, who started the whole trend of rings round planets just so that they could remember where they parked, and in the face of their glory, the Elakhon yawned.

Sagrada was chosen for the Grand Prix because, despite the Elakhon's mind-smearingly advanced military, they had stayed neutral in the Sentience Wars, as they did in all wars if they could possibly manage it without looking like a bunch of trustafarian art school seniors who weren't even going to bother with the group gallery show because, you know, the *system*, man. As Musmar the Night Manager, the greatest of all Elakhon rulers, wrote in his autobiography *Who Moved My Invincible Doomsday Device?* neu-trality was always a much more delicate operation than war or peace. Neutrality without a respectable bulge of firepower in your pocket was as good as telling the universe, *I am a helpless vulnerable fuzzy baby with a wet pink nose, please annihilate me at your earliest convenience.* But declaring neutrality from beneath an elaborate pillow fort of prosperity, military dominance, and a diverse entertainment industry made you look as enticing to all your postwar neighbors as a rich kid's lunch money. After all, it's always the fancy house that keeps its lights off and won't shell out for candy that's first pillaged on Halloween. (You might think that Musmar the Night Manager could not possibly have known about the regional human holiday known as Halloween, but by one of those many curious coincidences that comprise the only real evidence for a divine and wobbling hand in the design of the universe, some variant of Halloween is celebrated by every sentient species in the galaxy. There is, it would appear, something about the achievement of sentience that immediately fills the afflicted with the longing to become something else, something brighter, something wilder and more fearsome and morbid and covered in felt and glue and glitter, to escape into the mask of some other impossible life, and to afterward consume vast quantities of sweets.)

This carefully balanced neutrality was the second most significant factor in the longevity of their society. The first was Sagrada itself.

If you look up into the night sky, you will not see Sagrada. Not from Earth, not from Bataqliq, not even from Gakk-Gakk, Sagrada's largest and most socially toxic moon. The planet reflects almost none of the already miserly light from its shriveled, demented red sun. Rather, it greedily absorbs every photon until its surface shimmers with heat. That surface is wholly, utterly, indescribably black, from pole to pole, peak to peak, sea to shadowed sea. It is far blacker than coal or petroleum or the heart of a high school poet, far blacker than a mere total absence of light. It is surrounded by a mob of moons made of the same swarthy stuff, which block out starlight like bouncers at the hottest club in town. Sagrada is a study in darkness, an adoringly monogamous commitment to the gothic aesthetic. Beside Sagrada, ravens are as bright as parrots, widows are as flamboyant as cabaret dancers, and black holes suffer from crippling penumbra envy. For obvious reasons, in Elakhish, the word "black" and all its synonyms occupy the same linguistic niche as words like "cool," "sweet," "brilliant," "highly skilled," and "built like a brick shithouse."

In order to function in all this dimly red-rimmed darkness, the body of an Elakh is small, dense, nearly indestructible by anything that might be lying about, around, or in wait in the shadows, and mostly eyeballs. If a particularly melancholy child stacked a huge black ball of hard suet on top of a dainty black suet cone, gave it a lot of elegantly styled coaxial cable for hair, and stuck two enormous old-fashioned lightbulbs on it where eyes should generally go, they'd have a pretty solid approximation of an Elakh with which to horrify their parents. And yet, the Elakhon are widely considered to be a beautiful people. Their eyes quickly evolved to occupy nearly all their facial real estate, the better to devour any available light like starving beggars; their long, long lashes are powerful sensory organs like cat's whiskers, if cats could sense predators, weather systems, and other annoyances miles away. The hard, slightly greasy suet of their flesh is remarkably malleable, able to imitate a wide variety of limbs and other convenient protrusions. Imagine Sagrada in its earliest pastoral days, the Elakhon in their black villages, peacefully tilling black fields of midnight barley in the shadows of onyx mountains, carrying their tiny charcoal children to dig black clams from a black beach near a black sea, looking up into a sky so dark that it depressed itself, when the first alien starship cruised through their atmosphere and dumped a cargo hold full of state secrets onto their planet.

The Elakhon were able to advance technologically at a rate far faster than any other species to date because the rest of the galaxy used Sagrada as its personal high-end rubbish bin. What better place to hide something you didn't want anyone else to find than a planet so dark, it was practically invisible? The heavens rained down data-crystals, prototype vessels, unwanted furniture, spent weapons, drugs, bodies, treaties, vast sums of intergalactic currency, more data-crystals, and any commodities a governing body might want to remove from the market in order to create a sudden and profitable demand. Civilizations rose and fell and ran smack into walls, but the Elakhon went on, collecting, analyzing, improving, remembering.

In fact, in every language other than Elakhish, the word for the massively useful blackworld Sagrada translates to the Memory Bin, and to leave something there was to have it Binned.

After happily using everyone else's dirty little secrets to establish dominance over their sector and a continuous, lively civilization whose general tranquility Musmar the Night Manager famously attributed to the fact that light is a well-known irritant to all thinking, feeling beings, the Elakhon made the rather unexpected choice not to tell everyone to shove off and stop using their world as a collective toilet down which to flush any incriminating evidence the second the police come knocking. Instead, they became the great archivers and curators of galactic culture, hyperattentive beatnik librarian-salvagers combing every black inch of Sagrada for debris to analyze, label, and include in climate-controlled exhibits in the long, hexagonal, black granite halls of the Melanoatramentous Library, a palace of knowledge as large as Hungary, as well organized as a retirement home for executive assistants, and as well guarded as the meaning of life.

The first Metagalactic Grand Prix was held in the Melanoatramentous Library's Special Collections Room, as it contained the only stage with any real size or grandeur left standing after the war, and afterward, the whole thing could be immediately and efficiently Binned—a word which had come, over the millennia, to mean: "carefully, lovingly recorded for posterity by the Elakhon and preserved against the ravages of time, war, and the children's disrespect for history."

The winner of the first Grand Prix was an Alunizar ultratenor girl group called Glagol Jsem and the Death of All That Came Before, singing what would become the first interstellar smash single, "Maybe We'll Just Stay in Tonight Instead of Doing the Whole Intergalactic Civil War Thing, Wouldn't That Be Nice?" Five massive tubular sea squirts, protean tubes of golden and violet and scarlet veined flesh with a round, cilia-fringed siphon at each end that served as mouth, nose, face, cyclopean eye, and simple jet-propulsion system, undulated with passion. Their siphons, gaping with grief and ecstasy, hovered in the air above the weeping crowd, suspended in an orb of moonlit water rescued at the last possible second from their ruined homeworld. Naturally, it wasn't just the five of them. The Alunizars are the greatest practitioners of attachment parenting in the known universe. When an Alunizar reproduces, their children do not go out into the world to make their fortune and curse the urban dating scene, but simply *bud* from their mother or father, emerging out of their backs or their bellies as a complete and individual and rebellious bulge, but never leaving home. Each Alunizar is a colony, a generation ship, accumulated centuries of wisdom and experience and quick tempers and belligerent dinner conversations in one extremely lumpy, extremely lovely tube of glowing aquatic flesh. The death of a single Alunizar is the death of an entire nation, and the wars had gone on for years.

Glagol Jsem and the Death of All That Came Before sang in perfect bone-shattering five-thousand-part harmony, with the combined voices of their entire genetic lines, and they wept the rosy pink electricity generated by five thousand weaponized agony-ducts, and they performed the traditional Alunizar inter-dimensional two-step, which no foreigner had ever been allowed to witness before that moment in the black library, a dance half-way between Bollywood and Sea World, lit only by the biolumi-nescent fire of their tears and the transported moonlight of poor, far-off, still-smoldering Aluno Prime. At the climax of the dance there was a brilliant iridescent spiderweb of exploding light, and Glagol Jsem phased into a dimension where the whole notion of sentience had never gotten past committee, wriggled with delight, made a salacious gesture in the general direction she'd come from, and never came back.

They won by a single point.

10.

Don't Go Without Me

On a plush paisley couch in a large and tastefully furnished
suburban home outside London, Omar Caliṣkan, better known as
Oort St. Ultraviolet, the only one of the Absolute Zeros to make it
through fame and fortune and their opposites without a personality disorder, ambiguously employed royalty-collector, erstwhile
boyfrack, about to be ex-husband to a deeply alienated woman in
Cardiff, reasonably responsible father of two, and one-man band,
slept off the last bender of his marriage, the massive takeout vin-
daloo he'd ordered in, and through the invasion of Earth on a long
cool river of Ambien, absinthe, and regret.

Omar Caliṣkan, like all humans who found themselves asleep
at noon on a Thursday, spoke to the roadrunner in his dreams.
In the lounge room he shared with Justine and the kids, an ordinary lounge room belonging to an ordinary family, between the
well-worn blue-and-copper-striped couch they'd bought before
Nico was born and the black lacquered, vaguely Asian-styled end
tables they'd picked up for practically nothing when Justine's hotel
remodeled, the seven-foot-tall ultramarine fish-flamingo looked
far less alarming than it did in the real world, being only a dream.
The girls played on his mother's red and gold rug, squabbling over

a toy that looked very much like Planet Earth. Their cat, Capo, fortunate refugee from a local shelter and the birthday present he'd never outdo, hissed at the clouds over Australia. The ghost of his father sat in the leather recliner sipping a tropical drink from a glittery pink straw. And a giant bird was telling him he was going to have to save the world with his Oortophone. It was an ordinary dream for an ordinary man under severe emotional and dietary distress, nothing you wouldn't expect when you knocked back the acknowledged world heavyweight champion of sleeping pills.

"Remember, Omarcik," his father's ghost said in the dream, peering at his son over the sugared rim of his drink, just as he'd said when they were finally given permission to move into their flat in Manchester when Omar was six, just as he'd done every night that Omar had been sober enough to dream since. "We are ordinary English family now. When the world turns the wrong way round, ordinary is the best defense. Nobody bothers an ordinary Englishblokeman. Nobody makes a file on him, nobody asks him who his business is, nobody tells him come with me and don't make a fuss. If anybody bothers you, you just be so ordinary, *evet?*"

Omar stuck hard to his father's rules. Englishblokeman became a kind of untouchable superhero in his head, a man so normal, nothing abnormal could ever touch him.

And for a long time, nothing did. Faster than a well-ordered queue, more powerful than a muttered *tut*, able to walk right by police officers without being harassed. It's a bird, it's a plane, it's the fragile illusion of invulnerability inherent in being just like everyone else. No—it's Englishblokeman.

Even at the height of Absolute Zeros mania, Omar Calişkan saw nothing remotely out of the ordinary about his life. Oort St. Ultraviolet, for all his rhinestones and rouge, was simply the predictable outcome of practicing guitar more than multiplication

tables, more than talking to girls, more than looking old enough
to buy his own pints, of loving music like it gave birth to him, of
moving to London as soon as humanly possible, of doing time
in the club scene and at open mics and tolerating the person-
alities of people who could sing because they wanted to start a
band, but not like *he* wanted a band, of going home with random
artistically promising strangers because you never knew which
one was your future until you were ordering them ice cream at
five in the morning. Omar drew a straight line from their sold-
out world tour back and back and back to the day he'd started
school in Manchester, when the music teacher had set up every
instrument you could play in the band or orchestra in a big circle
on the thin, lowest-bidder gray carpet of the classroom that had
never been much better than concrete and let all the goggling
children go around and toot and twang and whistle and blow
on every one of them until they found something they liked or
shoved their hands in their pockets and said they only wanted to
play *football*, mum, and so refused to do the one thing that meant
anything in this world. Little Omar had approached them all with
enormous, worshipful dark eyes, the violin and the oboe and the
trumpet and the guitar and the drums and the trombone and
the clarinet and the cello, touching them as shyly as he would
one day touch Myra and Danesh and Justine, making them all
talk with his fingers and his mouth and his breath, and whirled
round to hug his parents desperately, whispering into their legs:
"But I want to play them all, Mum. I want them all. Don't make me
choose, I can't, I can't."

Everything that had happened to him afterward was the perfectly normal extension of that day, of that child. Even the trash-
fire that was *Ultraponce*, even rehab, even Justine getting pregnant
when they'd been so careful, even that horrible night in Edinburgh,

even their second daughter, just as unexpected and unimaginable as the first, even Justine's affair and his and then couples therapy on Tuesday nights for the rest of recorded time, and even working for fifteen years as a session musician like it was an office job, playing anonymously on other people's albums, other people's genres and styles and standards, in jeans and a T-shirt for someone else's band and only enough concealer to conceal his hangover, just as long as he was still playing. That was all fine. That was all normal. If you were writing a book about a failed pop group, that's how it would go. It was an ordinary story, the story of a thousand other musicians, the story of Englishblokeman. Omar felt safe inside that story, if not happy. If not much of anything else.

"Does it ever make you sad to only have one moon?" the roadrunner said, grooming Justine's long brown hair with its dark beak while she stared straight ahead into the nothing of dreams. "It would make me sad."

"It's the usual number, isn't it?" Omar asked, quite worried.

"Not overly," answered the fish-bird, and then Capo was pouncing hard on his snoring chest and licking him and kneading him until Omar Calişkan groaned himself awake. He opened his gunked-up eyes to find himself meeting the cool mouthwash-green feline gaze of the short-haired white cat that had stayed when his wife had not. Capo seemed to have brought company. Something was looming behind her. Two somethings. Two blurry somethings. Something neither cats nor daughters nor estranged wives nor curry deliverymen.

Something old. And something blue.

Omar's vision finally focused around the roadrunner and Decibel Jones. He had no idea what was going on, but it felt somehow inevitable. He had always been headed for something this unrelentingly, unforgivably stupid.

"Hiya, Oort," Decibel said as gently as he could under the circumstances.

The Esca cleared her long soft throat and asked in an eminently neighborly tone: "Do you think I might trouble you for a steak and a glass of milk? Whole, if you have it. But 2 percent would be fine."

11

1944

The Sentience Wars began and ended at a public bus stop.

Starships are frightfully useful and pleasant things, but not, strictly speaking, a must-have to get around town. Even the jankiest hand-me-down FTL-capable hoopty that couldn't pass a special relativity inspection to save its intrepid bridge crew is the neon-tracklit, fully stocked wet bar, stripper-pole-fitted superbass party limousine of galactic travel. It doesn't just get you from planet to planet, it gets you there in comfort, good company, high style, full of canapés, with a good buzz going, and looking like somebody to reckon with, which is very important to most young species trying to splash some cash around and make their mark on the nightlife.

But you could always take the bus.

In the early days of the universe, whether or not a habitable planet happened to have a wormhole nearby was as consequential to the eventual political map as whether or not a particular group of humans happened to be born on a continent with domesticable animals on tap or on an island the size of a doorknob where the only source of reliable protein was a semipoisonous tuber. Wormhole or no wormhole had just as little to do with the inherent superiority and/or possibly divine mandate of the smirking bastards who won the cosmic draw as cow or no cow, and yet, everyone everywhere will do, say, and stab nearly anything if it means they get to believe that they are blessed and their neighbors are basically toad-people.

Listen. The galaxy is a pretty damnably woolly place, and we've got a lot to cover in a short time if we're going to get through the whole war, but try not to forget about the cows. They're going to be important in a minute.

For the fortunate suns—the Utorak, the Keshet, the Voorpret, the Alunizar—the invention of space travel was as easy as building a big empty box and chucking it out of your gravitational well like a lucky shot Skee-Ball, straight into the 100-point hole waiting on the left-hand side of history. Everyone else had to grope around in the dark strapped to atomic bombs until they ran face-first into something other than more dark. It took the poor Inaki so long to invent FTL spaceflight that they actually skipped right over it and straight to medium-range instantaneous matter transportation, which is, in retrospect, much more practical for a species of parasitic fireflies so impossibly tiny that you can't believe they have enough room for an internal monologue, all clinging to the bodies of gentle-eyed, extremely itchy pachyderms on one perpetually cloudy rock in the constellation of Draco.

It wasn't fair. It wasn't equal. There wasn't anything to be done about it, since you could no more move an active wormhole than you could move a politician to pity. The distribution of wormholes and livestock with potential was an invisible lottery ticket, purchased long before the first primordial molecules got into the oozing business, which could only be won or lost, never exchanged, ignored, or tried again, and it determined the courses of lives beyond counting.

Now, these days, wormholes are galactic public transport:

taken for granted, run-down, underfunded, unsanitary, and unloved, crammed with commuters and pensioners, unruly young species and drunks who can't get home on their own power. The walls of any given wormhole are infested with indecipherable graffiti in ancient, impossible tongues, the only evidence of entire cauterized timelines and vast unspeakable intelligences trapped on the other side of the cohesion matrix, as well as whether or not Ursula Was Here. You are almost certain to get gum or vomit or causality or all three on your shoes.

For a few centuries there, the Alunizar got away with claiming to have invented wormholes. This allowed them to collect spectacular tolls, tax cargo, conduct random security checks and confiscate any particularly exciting items, and shut down routes for regularly scheduled repairs that, by innocent coincidence, happened to be popular with civilizations who objected to the Empire's habitual interstellar manspreading. Their story passed the smell test, at least: those blobby overgrown stained-glass sea squirts had been around longer than anyone except the Elakhon (whose entire society depended on never spilling anyone else's sociopolitical beans, no matter how piping hot and juicy), they did seem to know how to patch up the works when the system sprung a reality leak, and Aluno Prime was undeniably parked in just about the most advantageous spot in the whole quadrant, cozily adjacent to the N, F, R, L, and J lines. Besides, how else could they have colonized so much, so fast? Aquatic species have a notoriously tough time handling the usual technological transition from ruining their own planets to ruining whole solar systems. While mammals, insects, and enlightened lichen can zip about as long as they take along a few houseplants to micromanage the air cycle, the unlucky space whales of this universe have to sort out how to get a ship overburdened with the absurd weight of a personal ocean into high orbit. No matter the magnitude of science's triumph over nature, it will always be much easier to get a helium balloon to fly than a water balloon. Yet everywhere you went, the Alunizar were already there.

They lied, of course. Oh, how they lied! They lied through their *siphons*. They lied shamelessly, for generations, without a single ill-timed giggle to give up the game until the truth took out three Keshet frigates, six moons, a pulsar, an Alunizar mining colony as close to the border of Yüz space as they could manage and still get invited to holiday parties, a Yüz yacht containing the royal family on its way to their annual beach holiday, a bathtub containing Musmar the Night Manager (ancient ruler of the Elakhon, who was very surprised indeed to find himself naked and soapy and cold on the black floor of his ablution chamber) two of the Pleiades, a generous complimentary fruit basket provided to the Sex Pistols by Portobello Hotel in 1978, and the Inaki homeworld.

None of that makes the least bit of sense, naturally, because you've already forgotten the cows.

Up until that moment, the galactic scientific consensus wasn't too far off the human scientific consensus on the subject of wormholes, except that we thought they were purely theoretical, and everyone else got really irritated if they were closed for maintenance. A wormhole was a tear in the universe where space and time went to get well and truly hammered. They passed through every physical and temporal point simultaneously and dumped you out wherever the other end of the tunnel is, no worse for wear with only the *teensiest* bit of cancer. As long as you keep your arms and legs inside the vehicle, there's almost no danger of permeating the membrane of reality. In the drawing rooms of spacefaring society, the insectoids assured the silicon-based that the prehistoric Alunizar had probably done it with plain old explosives and almost certainly didn't know any more than anyone else except how to time a fuse.

They were wrong.

Despite their big lie, the Alunizar actually did know far more about wormholes than they were willing to share in mixed company. They had lived alongside them for the entire history of their soft and tubular race. They had used them to acquire an interstellar empire at a fabulously steep discount. They had tended and groomed and guarded the cosmic subway for thousands of years. They hadn't the first thing to do with inventing wormholes; it was the same pure imbecilic drooling luck that so many of the bloody things opened up just outside Aluno Prime's gravitational sphere of influence that dealt Europe a royal flush of luxury high-speed horses, butter-dispensing cows, jumper-shedding sheep, bacon-distributing pigs, and nonunionized donkeys, and Australia a full hand of fuck all.

You can't, after all, invent an animal. You can only domesticate it. It's all down to cows in the end, you see. Cows, and what wonders can be done with them.

The fact of the matter is, a great number of people have, for some time now, been merrily lobbing themselves both ways through the digestive tract of incomprehensibly ancient, infinitely unbothered beasts and paying handsomely for the privilege.

Life is beautiful and life is stupid.

The life cycle of a Quantum-Tufted Domesticated Wormhole (*Lacuna vermis familiaris*) takes place on a scale that beggars the imagination, kicks it while its down, and lights it on fire. Admittedly striking anatomical differences aside, of all the species in the known universe, they have the most in common culturally with the giant panda bear of Earth. They are large, slow, solitary creatures whose natural habitat is relentlessly encroached upon by the implacable advance of civilization, and, improbably, if you could ever see a whole wormhole all at once (which you can't), you'd find them just as chubbily adorable. They spend most of their time sleeping, can only consume a widely available but barely digestible substance that gradually poisons them, and respond to the process of reproduction, which everyone else finds pretty exciting, with little more than a vast, cosmic ennui. They can only mate and give birth at the heat-death of the universe, when all this expanding matter takes a long, hard look at its choices, peels out into a hard reverse, and rapidly compresses itself back down into a ball of white-hot everything, ready to reboot the Big Bang and start the long march of reality all over again, only this time without anyone ever inventing paper clips. The first thing that ever happens to an adorable baby wormhole is that it rather traumatically explodes, so it's hardly any wonder they're not terribly good at parties. Like kudzu roots, some small part of them remains forever in that continuous moment of detonating lava and life while the rest of them is flung into every part of space and time by the sheer physics-pummeling force of the beginning of everything. At which point the poor things are so tuckered out that they promptly lie down for a trillion-year nap.

You can only see a wormhole if it happened to fall asleep with its mouth open. Otherwise, being mostly composed of minimally corporeal time and space and entropy and memory with a sprinkling of platinum molecules and a dash of radioactive PTSD, they are perfectly camouflaged by the darkness of the interstellar void. They dream in sixteen dimensions. They breathe once a millennium. Their language is nothing but umlauts. They drift mindlessly through all that ever was or is or will be, drawn this way and that only by the smell of food that might flow effortlessly into their sleeping mouths.

The giant panda eats bamboo. The wormhole eats regret.

As anyone with a passing interest in self-help books knows,

new quantum realities are being formed all over the place, anytime some collection of hyperactive molecules decides between sushi and curry for dinner or whether to marry their childhood sweetheart or see what else the world has to offer or whether to sort out how to derive energy from chlorophyll or meat or both or neither. The universe is a very large and very complicated demonstration of having one's cake and eating it too. It sees no reason not to have it all. But most hyperactive molecules must proceed linearly along their own fork, unless they are a Keshet, only grazing the surface of other timelines as they yearn and brood and wonder what could have been, if only they had chosen the yellowfin sashimi, if they could have been satisfied with loving that one gorgeously familiar face, if they could now stand green in the warmth drinking down the sun. It takes energy for new roads to diverge in new woods, and no energy is spent with complete efficiency, without waste. Where wood has burned, there will be ash. The waste product of the constantly dividing multiverse is a fine, drifting mist of regret, and no wormhole has ever starved.

A handful of these gentle space yaks found Aluno Prime, a watering hole too good and too deep to ever leave. Two or three fell into a food coma so deep that their gaping mouths shut as they rolled on their sides, snoring soundlessly into oblivion. That's all. That's the reason behind the utter cultural and spatial dominance of the ooey, gooey Aluzinar. They screwed up and chose poorly so often; they were so majestically sad that they drew a herd of wormholes to them like the steam from a fresh pie levitating a snoozing dog toward the windowsill on *Mr. Looney of the Tunes.*

So what happened that day that whiplashed all those frigates and deep-space miners and moons and pulsars and Musmar's black bathtub and firefly-encrusted green elephants and Sid Vicious's complimentary Anjou pears?

One yawned.

A wormhole yawned in its sleep and the yawn ricocheted through a stack of realities like a snapped powerline, and suddenly everyone could see a new glittering gap in the sky and on the other side of that gap lay the far side of the galaxy, unexplored, untapped, unreachable by the usual party ships until that moment. On the other side lay the Sziv and the Voorpret and the Vulna and an intelligent twilit mega-hurricane called Hrodos and the Ursulas and the 321 and the Smaragdi and, far beyond even them, a small, watery, excitable planet called Earth.

Unfortunately, the Yüz thought the Alunizar had blown their royals out of the sky, the Alunizar were convinced that the Yüz had decided to push back their colonies for no good reason at all, a band of Keshet single-timeline-separatists took credit for the moons but blamed the frigates on the Slozhit, the Utorak and the Meleg had disputed ownership of the pulsar for generations and each assumed the other had finally gotten sick of messing about discussing things like adults, and the Elakhon quietly seethed about the theft of their long-dead emperor's bathtub but, in order not to compound the offense by dishonoring Musmar's philosophy of neutrality, simply started selling weapons to positively everyone. Half the Milky Way was already steaming by the time they encountered the meat of the other half, and the Sentience Wars progressed at record speed from confusion and posturing to, in technical terms, an intergalactic shitshow.

Thankfully, the Sex Pistols weren't really much for apples and pears anyway and never noticed anything amiss.

12.

Come on, I'll Give You a Flower

In the thirteen minutes and eleven seconds that elapsed between Oort St. Ultraviolet waking from dreams of his daughters growing up and refusing to visit at Christmas and the abrupt disappearance of Decibel Jones from the backseat of a gently used BMW 760Li, the entity known as the roadrunner built a ship capable of traveling at many times the speed of light, engaging in a mild spot of dogfighting, providing roomy accommodations with plenty of lunch, life support, and legroom for four, and making the most advanced human aircraft wet itself and crumple into a heap wondering just what had it been doing with its life.

Aerospace engineers around the world, take note.

The tall blue flamingo-fish reached up and scooped the gelatinous green hair accessory off her head like a woman removing an earring at the end of a long day. The alien presented the gummy flower to two of the three Absolute Zeros with obvious pride, though it was no bigger than a paper watercooler cup and parts of it were crusted over with tiny yellow and pinkish warts and all of it smelled like Brighton Beach at low tide.

"I require a substrate," chirped the Esca happily. "Are you terribly attached to your headphones?"

Oort St. Ultraviolet, deeply apologetic creator of the maddening earworm that was the current West Cornwall Pasty Company jingle, "Live and Let Pie," somewhat reluctantly handed over his bespoke Kuu & Co. oversize, overear, oversensitive headphones in the limited edition Phantom Pearl color scheme.

"I promise you, Oort," said the roadrunner with soothing protectiveness, "in terms of audiovisual equipment, anything you have down here, we can do better up there, and . . . well, everything else, too. It's not your fault. No one expects more from a species that still uses electric kettles."

Very carefully, the roadrunner slid her jellied barrette onto the left cup of the headphones and set it all down on Oort's coffee table. It wobbled there for a moment, then thin gluey tentacles shot out and covered the space where a human head was meant to fit with a fleshy semitransparent spiderweb. The mouth of the flower suckled at the air expectantly. The Esca poured a pint glass of whole milk directly into that almost obscene little polyp, then fed in a large, raw, well-marbled rib eye steak that Oort had fished out of the freezer and shoved into the microwave, whereupon the most piercingly awkward silence of his life descended as his estranged former bandmate and a giant feathered alien waited for the defrost cycle to finish.

"It's a kilo steak. I bought it to share with the girls on Saturday," Oort had mumbled sheepishly. "Cheaper than buying three." Capo meowed and glanced meaningfully at her empty food bowl. "It takes twenty minutes." He'd picked at his fingernails and prayed for death. "Sorry."

The phlegmy flower chewed the defrosted meat down, inch by inch, with obvious satisfaction.

"Lucky thing you had rib eye," the roadrunner mused, unsettlingly, in Oort's mother's voice. "We might have had to waste time popping down to the shop. Sirloin doesn't have the necessary fat content, you know. Fat's just the thing for spaceflight. Fat, and calcium."

"I should call Justine," Oort said suddenly. "The girls will worry—"

But the man *Rolling Stone* once called "Orpheus reincarnated as the holiday decor section of Debenhams" did not get to say what he wanted to tell his daughters or the wife he'd ignored in favor of a music studio far too many times, as things began to happen at an astonishing rate.

Razor-sharp metallic snowflakes erupted fractally out of the seaflower-headphone combo platter. Fluorescent black coral shot out of it like parachutes deploying. Those thin tentacles or stamens or vines or what-have-you shot out everywhere, grabbing whatever they could find and cramming it into a rapidly expanding mint-jelly maw. In went delicate glass sculptures from Baku, Paris, Lodz, Prague. Out burst pitted, rough red prongs that reminded Oort of the reef he'd snorkeled in the Maldives with Mark Ronson just before Mark, and the Maldives, died. In went his juicer, his espresso machine, his electric kettle, his microwave. The thing on his coffee table vomited forth ropy sapphire starfish-legs that wrapped around the table and gobbled that up too. The whole rubbish heap crashed to the floor, hauling in table lamps and the hallway chandelier after it. Tongues of spiral wire coral snatched his tablet projector, his wafer-screen television, his gaming rig, his wineglasses. The little crusty warts polka-dotting the flower's distended gullet detonated, covering the now more or less Volkswagen-size love child of the Great Barrier Reef and Oort's tastefully appointed suburban home in a swarm of what appeared to be yellow-and-fuchsia-striped fish. More polyps gushed out of the holes in the coral, some the same gummy jade color as the original, others in new and exciting wine pastille shades. Now their horrifying round mouths were ringed in a wild tentacular fringe, lurching down the hallway in search of pillows, linens, mobile phone chargers, and electronic readers.

Oort St. Ultraviolet watched in abject despair. All the physical evidence of his life on Earth was being torn to pieces and keel-hauled into the maw of a hungry space flower as though his marriage, his children, his stable work life, his healthy income and investments achieved through years of prudent selling out, and his study of good interior design had just been a long, long setup for a truly mean-spirited punch line. He'd no idea what to do. He'd seen their band's name at the bottom of the alien's list, even if, at the time, he'd thought it was a curry-induced dream. If Dess was here, he'd probably already drafted them into an army of two to save the planet. Dess would do anything you asked if you fluttered your eyelashes and told him he was good. And, Oort supposed, he would as well, only no one had fluttered anything yet. If he hauled off and told them to leave his things alone and get out, would that doom humanity? It had to be taken as a serious possibility. In the face of the wanton destruction of all he had ever held dear, Oort uttered a furious *tut* under his breath and, as that produced no result, gave up.

Oort barely escaped becoming one with the volcanic steak-fueled repo-beast. His beloved Oortophone was not so lucky. Ultraviolet watched it get sucked down into the biological sinkhole in total horror. In went the hallway mirror, a vase full of Venetian glass dahlias, and Capo's water bowl. It was slowing down now, but only because it was running out of fuel and room to maneuver. It reminded Oort suddenly of those little brightly colored pills he'd loved as a kid. You put them in a sinkful of water and in thirty seconds they swelled up into a big foam dinosaur you could play with. However, this was not a foam dinosaur you could play with. It was a bespoke late-model oversize, overhauled, overtorqued, guaranteed to work even in the most inhospitable environments Wearable Instant Short-Range Combat Shuttle in the limited edition Kaleidoscope of the Sea color scheme, 100 percent manufactured on Bataqliq by your ever-discreet friends at the Üürgama Conglomerate.

And it was almost finished.

Two mauve sea cucumbers shot out of the top of the infant ship and seized the gas range. Four tangerine anemones ripped down the roof, leaving them standing in a gaping sinkhole in the middle of his once-respectable neighborhood. Capo scrambled up his pant leg in a desperate panic, shrieking and leaving serious stab wounds in his calves. The Esca frowned, inasmuch as a beak like an upside-down boomerang can frown. She reached out one long, silvery-blue frond and inserted it directly into the shelter-cat's pink ear. Capo's eyes went wide; her pupils blew out. She didn't shriek again. Her claws retracted and Decibel caught her as she dropped like a rock off Oort's shoulder. Capo stared up at him, blinking furiously. Then she yawned.

The ship rose high above them now, a mass of living coral and understated style, swathed in translucent cerulean jellyfish-bells and swarming with every ounce of symbiotic life you could cram into a flying ecosystem the size of a blue whale.

The roadrunner trilled joyfully. Her eyes filmed over briefly, just licking the surface of their memories. "Your Uber has arrived!"

A hatch in the underside of the Üürgama Conglomerate Instant Short-Range Combat Shuttle that had, a moment ago, been a white leather couch, opened before them. Six carbonated gluco-amino exhaust ports ignited in the belly of the stern with a sound like overexcited jacuzzi jets, casting candy-cane-colored shadows on the ruins of a very nice place to live.

While Decibel Jones and Oort St. Ultraviolet still managed to stand next to each other long enough to do the occasional *Where Are They Now?* photo shoot, Danesh Jalo and Omar Calişkan had, in fact, not spoken for several years. Something about their never-completed third album, variously reported as having been titled *Absence Leaves the Tart to Wander, Shag and Bone Man,* or *Papa Needs a New Pair of Prudent Investment Portfolios.* Something about an autumn night in Edinburgh.

"Dess, *what* is going *on?*" shouted Oort St. Ultraviolet in the sudden quiet, unable to maintain an upper lip of any kind for another second.

"We're going to save the planet," Decibel Jones said in the voice that launched a thousand sexual awakenings. He slung his arm round his old boyfrack's waist. "I thought you'd want to sit in."

A moment later, all three of them, plus one white cat, ceased to occupy Planet Earth.

Remember that friendly, bouncing disco ball you were following? Hold on tight with everything you've got, because now that the band's back together, that shiny little minx is about to break orbit.

13

Everything Has Rhythm

The question has never been: Can you build cities?

Ants do that.

The question has never been: Are you capable of considering your own existence and getting kind of depressed about it?

Any animal in captivity does that.

The question has never been: Can you use tools?

Crows do that. Otters do that. Apes do that. Good Lord, everybody does that.

The question has never been: Can you perform complex problem solving?

Dogs do that.

The question has never been: Can you experience love?

Nobody doesn't.

The question has never been: Can you use language?

Parrots and dolphins and cuttlefish do that.

The question has never even been: Do you understand object permanence, can you recognize yourself in the mirror, do you bury your dead, do you bond emotionally with your young?

Elephants do all those things, and some humans definitely don't.

The only question is this:

Do you have enough empathy and yearning and desperation to connect to others outside yourself and scream into the void in four-part harmony? Enough brainpower and fine motor control and aesthetic ideation to look at feathers and stones and stuff that comes out of a worm's more unpleasant holes and see gowns, veils, platform heels? Enough sheer style and excess energy to do something that provides no direct, material benefit to your personal survival, that might even mark you out from the pack as shiny, glittery prey, to do it for no other reason than that it *rocks*?

Everything in the universe has rhythm. Everything pulses to a beat laid down by the Big Bang. Everything feels the drumline of creation from star to sex to song. But can you *make* that rhythm? In order to create a pop band, the whole apparatus of civilization must be up and running and tapping its toe to the beat. Electricity, poetry, mathematics, sound amplification, textiles, arena architecture, efficient mimetic exchange, dramaturgy, industry, marketing, the bureaucratic classes, cultural critics, audiovisual transmission, special effects, music theory, symbology, metaphor, transportation, banking, enough leisure and excess calories to do anything beyond hunt, all of it, everything.

Can everyone else trust that, if you *must* declare war and wipe out half a quadrant, you'll at least write a sad song about it?

Yes?

Well, even that is not quite enough.

Are you kind enough, on your little planet, not to shut that rhythm down? Not to crush underfoot the singers of songs and tellers of tales and wearers of silk? Because it's monsters who do that. Who extinguish art. Who burn books. Who ban music.

Who yell at anyone with ears to turn off that racket. Who cannot see outside themselves clearly enough to sing their truth to the heavens. Do you have enough goodness in your world to let the music play?

Do you have soul?

Air

Go sing it like a hummingbird
The greatest anthem ever heard.
—"Heroes," Måns Zemerlöw

14.

Vampires Are Alive

Mira and Oort were wrong, by the way, on the night they met
Decibel Jones and discussed the nature of extraterrestrial culture
and determined the course of their entire lives via scoops of pistachio, coconut, and mango gelato. There are shy, nerdy predator
scientists. The Things of Thing-World will, very occasionally, ven-
ture beyond the opportunities afforded to them by 24/7 slaughterparties and exploding blood.

Scorpions do go to the moon.

Take, for example, the Yurtmak of Planet Ynt, a deranged gut-
ter ball of gas-jungles and carnivorous rivers hurtling through the
beer-bottle-strewn lanes of the gravitational bowling alley that is
septuple star system Nu Scorpii. Improbably, the body of an adult
Yurtmak is basically the same as a human's, if slightly a snailier
color and capable of producing a pernicious pheromone from its
nipples that has an effect on the IQ of any foreign visitor similar
to the effect of a folding chair on a professional wrestler. Unfortunately for all of us, they also have heads. The head of a Yurtmak
can best be described as what you would get if a hippo mated with
a chain saw and produced something you wouldn't let into public
school even with a hat on, who then went on to have an unhappy

affair with a spiny puffer fish, whereupon, at the height of a particularly pustulant, turgid puberty, the resulting grandchild's face
exploded. The Yurtmak are obligate carnivores for whom murder
occupies the same cultural space as football does for humans in
a World Cup year, complete with merchandising, celebrity players
followed by hordes of fans, and families gathering of a Sunday to
bond over the spectacle, maybe hitting the backyard to show off a
few trick shots for the kids.

Yet the famed philosopher and beloved children's author
Goguenar Gorecannon was Yurtmak. Even as a juvenile, her carnage was workmanlike and derivative at best, leaving her out-
cast, underemployed, and unpopular with men of her peer group,
despite the best efforts of modern Ynt-wide dating services.
Goguenar took this reasonably well, for a Yurtmak. Carefully
avoiding major organs, she fondly stabbed her mother and father
good-bye and vanished into the wilderness. Eventually, she settled
down, built herself a traditional heartvalve-hut in the depths of
the fluoro-chloro forest of Yllir and buckled down to invent a way,
any way, to get off that rock full of socially challenged chain-saw-
faced hooligans.

That is what Mira and Oort forgot, having been, if not popular,
always cool. No matter how mad, bad, and dangerous to know a
civilization gets, unto every generation are born the lonely and
the uncool, destined to forever stare into the candy-store window
of their culture, and loneliness is the mother of ascension. Only
the uncool have the requisite alone time to advance their species. And so it was that, eventually, between drawing meatship
schematics in the dirt and dreaming of a world where she didn't
hate literally everyone, the shiest and most sensitive of Yurtmaks
began to plan the most ambitious massacre in the history of the
galaxy: the murder of stupidity.

The fateful weapon? A large-print, mildly venomous picture book for which the general galactic population feels a level of affection and tender attachment that falls somewhere between Newton's *Principia Mathematica* and *Goodnight Moon*. *Goguenar Gorecannon's Unkillable Facts* contains 99.9 percent pure reliable and comprehensive laws of the universe as observed by an underachieving socially anxious mutant murderhippo and is considered to be as essential to a healthy, balanced childhood as hugs, nightlights, and cellular division. It is nearly impossible to forget one of Goguenar Gorecannon's Unkillable Facts. The gently envenomated pages produce flashes of temporary but breathtakingly colorful pain as you turn them, so that the simple, heartfelt prose is charred into the reader's sense-memory with incredible efficiency.

This is Goguenar's Second General Unkillable Fact: *For everything that exists, somewhere in the universe, there is a creature that eats it, breathes it, fucks it, wears it, secretes, perspires, exhales, or excretes it. If you want to argue with me on this one, consider the Brick-Breathing Beast of Ballun 4 and shut your cakehole.*

You have already heard the First General Fact: *Life is beautiful and life is stupid.* It goes on to add: *You can only ever fix one of these at a time, and wouldn't it be nice if anyone could agree on which one is the bigger problem?*

Given her sales numbers, Goguenar Gorecannon, Assassin of Ignorance, is, to this day, idolized among the Yurtmak throughout the seven slaloming stars of the Nu Scorpii system as the greatest serial killer ever to play the game.

Perhaps, if humans had been able to read Goguenar Gorecannon and the First General as a bedtime story like everyone else, they wouldn't have had such a terribly tough time figuring out the whole trick with interstellar spaceships.

15.

The Ship Is Leaving Tonight

Every civilization comes to the creation of an iconic ship design in their own way and in their own time, just as methodically and tenderly as a planet comes to the configuration of its favorite species. It simply cannot be rushed and, once arrived at, is rarely abandoned. Ask any child to draw a house, and though there may be variations in chimney placement or door shape, it will be recognizable to anyone with as many limbs and lobes as that child *as* a house. A ship, lovingly crafted by the gravity, raw materials, anatomical pluses and minuses, architectural traditions, and functional-to-fabulous score of its species at the time of mass driver invention is no less cozy and relaxing than the drawings of a house made by the innocent hands of untraumatized juveniles.

It is, therefore, entirely impossible to mistake one world's fleet for another. No matter how tactically advantageous such camouflage might be, it's just not *comfy*, so why make things more unpleasant for everyone? One would never confuse the soft stacked bubbles of an Alunizar Tuftship for the single hollowed-out moon-gem of an Utorak Octahedro-Sloop or the living wicker-ball of a Keshet Chlorophrigate for the classic silver saucers of the Smaragdi. And no one could ever see an aggressively colorful coral reef floating in space and not know that the Esca had come to town.

The one vehicular commonality among all the millions of spacefaring species past, present, future, and Prefer Not to State is that it is easier, cheaper, and more fun to grow than to build. This is what Goguenar Gorecannon discovered in the carbonated shadows of the fluoro-chloro forest of Yllir as she tried to invent a way out of loneliness, and it led to both the impressive horror-tonnage of the Yurtmak Meatship and that marvelous Second General Unkillable Fact: *For everything that exists, somewhere in the universe, there is a creature that eats it, breathes it, fucks it, wears it, secretes, perspires, exhales, or excretes it.* Somewhere on Ynt, there was a mammal the size of a convention center, stuck taxonomically between a bear and a crocodile, the decomposition of whose fresh corpse produced the exact type of gases necessary (when combined with the electrostatic ion acid-sap of Yllir trees) to propel the entire disgusting mass of itself into orbit. Somewhere on Earth is an insect that excretes a golden antibacterial ooze that also does a splendid job sweetening your tea; a terribly picturesque tree whose bark will fix your malaria right up; and a large four-legged, two-horned mammal whose reproductive system dispenses ice cream, brie, and buttercream frosting.

But somewhere on Bataqliq was an invertebrate coral polyp who, when combined with the profit-motive of the Üürgama Conglomerate Research and Development Bog, could digest a sudden overdose of fat, iron, riboflavin, calcium, and whatever else was unlucky enough to be within a roughly six-meter radius, and crap out a spaceship. And, like overbearing parents pressuring their introverted, artistically inclined children into becoming rich doctors who jump the karaoke queue, the Esca managed, with a little positive reinforcement and an orgy of gene-splicing, to railroad their local bioluminescent moon-jellies into inhaling stellar radiation through their translucent bells and exhaling a healthful oxygen-nitrogen mix, their version of sea cucumbers into ejaculating explosive saltwater plasma at any nearby enemies, their brand of furry brine shrimp into eating space debris and vomiting defensive shields, their six-eyed mussels into filtering solar energy and converting it to usable propulsion, schools of something very like overemotional clown fish into flushing bright green in the presence of foreign long-range radio waves or working FTL drives, and, perhaps most impressively for an aquatic creature lacking anything like the proper glandular setup, their freshwater starfish into sweating gravity.

For an Üürgama Conglomerate Wearable Instant Short-Range Combat Shuttle, the trip from Earth to the moon took approximately the length of time necessary for the roadrunner to explain all this to her cargo of aging rock stars, look puzzled at their response, and ask: "What do you mean nothing on your planet excretes spaceships?" The "small ambassadorial vessel docked in lunar orbit" loomed up outside a porthole punched in the fluorescent coral wall at "What," drew closer at "planet," and by the time of the question mark, they could see nothing but the massive bulk of the Esca frigate.

If their shuttle was a nice reef in the Maldives, the real interstellar cruise ship was the Great Barrier Reef touched by the drunken god of space, time, and saltwater aquariums. High above the dark side of the moon floated a hypercolored goulash of coral only slightly smaller than Sardinia, studded with all of the above. The unfiltered light of Earth's familiar yellow sun sparkled on the electric blue and sizzling pink bells of jellyfish who had clearly cleaned their plates at every supper. They were absolutely massive, encasing the entire reefship in a protective barrier of neon mesogleastic skin, their tentacles clustering beneath the craft like a sloppy Christmas bow, ready and eager to dock with any vessel secreting a friendly venom formulation.

On the starboard flank of the ship, in pristine, enormous English letters, a swarm of phosphorescent sea worms spelled out the name of the great Esca interstellar ship: *Cake in the Rain.*

The roadrunner trilled joyfully in the distinct tones of a movie trailer voice-over. "Look, friends! It's not *such* a big, scary galaxy out for blood! We respect your primitive culture so deeply that we have named an entire reefship in your honor! You see, even if the song of your people falls flat, we will carry on the best of you into the universe's promising future!"

Oort St. Ultraviolet took a breath to say something about the utter and complete nonsense of the entire London Aquarium hanging out on the unfashionable end of the moon with the most rubbish lyric in history blinking on and off on its side like a broken pub sign and demand, once again, that someone explain the last twenty minutes to him, but slowly this time, and with short words. But before he could turn that breath into words, a gulping sound, halfway between a champagne bottle opening and an octopus-sucker latching on, popped their ears painfully as the shuttle corked itself into the mother ship's mollusk-encrusted cloaca and the air lock began to equalize the pressure between the two ships. On the wall of the shuttle, the encorallated remains of Oort's microwave display counted down helpfully in large blue numbers.

On the other side of the jelly-glass docking hatch they could see, improbably, impossibly, a hyperactive red panda jumping up and down and waving his paws at them.

"That is Öö," said the blue flamingo. "He is our Mandatory Keshet and my extremely best friend. You will probably like him better than you like me. Everyone does. I accept that."

The microwave numbers ticked down slowly. There was nothing to do but wait until the next insanity rushed in with the airflow.

Decibel tapped his foot awkwardly. "You look great, Oort. Er . . . em. Still teaching?"

"I have two kids, you arse," Oort replied.

You couldn't ever really get mad at Dess. He didn't *mean* anything by not being able to retain information that didn't concern himself, music, sex, movies, or, bizarrely, Oort had found one night on the tour bus to Dublin, nineteenth-century literature for more than an hour or two. Especially when he smiled sheepishly and dragged that million-watt focus back onto you. That sheepish smile killed him every time. Oort used to find it endearing and even enviable—Decibel Jones always lived in the moment; Omar Calişkan always lived in an uncertain future. Mira, he supposed, had always lived in her own head and allowed others to visit once in a while. With advance notice. And extensive decontamination protocols.

"Excuse me, babies," said the roadrunner, in what both of them instantly recognized as the voice of their old manager, Lila Poole. "But you gotta supper up before a show. How many times have I told you? I swear, you can lead a punk to stardom, but you can't make 'er *eat*."

The Esca held up one of Oort's much-used white lacquered tea trays, the handles of which were now fully colonized by vermilion brain coral. On it lay three glass saucers, and on each one of those sat two servings of something that looked a lot like a very expensive mushroom, something that looked like a squashed licorice Allsort from the bottom of the bag, and something that looked like a cappuccino, if the barista had won several prizes

for latte art but had an unfortunate seizure while drawing a qua-
dratic equation in your milk foam.

"This is some hard-core, triple-X, keep-it-in-the-back-room-
under-a-curtain, *Alice in Wonderland* action is what this is," Decibel
said with total delight. "Is it lunch?" His hand was already halfway to one of the mushrooms. That was the power of Lila Poole's
indefatigably upbeat boardroom-mum North Country voice. If Lila
said to do it, it was good for you, good for the band, and probably
good for humankind at large. And it had been so long. A feeling of
oceanic calm he hadn't felt in years descended over Decibel Jones.
Someone else was taking care of the details. Someone else was
handling logistics. Thank Christ.

"I really, *really* think we need to have a serious discussion about
food allergies before we start eating space-Allsorts," Oort fretted,
but he too was under the spell of their old Lila-fueled agreeable-
ness. "Because peanuts are nothing compared to what, I presume,
grows on some artisanal asteroid on the underside of the universe.
Do you cats have an MHRA? FDA? Anything?"

"Don't whine, kittens. It's not lunch. Think of these as the jabs
for your Pan-Asian tour—there's your hep A, there's your hep B,
and there's your typhoid vaccine. Not everybody you'll meet is
as conveniently mnemonopathic, oxygen-breathing, and gravitationally compatible as your girl Friday here. The mushroom's
actually a dormant fungal agent that will infect your brain stem
with a pretty laid-back strain of Yoompian encephalitis—"

"Whoa, whoa, whoa!" shouted Dess and Oort. They leaped
back as though the tea tray were full of spiders and credit-card
bills. Decibel tried to recover quickly, telling himself that he really
ought to have gotten over any squeamishness with regards to
alien biological compounds back in Croydon. But it was instinctive, as deep as dirt.

"Take it easy! Jesus Christ, you gotta learn to trust a little! You'd think I'd threatened to wipe out your whole planet! Ha-ha, my little joke. They're all completely safe, I promise. Look, my whole job is getting you to Litost in one piece and ready to shine, so I wouldn't hurt you for love nor money nor sociopolitical advantage. Friends, Decibel, Oort, lend me your ears! Only speaking languages you've actually learned is a sign of a healthy mind. Where's the fun in that? Once your cute wee antibodies get a load of Yoompian encephalitis, they'll start working like the rent's due *tonight*. You know how your nose gets all snotty and your throat swells up when you have the flu? Well, turns out, as long as you're carbon-based and keep your brain on the inside, the body's natural immune response to this is to produce a kind of linguistic acid reflux that blows out the bits of your brain that insist on having to conjugate and decline and punctuate things before it can understand them like cheap subwoofers. Doesn't work on the Yoomps, though, poor sods. They're *pretty* resentful about it. You haven't seen anything until you've seen potbellied plesiosaurs trying to speed-read through sixteen local phrase books at once. Oh! You two are now officially allergic to penicillin. That shit clears the infection right up. Right. So. The Allsorts is just gonna paste in some of the Ursulas's junk DNA and mutate your lungs into being a *bit* less closed-minded when it comes to respiratory partners, and the coffee is just a caffeine jolt to your inner ear with a nice foamy agile-gravity agent so you don't barf, drift off, or explode when we land. Thank the Yüz— it's mostly their toenails. We share up here, you know? Makes it a homier galaxy for everyone. Plus, if you don't open source your assets, we quarantine your planet and any further attempts to holiday outside your system will be met with big, big cannons. I mean, giant. Huge. Still! It's all right, isn't it? Couple of bites and a slurp and you're ready for anything. It's like Goguenar's Fourth General

Unkillable Fact says: 'Everyone's always saying love is the element that binds the universe together, but that's a load of bollocks; it's convenience. All things, from evolution to municipal sanitation to marriage to the Big Bang to diplomacy to the distribution of shops in urban centers, trend toward the most convenient outcome for the greatest number of lazy bastards, because the inconvenient stuff ends up alone without any friends and a foot growing out of their head and who has the time?'"

"This is disgusting," Oort Ultraviolet snorted.

"This is *amazing*," Dess whispered. "Much less invasive than Heathrow customs, anyway."

Oort's microwave chimed. Their docking procedures had finished defrosting. A cheerful blue popcorn kernel made of asterisks signaled the completion of the decompression cycle.

"You know I'd never hurt you," Mira's throaty voice came pouring out of that dark alien beak.

"Hey," said Oort quietly. "Don't. You don't have to do that."

"Do what, baby?"

"Talk like Mira. Or Lila. Or my dad or Dess's nan or anyone."

"Do you not enjoy it? Does it not put you at ease?"

"No. Just be normal. Just be yourself. Just be . . . whatever passes for an ordinary sort of bloke where you come from. Like me, see? Decibel can swan about, and, well, if you'd ever met her, Mira could make eyes at you and turn you to jelly in an instant, but I'm just Omar. I like music and football and a laugh, and half the reason the band lasted as long as it did is that I'm so easy to get along with that those two only ever had each other to pick on. It's fine, we don't need to be at ease. This isn't an *at ease* kind of gig. And honestly, it's really, *really* creepy."

The bird's fishy eyes narrowed. "You don't really like football. I can see it in your cerebral structure."

"But I *want* to like it, and that's just as good in the end. Just . . . be the roadrunner. Be like me, and when he starts up being Dess again, which he will, you and I can go smoke a ciggy together and make fun of his accent. Deal?"

"Deal, Mr. Ultraviolet."

The air lock released, a seven-foot-tall blue bird punched a gold-plated starfish, and Decibel Jones and the last of the Absolute Zeros stepped from obscurity onto the biggest stage in the universe.

16.

I Am a Real Boy

The nineteenth Metagalactic Grand Prix was held on Pallulle, the Smaragdi homeworld.

It was the first time a species who did not fight in the war, on account of their having been minding their own business at the time, toddling about with endearing hesitance on their own moons, and not bothering anyone except the moon-bears, attempted to sing their way into the upper echelons of galactic society.

Contrary to popular opinion concerning the desirability of getting in early on Alpha Centauri real estate development, Pallulle is the nearest planet to Earth that wouldn't *entirely* murder any human being who set foot on it. At the very least, you'd have time to get a nice shark's heart sausage in at one of Blue Ruutu's finer bistros before the low-gravity, high-pressure atmosphere and the global, rather well-founded cynicism on the subject of strangers started rather dramatically forcing blood out of the ends of your hair. Some forty light-years away in the constellation of Aquarius, Pallulle revolves around an ultracool blue dwarf star that humans have designated TRAPPIST-1. The Smaragdi, however, call their pale, minimalist sun Lagom, a word that means, in their exceedingly specific language: "a spouse who habitually withholds affection but comes through with a squeeze when you really need them and always pays the bills on time." Pallulle itself means: "the parent who gives and gives, but it is never enough for their ungrateful children, who will probably never amount to anything, anyway."

Among the Smaragdi, self-deprecation has been refined into an art. You have not truly embraced the possibilities of intergalactic life until you have awkwardly nibbled vapor-cheese and drunk platinum wine at a stand-up modesty show on Pallulle. It is a cold crystal place covered in cold crystal oceans and warm crystal people.

At least it was.

Because Lagom is never much in the mood for the whole sensually nurturing solar warmth gig, Pallulle is a semihollow world. If you were to stand on the opal-crusted peak of Mt. Ailinin, far from the lights of the great Smaragdi cities, and look into the sky, you would see, just before your eyelashes started bleeding, what the ancient Smaragdi were doing while life on Earth was just sorting out whether two cells could ever *really* be better than one. Even the Alunizar were astonished when they careened drunkenly into this little world of grotesque monsters surrounded by engineering's answer to the Sistine Chapel. (Unfortunately for them, the Smaragdi seemed to have been created in a lab for the express purpose of scaring the salt water out of an Alunizar. A Smaragdin looks very much as though someone built the most unnecessarily elaborate set of eighteenth-century Spanish plate armor out of bleached ivory and quartz, gave it a head of blue-white hair like a 1970s shampoo commercial, stretched the whole thing out to nine or ten feet like particularly stern and judgmental taffy, then thought it might be a *bit* intimidating and painted a bit of pastel green and lavender on the joint-blades for a more festive spring look. The overall effect would seem quite beautiful and haunting to a human, but to a short, Technicolor invertebrate Alunizar, they look like the devil's own skeleton.)

Pallulle is snugly encased in Old Ruutu's Bindle: a cross-hatched topiary of translucent solar rods designed by the classical poet-engineer Old Ruutu to catch Lagom's emotionally unavailable light, beef it up a bit, and direct it usefully to the most inhabited parts of the surface. The glaciated surface of Pallulle was suddenly polka-dotted with pools of Ruutu-blessed artificial alpine climate full of silver ferns, blue-gray orchards heavy with gin-fruit, and liquid oceans in which the neon-blooded *suflet* shark swims free. The name of Old Ruutu is, among the Smaragdi, spoken with an awe equivalent to Jesus Christ and Nikola Tesla borrowing Buddha's tandem bicycle for a quick Sunday ride through Shakespeare's back garden. On Activation Day, every city on Pallulle scrambled to rename itself after him, which caused a great deal of confusion, upset feelings, cancelled family reunions, Ruutu absolutely forbidding anyone to do any such stupid thing as it was *no big deal, I was up there anyway, might as well do a spot of DIY while I've still got my health, you know if you have someone in they'll only rip you off, and besides, you'd all do the same for me, anyway it's a bit rubbish, I was in a rush,* two regional wars, and a small but feisty economic crisis until it was decided that everyone was pretty, they all loved the old man equally, and there was quite enough Ruutu to go around and the mapmakers would just have to seek out anxiety medication. Hence, on Pallulle, you will find no London, Paris, Vlimeux, or Alun, but only Blue Ruutu, White Ruutu, Little Ruutu, New Ruutu, Ruutu-by-the-Sea, Dirty Ruutu, Broke-down Ruutu, Backwoods Ruutu, and so on and so forth.

Controversially, the twenty-second Metagalactic Grand Prix

was held in Dirty Ruutu, the Smaragdi answer to Prague—once the capital of a great empire, torn apart by war, religion, vanished industry, and tourists who know in their hearts that it's not wrong to get so phenomenally plastered that you punch a police horse because everyone *knows* horses vote Tory, just so long as you do it while ignoring some of the most sublime architecture in the universe. The general idea was that, whether or not the Yurtmak turned out to be sentient, it would be rather poor form to rub their alleged noses in the cosmopolitan delights of Blue Ruutu and then send them home full of envy and the slow, wistful poisoning of a farmboy's dissatisfaction with his pigs after he has seen palaces. Even if they ended up having to roast the poor things shortly afterward, it just didn't seem very *nice*.

No one expected much of anything out of the Yurtmak in the way of danceable pop hits. The Utorak had discovered their world by accident and immediately wished they hadn't. The first officer on a deep-space fishing boat, hunting the vast, delicious, and deadly *zabok* crabs that scuttled through the galaxy suckling at hidden tide pools of dark matter, picked up the faint broadcast of what their xenothropologist surmised was a folk festival emanating from a little planet by the name of Ynt. Had the Utorak then required all *zabok* trawlers to carry accredited translators on board as they do now, the poor Utorak commander would have known right away that the folk festival in question was the Yurtmak Super Murderderby 9000 and very likely turned right around and headed toward the safer embraces of giant dark-matter crabs in the lonely depths of the void. The Yurtmak were clownishly violent, disgusting to look at, in possession of a language that sounded like someone enthusiastically smashing pots and pans together in a hot tar pit, and hadn't even gotten around to inventing agriculture before somehow, bafflingly, managing spaceflight.

They were exactly the sort of species the Sentience Wars had raged across the known cosmos to prevent from getting too big for their interstellar trousers.

But rules are rules. No blowing up the horrifying deathgoblins next door without a bit of song and dance first.

The Sziv won that year. Being a group intelligence comprised of hot pink algae genetically fused with nanocomputational spores, the Sziv never formed rock bands per se. They sent the same supergroup to the Grand Prix every year, some 60 percent of their species, decanted into artful vases and simply called Us. They sang by pheromone, a crescendo of infectious hormones that maddened the mating instincts of every species in the Dirty Ruutu Flophouse and Grill—a vast, glittering, state-of-the-art performance arena seating over one hundred thousand—until the slightest whisper sounded like a techno-erotic laser light show of the soul, at which point Us spilled out of their vases in an undulating rosy wave, spun up into a towering spiral of velvet sparkling life, and sang an ancient Sziv folk ballad called "Love Is Easy When You're a Hive Mind" coupled with a thumping, thrusting, subwoofer-slaughtering beat, dispersing on the downbeat, slamming back into their magenta spire on the upbeat, and bringing the house all the way down.

Iatagan Yoomp, Murderderby champion and celebrated torch singer, walked across the spotless frozen floor of the Flophouse dressed in a traditional Yurtmak lung-gown, her dripping, pustulant face hidden beneath a black veil so long, it wrapped twice around the stage. She held something in her arms. The lights turned red and heavy and dim. A slow drum pulsed. Iatagan tore open the veil with her claws and revealed her instrument: the skeleton of her mate, cleaned and polished and hollowed so that when she wrapped her arms around him and tenderly kissed his fangs, her breath filled up his bones and emerged from his rib cage as a savage and anguished melody called "Death Is a Wish Your Fists Make." *It's not what you think,* went the chorus, *don't be afraid. To love is to slaughter, to slaughter is to love, but by the rocks below and the rocks above, you don't do either one unless the other guy's really into it.*

At the conclusion of the song, which went on to become a popular choice for wedding DJs, Iatagan set herself on fire and burned to death in front of everyone with a smile on her face, waving delightedly to her fans as the audience threw flowers into her pyre and watched them sizzle up into the heavens.

The judging was not quick. A hundred thousand dinners were ordered in from neighboring Ruutus. In the early hours of the next morning, it was decided, by a very slim margin, that Iatagan Yoomp and all her people were undeniably alive, intelligent, and possessed of a complex inner life, especially since the Utorak had really phoned it in that year with the entirely forgettable "Shall I Compare Thee to a Dark-Matter Crab?" Yet, if not for Iatagan Yoomp's sacrifice, the galaxy's children would never have grown up under the not-terribly-gentle ministrations of Goguenar Gorecannon's Unkillable Facts, the twentieth of which, penned for the occasion of the twenty-third Grand Prix on Ynt, is: *No one is ever really satisfied with what they've got, look at that skinny bastard Old Ruutu, he heated up his whole planet like a leftover takeaway, and he still wasn't really that happy, if you ask me. People are mostly happiest when they think they're just about to get the thing they want most.*

Before and after, they're all monsters.

17

Every Way That I Can

"Hi! Hi! HiHiHulloHi!"

Oort St. Ultraviolet and Decibel Jones, individually and collectively, assumed the time-traveling red panda called Öö leaped up as they boarded, made a high-pitched squealing noise, and careened over backward waving his paws in the air because he was just so feverishly excited to meet them. However, among the Keshet, this is a cool, eminently diplomatic, even standoffish greeting. Down to the soles of its cells, a Keshet is a constant atomic, temporal, and emotional ball-pit into which an infinite army of cake-addled toddlers jumps, over and over, and it is every single one of their birthdays, forever.

And he wasn't happy to see them at all.

"Öö! ÖöÖöÖö is me and you are them and we are all—but whoooooooa waitwaitstopwait are you *not* Yoko Ono? Whatwhathowwhat the fuck, Al? I gave you a picture of her and everything! Do all primates *still* look the samesameidenticalsame to you? We *practiced,* Al! We practiced all the way here! It was so boring!"

"Al?" Dess asked. "You're not Al. Al runs a chip shop on the corner. Al fixes the furnace. You're the roadrunner."

"That's what *you* call me, and look, Dess, I like you a lot, but

I've nibbled heaps of memories in the last twenty-four hours so I know what a Looney Tunes is, and frankly, I think it's a *bit* insensitive. Öö's time is far too valuable and volatile to dribble it away calling me Altonaut Who Runs Faster Than Wisdom Down the Milk Road, but at least he uses part of my actual name, because that's *respect*, isn't it?"

"Sorry," mumbled Decibel.

"Sorry," Oort Ultraviolet repeated with a shrug.

"Nononoyesyesno, I lóve it, it's perfect, farwayfar better than Al. We received the dogandbirdandbombandcanyon show in the big radio wave haul off this world. It was excellentgreatexcellent-allright. A song of nihilism and the hopelessness of desire. At first we thought it was such an obvious allegory for the war that we ignored it. Must be one of us, youknowyeahyouknowno? Some pirate cartoon channel out of Octave space junking up the signal. Nope. Coincidencechancechancefatechance. An echo in the great unconscious. I *hate* that. Makes my job harder. But it's perfect-perfectcorrect—that's *you*, Al, you're the roadrunner! I'm gonna call you that from now on. I'll alert the other Keshet when I get back into the continuity. They won't be happy about Yoko Ono, though."

"It seems Mrs. Ono died, Öö," the great blue fish-flamingo went on, in what Dess could only assume was her own voice. Or perhaps one of the hyperactive red panda's school friends. He wondered, suddenly, if it was very tough to keep it all straight, to skim for the right voice every time you talked to someone. Decibel Jones rather wished he could scrape off the top of an audience's memory and sing however the fuck they wanted him to sing. He'd supposed he'd known how, once. Once. "Very sorry, I did try. And I *can* tell them apart! They all have different thumbnails, it turns out. You didn't tell me that. And you told me Yoko Ono was alive. That's *two* major stuff-ups. If you'd use even one of those day planners I keep buying you, we wouldn't keep having these embarrassing mistakes."

"DIED? Whenwhenwhy? How could this HAPPEN? Oh no! Oh NOOOO. What about KYOKO? Did she ever find her mommy's hand inthesnowinthesnowinthesnowintherain . . . ?"

"Three years ago, I think?" Oort Ultraviolet said helpfully. "She died of . . . well, of being an old lady, really."

Öö blinked his adorable brown eyes and rubbed his fuzzy apricot-colored cheeks with his paws. "I don't get it."

"What's there to get, love? She was ninety or something, wasn't she?"

The red panda wriggled his button nose. "No, butwhybutwhybuthow should that killkillhurtkill anybody?"

Al let that question drift pointedly unacknowledged among them like a fart at a dinner party. "This is what's left of the band. Decibel Jones and the Absolute Zeros, Öö. They'll do fine. Probably."

The Keshet made a face like he'd just eaten kale for the first time and scrambled down a long corridor lit with a calming dappled undersea light that flowed out from holes in the thick black coral. He spun around in circles, found things to eat hidden in his striped tail, and bounced over himself several times.

"'Kay, 'Kay, 'KayKayKay. Pay attention! I'm not going to go through it twice! Well, wellwellwell, I *will* go through it twice. More than twice. WAYWAYFARMORE. I will conduct your tour of the good shipship *Cake in the Rain* 10^{47} times before the waveform sets and this whole timeline gets served at the table." Öö stopped, fell over backward, and looked up at them, clasping his little black paws. "You see, gentlemen, *time* is a *cheesecake*. It must be *whipwhipstirred* and *mixed* and *creamed* and *frappéd* by someone who knows whatwhathowwhat he's doing, and then it must be LEFT to set in the refrigerator until all the chronologies gel into something the multiverse can sink its teethtoothsteeth into. Though to be honest, even after it's set, the whole thing is quite jiggly and wobblyobbly and you can stick your fists right THROUGH it and cram HANDFULS and HANDFULS into your MOUTH because TIME is so YUMMY and FATTENING. But YOU won't go through it twice, so heads up, sailors! Well, you *will* go through it twice, but you won't know it." Öö, the ship's Mandatory Keshet, tumbled off down the hall. "Lookseelook if you see this fluffy orange ice cream-sherbetcreamcreamy-looking coral, don't eat it, that's a doorknob. Lifts are clearly marked by the angry squids. Command's that way, cafeteria's on reef four, cocktails at seven p.m. on the observation deck, that's the engine room, don't look in there—"

"Jesus *Christ*," Decibel Jones cried out as they passed a round jelly-glass window into the engine room.

Inside, they could clearly see a lovely Victorian-looking bedroom with green curtains and a splendid four-poster bed on which two undeniably naked and undeniably human people were rather vigorously going at it.

"Not an engine," Oort shouted, as if to summon someone who could fix it up. "Not an engine! Sorry. Sorry, Miss. Sir. Sorry."

But it was an engine. It was, in fact, the absolute pinnacle of propulsion technology.

The Keshet Effulgence owes its exalted position in galactic society to its patent on the Paradox Box, simply the most efficient FTL drive ever imagined by any species. A ship that wishes to avoid the unpleasantness of the public wormhole system is required by corporate law and the desire for self-preservation to have a Keshet representative on board, as anyone else attempting to work the Box would find their molecules subjected to all manner of assault in defiance of time, logic, and propriety—for example, summarily rearranged to resemble a painting by Picasso after it has been shat out by a sexually frustrated emu and delivered to the doorstep of a wholly perplexed pre-asp Cleopatra.

The Paradox Box is a simple enough concept that could only have been discovered by a species born with the chronochondria of their cells set to *fun*. The splitting of an atom is nothing compared to the energy released by even a small, unassuming, paint-by-numbers time-travel paradox. This is why the prudent time traveler avoids, at all costs, meeting their younger selves or killing the inventor of time travel (a very nice little girl named Malinda Moss, who was, not coincidentally but definitely improbably, also the progenitor of the Keshet, who will have once someday had a terrible accident with a wormhole, a zoo, and a lifetime of emotional neglect) or buying, selling, or gifting strange pocket watches without a properly established chain of provenance or stepping on any important butterflies or, really, any insects at all if it can be helped.

However, for a starship, such horrifying temporal train wrecks are a quick fill-up at the petrol station. The Keshet, luckily for travel agents everywhere, are born flitting from timeline to timeline like hummingbirds from flower to flower to the invasion of the Mongols to flower. They don't have to expend any more energy to do it than a human expends maintaining enough muscle tension to keep them from being a meat aspic. They cycle through every version of every timeline they come into contact with until all permutations are exhausted and the infinite forking decisions of everything ever have firmed up into a cool, refreshing reality. All of this takes no time whatsoever relative to the friends, loved ones, and office furniture of a Keshet, and the entirety of all time multiplied exponentially relative to the Keshet themselves. Öö's attention-deficit-disordered dialect wasn't actually a stutter, but the only visible effect of all this constant cosmic channel surfing—each time they get stuck repeating a word, it is a slightly different Keshet in a slightly different timeline trying out different linguistic paths through the mess of it all.

All of which is to say, whenever they're short of cash, an enterprising red panda will go scurrying about snuffling up a paradox, pack it carefully in quantum bubble-wrap, and deliver it to the nearest ship, installation included, where it can be safely held in a stasis field until someone presses the big red button. The cosmos-shredding energy released by the paradox then dutifully shreds the cosmos, just a little, in the back where no one will notice, allowing a vessel to cruise happily through the high-occupancy vehicle lane of space and time and come out the other end when the iterative cycles of the paradox exhaust themselves and become a cheesecake. Therefore, it's very important to select the right-size paradox for the journey at hand.

As the gardenworld of Litost was a hefty journey of some sixty-five hundred miles, Öö had had to find something juicy in the local pantry. Thus, in the engine room of the *Cake in the Rain*, a Mr. Walter John Pritchard of Virginia Beach, Virginia, was busy becoming his own grandfather.

"And HERETHERERIGHTTHISWAY is your recordingstateroom-studio for the remainderdurationremainderelevendays of the flight. I know you'll want to get started right away writing the bassline of the total salvation of your species, so we've just stuffed it full of anything we thought you might need. Please pull the eel in the lavatory if we missed anything."

Lilac-colored brain coral subwoofers studded the walls. Sea slug soundproofing rippled orangely across the ceiling. The floor was a lime-green anemone shag carpet. A vast glittering soundboard dominated one corner. Three jelly-glass doors led off into bedrooms that could plausibly be comfortable for a human being. A swim-in closet overflowed with fabric in every type but matte and every color but brown next to a bank of mirrors. Dess and Oort caught their reflections and did a proper slapstick double take.

"Look at you!" crowed Decibel. "You've gone all first-year art project! And so have I!"

All down the sides of their necks and across their collarbones, a spray of deep scarlet leopardy spots had sprung up, if leopards were too glam for the veldt and soaked their spots in glitter before padding off to the club.

"That's the encephalitis! Coming in nicely!" the roadrunner said approvingly.

Oort St. Ultraviolet looked as though he was about to be sick. He rubbed at his spots, but they weren't going anywhere. Decibel Jones preened. He pulled out his collar to see how far down they went, which was *quite* far.

The whole place was lit with glowing purple-striped sea nettles that hung from the long encrusted ribs of the ship like party lanterns. Mira's drums and old Casio sat proudly in a corner. Guitars lined one wall, normal noncoral guitars, famous guitars: Hendrix's, Clapton's, Page's. Beneath them was Oort's petting farm: double-necked cello, electro-glass hurdy-gurdy, übertheremin, Moog—and a perfect glass Oortophone.

It was gorgeous. It was grotesque. It was an exact replica of their first recording studio in Hoxton, reclaimed by the sea. Mnemopathy really was was a hell of a thing, Decibel thought as he ran his fingers over the cymbal on Mira's drums.

"Mushy, mushy, Wonderful," he whispered.

"I don't see any of *my* toys," sniffed Capo the short-haired cat, padding superciliously into the room after having thoroughly inspected the hallway.

"Hell-o," said Jones.

"*What* did you *do* to my *cat*?" Oort exploded, pointing at the unconcerned feline like a Salem girl at trial. "Not okay! That is not okay! I agreed to spaceships and aliens and the possible end of life on Earth. I did not agree to tolerate *talking cats*. This is too much. It's too mad. It's *out of genre*. Undo it immediately!"

"I gave her the ability to talk," said the tall, graceful Esca as she stepped gingerly into the room. "It's very easy. Through the ear. Just a little strobe lighting in the hippocampus. A . . . gift. I thought you would both enjoy it."

"Eh," said Capo, licking her paw and whacking it over one ear vigorously.

"Also, it rather neatly proves a point," the roadrunner went on. "You keep saying that we converse, and therefore sentience is not in question. Now your pet converses. So perhaps you can see that speech is not the determining factor. Any animal can talk. But Capo cannot assemble a band and sing a heartbreaking work of popular music. She hasn't got the thumbs, the postproduction skills, or the vocal range. We did think about this sort of thing, you know. We did discuss it for more than a second or two."

"Could if I wanted," Capo sniffed. "You don't know. You're just a bird." A hungry look came into her green eyes. "A *big* bird."

"Look, birdie," Oort said with a nervous laugh. He reached out to put his arm around the roadrunner, as he'd do with any hard-arse producer who just didn't understand what he was all about. "This is all a laugh, right? What I mean is, you're not *really* going to incinerate our planet if we don't sing better than anyone has ever sung in the whole history of humanity, right? It's just a bit of hazing. Messing about with the new kid in school, yeah? Well, you got us good! Honestly! Scared shitless, me. I might've peed a little. The Yoko stuff was a deep cut, really subtle comedy. But I get you, all the way. So let's have a drink and skip to the part where everyone jumps out and yells, 'Surprise, fooled you, you pronks, you should see the look on your face,' all right?"

The roadrunner blinked her gorgeous Disney eyes and looked

away with something that could almost be mistaken for shame.

"I've got *kids*, mate. You didn't even let me call them. You turned my mobile into the left tit on your spaceship. What is *wrong* with you?"

Decibel Jones sprung into action. Yeah, sure, he was a drunk and a fool wearing last night's rhinestones and tomorrow's hangover, long past his salad days or even his soup days. He was, in fact, approaching middle age at the speed of paradox. But if he could still do anything in this universe, he could get his band onstage when they got the Eeyores, which had been, if he really thought about it, mostly all the time.

"Okay, okay, Oort. Omar. My darling. My Arkable love. It's *fine*. It's fine! You don't need to call little Sarah and Samantha—"

"Nico and Siouxsie."

"God, really? Bit on the nose, don't you think? No, no, of course. Lovely names. Good old Sue," Dess said soothingly. "Anyway, you don't need to call them because we'll be *fine*. Write the greatest song ever composed by man, beast, or polyp in eleven days? No problem! Don't you remember when we were writing *Spacecrumpet*? Days laid out on the floor of some godforsaken flop, nights on the floor of some godforsaken nightclub, and all of it paradise. All of it *us*. The lyrics came like *honey*, my dearest darling space oddity. The melodies came like wine. So we just do it again. Wind back the clock. And you know what? We save the world like motherfucking caped crusaders and the history books get printed in *glitter* from now on, and on page one they all say: THANK YOU DECIBEL JONES AND THE ABSOLUTE ZEROS! They chose us, gorgeous. Don't forget it. Out of everyone singing and playing and Auto-Tuning their hearts out all over the sodding stupid planet. *They* chose *us*."

"Only because everyone else was dead," mused Oort, stroking his cat's silky head and watching Dess do what he always did, which was to shove everyone else's feelings into a sack and drown them in the ocean of his own enthusiasm.

"So what? So *destiny*, that's what. So immortality! So me and you and Mira." Decibel's face fell. "Well. Me and you. So your stupid cat. So flying a fuck-fueled aquarium to Planet Music and rocking so hard and so true, they'll know just how alive glamkind is. I can already hear it, Oort. I can hear the song that's gonna save us all, and you are gonna blast it from the quasars to the Queen's ears, and you and me are gonna sing it till the stars rain down like applause, my glorious, gloomy boyfrack."

"Öö and I will leave you to it," said the space flamingo, bowing with the space panda and beating a surprisingly sensitive retreat.

Oort looked up at Dess with moist eyes. Almost like they used to look at him, when he'd believed they'd find a manager, a label, a venue, a place on the charts, a place in the world. When he'd believed and they couldn't quite yet. When his belief and a kebab shared among them could keep them going through a thousand and one Brobdingnagian nights.

"I'm not your boy-anything anymore," Oort said stonily as soon as the cabin door shut. "So just don't."

Decibel blinked in hurt confusion. Hadn't Oort heard him? Hadn't he just been giving him the old eyes?

"Okay, Dess," Oort said, playing the reconciling middle child between Decibel and the ghost of the Zero who'd missed the flight, as he'd done a hundred thousand times before. "Okay. Let's hear it. Let's hear the song that's gonna get me back to my girls. Give us a few bars."

Decibel Jones clapped his hands together and broke into a smile that once graced the cover of every magazine worth its gloss.

"Oh, sorry, that was a lie. I have no idea."

18

All the Things That Nobody Sees

It takes eleven days, give or take, to reach Litost from Earth via paradox-fueled aquarium. Back in the mango-colored days of Hope & Ruin, this would have been more than enough time for the Absolute Zeros to knock out a pop anthem that would drench the world in a tsunami of glitter and meaning.

Now it was just long enough to write absolutely nothing—reveal two things better kept secret and one that should have been laid out ages ago; set three accidental fires; send back seventeen separate meals for being far too surrealistic; pitch six screaming matches; consider suicide by air lock at least once or twice; reject hundreds of potential lyrics and riffs; form one extremely unlikely, inconvenient, and non-Euclidean friendship; invent four entirely new swear words; request separate accommodations; quit in tears; make up in tears; get in a few quality depression sessions; seriously annoy one large, usually serene white cat; and remind them why they'd broken up the band in the first place.

Capo napped almost the whole way across the galaxy.

Nico and Siouxsie Calişkan's enormous four-year-old Maine Coon–Angora-somebody's-barn-cat-possibly-a-stray-albino-panther mix was entirely unbothered by suddenly achieving the ability to speak rather posh English. Oh, certainly it had been alarming at first. But adjusting to sudden changes in your circumstances was easy when you didn't really care about anything. As far as she was concerned, she'd always talked. By some miracle, everyone else had recently achieved the ability to listen properly. She was over the novelty within half an hour. No one listened to her or asked for her input or attended gratefully to her needs any more than they ever had. They were too busy making big monkey fusses over their big monkey problems. Capo didn't see why it was *ever* necessary to make a fuss. Fussing was for dogs and babies. This new house smelled like delicious fish; the steady rumbling of the engine vibrated at almost the exact frequency of a purr; there were *scads* of birds and scurrying, red, squirrel-type things roaming about; and whenever she was hungry, she could just gnaw on the walls till little shrimps came out to investigate. It was a vast improvement over their old house in terms of cat-comfort.

The key to a happy life, Capo devoutly believed, was never giving much of a damn what happened in any given day so long as you got in a nap, a kill, and a snuggle, and the snuggle was optional. When Oort and Justine had adopted her from that shelter and taken her to a nice house where she was expected to be a civilized, well-behaved indoor cat despite the whole joint lacking anything like a population of murderable sparrows, field mice, bunnies, and whatnot, she hadn't run around making grand speeches and crying and questioning the meaning of it all. She'd just carried on and contented herself with spiders, pieces of lint, and occasionally scratching or biting one of the kids just to keep in practice.

The nap was the really important thing. The nap was all.

Capo quickly triangulated the prime sleeping spot in their stateroom: a tall coral plinth with a decorative pot of flowering seaweed on top. The pot made a fantastic sound when it smashed against the floor. The massive white cat settled in for what might have been an hour or a lifetime or eleven days. It simply wasn't any of her concern how long. Occasionally, loud noises or hunger or a drum riff or the blort of an Oortophone or Decibel trying to coax her into eating something that looked like a licorice Allsort woke Capo from her long day's journey into snooze. She opened her bright green eyes, investigated, protested, or ingested as necessary, turned her rump to the offending thing, and went back to sleep. Thus, for her, the voyage passed by like a training montage in a hastily made feel-bad film, in bits and flits and pieces the feline found it far too much work to understand or care about.

➤

"I think it's time for a radical suggestion, Oort. It's time to bring back Ultraponce."

"NO."

"What? I don't care what the critics said. The critics are all back on Earth, praying they were wrong about us, and they were. The literal heavens opened, and magical beings descended and said we rocked. This is what those birds and pandas and whatnots want to hear! Ultraponce, King of Time and Space, shooting sadness in the face and snogging gods and lighting up the dark. It's perfect! It was our opus!"

"It was your opus. That was the whole problem, Mr. Wee Tate of the Modern. Spacecrumpet was us, all of us, passing a napkin around at three a.m. and writing out a song line by line by line and humming together till something real came out; writing lyrics for one another's tunes, and tunes for one another's lyrics. It was communal, you prat. That was the point. Ultraponce was you. Just you. Inventing this bigger and better version of yourself in a superhero cape and making us your *fucking backup band. Oh, no, it was better to have a unified voice, wasn't it? But unified just meant your voice. Your words. Even though the second-biggest hit off Spacecrumpet was Mira's, and you know it, and it just eats you alive inside, doesn't it? You don't get to do that again. You don't get to ignore us. Me. We were on that list too. Remind me how well Decibel Jones has been doing without the Zeros?"*

"I don't know, Omar. How's writing pie jingles coming? Having fun playing bass on some reality star's vanity album, are we? Writing a jingle for a luxury-car commercial? You fucking sold out. At least I'm still trying. God, they always go straight at the end, don't they? One way or the other or both. Excuse me for not sticking around your little one-man misery society."

Capo's ruff rippled. She flexed her claws and rolled over, paws splayed out, white belly to the ceiling, and soon enough she was snoring tinily. Eyes shut. Eyes open. Eyes shut again. Eyes open.

"C'mere, ya fuzzy redness. It's late, and Dess and the roadrunner are at it again, and I miss my wife and I miss my kids, and I've got this feeling in my chest like I'm going to have a very undignified nonsentient freak-out if I don't focus on something other than the fact that the chandelier is staring at me and there's nothing outside but empty all the way down and everything I love is probably going to get burned to the ground. I'll sing you some Yoko. I think I remember 'Walking on Thin Ice,' more or less."

Mandatory Keshet Öö scrunched up his cream-colored face and wrinkled his black nose. Capo wanted to bite his cream-colored face and his black nose so badly her fangs itched. "That's got Lennon all over it," the uncatchable time-traveling prey animal said doubtfully.

"Yeah, well, so do I, mate."

Oort St. Ultraviolet began to strum softly in the long dark between worlds, singing about a lake as big as the ocean.

"Do the scream, though," the red panda insisted.

"Come on, that's the worst bit. I'm more of a cerebral crooner than a screamer."

"This is why we're worriedworriedconcerneddubious about your sentience. How can you sing a song without a scream from the gut of your soulmindbodyheartsoulsoulsoul? What even is a songsong-anthemchantsong without the screamy bit? Listen, this will be very awkwardweirdawkwardsociallytwisted for you, but I hatehatecan't-bear this part I want to skip pastpastfuturepresentpast it as fast as we can. Come on, let's go fasterfasterfaster. We are always already friends. I have had this interaction with you twelve thousand six hundred and three times alreadybeforealreadyalready. I have already scrambledclimbedwiggled back and forth through every interaction we have ever had or ever will never have but might, every permutation of our mutual sympatheticemotionalempathicintellectualsnuggle experi-ence, every outcomewinlosedrawnuclearannihilation of the Grand Prix, of your band, of your marriage, of every cell that makes up you and me and the future and the past. This is our first real conversation for you, but it is the billionth for me. I currently rank you fifthfifthfourthsixth of my favorite entities of all time. And I know you can do the screamy bit really really good. You can. I don't know about your crooning. But I believe utterly in your screamy bits. Do the thing, Englishblokeman. Just onceoncetwiceinfinityforever."

Oort St. Ultraviolet shut his eyes in the depths of space, took a deep breath, and screech-sang the ghost of Yoko Ono proud. He stopped short.

"Lennon got shot right after he recorded that, you know. Played away the afternoon, didn't make it through the night. He was holding the final tape in his hand when he died."

"I knowknowwentsaw. I was thereheretherethereeverywhereallthe-timenowheretherehere."

Oort's eyes went dark and wet and pained. "You might have a point about us."

"I know that, too."

Whiskers quivered. Eyes shut. Eyes open again.

"I'm sorry, Oort. I'm so sorry. You're right. You're always so bloody right. I hate that about you. I was just . . . I was happy, then. For one stupid minute. I was happy. I was in the middle of things and I wanted to stay there, I wanted it to be like that forever, and Mira wanted to write all these Important Songs about What's Going On and you wanted to do, like, concept jazz or something, and I felt it slipping away. I felt like I was the only one who understood that the only wall we could ever build against What's Going On was the glitter and the shine and the synth and the knowing grin that never stops knowing. The show. Because the opposite of fascism isn't anarchy, it's theater. When the world is fucked, you go to the theater, you go to the shine, and when the bad men come, all there is left to do is sing them down. You didn't get it, I didn't think you understood, you can't sing a dirge to the reaper, he's already heard them all. You gotta slaughter him with joy and a beat like the best of all possible shags, and because somehow, somehow, my nan's cartoons always had it right and the Care Bear Stare is the most powerful force in the world, and I wanted to shine and you wanted to scream, and we just failed, we failed at both and neither because of me."

"It's always all about you, somehow. Even when you're apologizing. It's kind of impressive."

"I'm trying."

"So you were an arrogant, selfish arseface because 'the world, man'? Or because me and Mira were just too thick to comprehend your genius?"

"God, you just do not crack, do you? What is this about? Why do you hate me so much? You used to love me. I still love you."

"I don't hate you. I just don't like looking at you too much these days."

"Fine. Don't tell me. Don't use your outside voice like a grownup. Go back to interfering with your panda friend. Is this because of Edinburgh? Do you really still hate me for that? Because I didn't marry her?"

Capo watched her human set the device she was named for down carefully on a knob of black coral. He spoke very quietly and clearly. "Go fuck yourself, Funshine Bear. You're the stupidest man I've ever known. Even if the rest of us are sentient . . . And you? Are decisively not. She didn't want to marry you, you arse. Everything was on fire and all we could do was watch it happen on TV. It was a weird night. She got weird. It was a natural reaction."

"None of us stopped her. None of us even saw her leave. You didn't either. Neither did Lila. How is it still my fault?"

"It's your fault because if you'd just told her you loved her, because you did, and not to cry, because that's what a human being does, and that everything was going to be okay, because who knew, maybe it would have been. Instead of laughing in her face like a goddamned monster, she wouldn't have had to go calm herself down by driving, and she would be here in this horrible, stupid, gorgeous, fucking spaceship with us, and the song would already be written and nothing bad would ever have happened to us. It's your fault she's dead, and I've never much felt like forgiving you so just leave me be."

A long silence. Long enough to lie down in. Long enough to forget you ever knew how to talk.

"We're not, you know."

"Not what, Oort?"

"Sentient. Nobody sentient would have let any of it happen. Would have let that night come, or go on after. I'm not either. Nobody sentient would have let Mira drive."

Eyes slid closed. Eyes slitted open.

Decibel Jones lay in the dark alongside the roadrunner's long, lithe, blue body. "Were you afraid, before the Grand Prix?"

"Very much."

"I shouldn't have come. I'll just sludge it up. I'm already sludging it up. All I've ever wanted was to make something beautiful, and everything I touch just disappears in a poof of fuckery." Capo wrinkled her muzzle in distaste. She was, as all cats, ultimately conservative on the subject of interspecies relations.

Decibel changed subjects like a drunk changing lanes. "Look, are we a thing? An item? I don't know how this works."

"I'm sorry. There is only one of you. Esca do not pair-bond. Perhaps if all the Zeros were here, we could manage a flock, but as it is, you and I are just friends with a short-term benefit plan. But I do like you. Even if you're only plausibly sentient."

A long silence.

"How long do Esca live?"

"If we're careful, around three hundred years. I am one hundred twenty-one, if you're asking. Not too old for you, I hope."

"It's . . . less. For us. A lot less."

The Esca nuzzled him with her thick black beak. "That's because your science is tiny and ridiculous and adorable like a plush toy."

"You shouldn't come round anymore. It's not good for you. I'll sludge you up too. I won't mean to, but I will. Plus, I think it really bothers Oort's cat."

The great ultramarine fish-flamingo made a soft, awful sound with her rib cage. "I am having fun. Please do not make me go."

"I loved Mira and she left. I loved Oort and . . . well, Oort seems fine. But I loved my parents and I loved my grandmother and I loved Lila Poole and I loved my life, and it's all gone. Being around me is a high-risk enterprise."

"'Dying happens to everyone, even stars. Even the stuff between the stars. But if you believe in yourself and achieve your goals, you can die so hard that no one will ever forget you, and that's almost as good as not dying at all. Well, it isn't, really, it isn't at all, and believing and achieving is just something sportscasters say, but what are you gonna do, not die? Try it. I'll wait.'"

"What?"

"It is Goguenar Gorecannon's Seventh Unkillable Fact."

"Who the hell is Goguenar Gorecannon?"

"I will bring you my copy," the roadrunner said softly, and when she said it, she said it in Mira's lilting, amused voice.

Capo hissed in her dreams, chasing red pandas and blue flamingos through an infinite suburban garden. Eyes squeezed tight. Eyes blinked open.

"Heya, Öö. Roadrunner."

"Heya, Oort."

"So . . . I think we have a melody. It's . . . it's good. Hairs-on-the-back-of-your-neck good. It's something."

The red panda scratched his hind leg. "That's nice."

"And Dess has a plan for lyrics. It's pretty clever, actually. We agreed we were never going to write the perfect song to encapsulate ourselves and our species and our hopes and dreams for the universe, for the future, for everything humanity ever has been or hopes to be, but that also has a great beat and summer pop chart potential. Using pyrotechnics we don't have, costumes that somehow magically manifest without Mira, and a hope and a prayer that an Oortophone is compatible with the local voltage. It would have to be the greatest song ever written, and let's be honest, even our best was never Mozart. So we're going to copy off humanity's homework. Every poem brilliant enough for us to remember without a Wi-Fi connection, every line, every immortal pentameter. We'll string it together with a few prepositions and voilà: instant genius."

The stranger that was so good at upsetting Capo's human picked at something on his shoe. A mouse? A spider? Ah, no, nothing. Of course. Humans were the worst. The stranger spat out a few lines like he wanted to be anywhere else:

Quoth the Raven: to be or not to be

that is the question

whether I am the master of my fate

in form how like an angel

in apprehension how

to strive to seek to find and not to yield

and though I could not stop for Death

O love there is no other life than here

burning bright in the forest of the night

calling for our fiddlers three...

"I'm still working on the bridge."

"Come on, Dess, give it something. A bit of the old oomph."

The bird talked, which irritated Capo because she was reminded that she hadn't yet eaten the bird. "It's . . . a bit awkward. I'm not sure I follow the sentiment completely."

"It doesn't matter anyway," Decibel mumbled.

"Look, Dess, I'm sorry about last night. You don't have to be like that. It's me, remember? Your old Oort. Do the part with *dulce et decorum est.* Come on, it's good, I promise. I wouldn't tell you it was good if it wasn't; that's not me."

Decibel Jones pushed a mauve anemone on the wall. A clear jelly-glass screen flickered on, half swallowed up by the coral hull.

"It's not about that. I was a rotten little brat, all right? I was Mr. Devil of Tasmania. But it doesn't matter now. I've been up all night while you were in Snoozepool. Doing reconnaissance. Research. I used to be good at that, you know. At a lot of things."

Decibel Jones and Oort St. Ultraviolet watched on the screen as a century of Grand Prix performances began to play, one after the other. Glorious golden tubes of sea-flesh pulsing; huge-eyed, childlike black

creatures chanting; some kind of horrific monster dancing with a skeleton; a pale thorny suit of armor blushing, somehow; out loud, seven
graceful blue Esca sieving the wind through their bones. And there was
the roadrunner, at the head of the band, projecting a waterbird made of
light from her lantern; another Esca, dancing silently on another stage,
somewhere else, somewhere far. Behind her, others moved like eggs floating in a marsh, waiting to become alive. When the lantern-bird opened
her throat to sing, another light shone—light within light, light from its
own lantern streamed out and shaped itself into glowing, glittering, horrifying ruins. Planetary ruins, the ruins of constellations. Alunizar ships
crushed to death and drifting among the stars; the crystalline cities of
the Keshet turned to rubble; the starlit weeping of the Yüz over the molten surface of their homeworld. And over all this stretched the wings of
the Esca—their Esca, the roadrunner, the infrasound, vibratory, kindly
voice of her people with their huge eyes begging for protection, their
soft throats that anyone could cut at any moment. With her wings and
piscine fronds and lantern light, the Esca lay herself over the ruins, gave
up her body and her song to keep what was left from harm, took the terrible fire still raining down from the ultramarine biolamps of her backup
dancers on the silken feathers and scales of her back until she was gone;
she was gone and her voice vanished, but the galaxy remained. Civilization remained.

And then another song began, better than that one. Each song was so
impossible, so perfect, so complex, so anatomically baffling, and they only
grew more heartbreaking and piercing, the special effects more dazzling,
the fire and the ice and the psychic manipulation of the audience, that
both of them sobbed and sobbed as if they had lost every last thing in the
world. Hours passed.

The humans watched in an agony of feeling, in a rictus of involuntary ecstasy and horror and grief and artistic nirvana, their bodies
shuddering, their brains a sea of flaming blue emotion.

The cat watched with semi-mild interest. It was all right, she supposed, if you were into that sort of thing.

When it was over, Decibel Jones turned to the last Absolute Zero and said:

"So . . . I suppose what I'm saying is we're all going to die."

19.

The War Is Not Over

The twenty-ninth Metagalactic Grand Prix was held on Fenek, the homeworld of the Voorpret Mutation.

It was the first time a member species of the Great Octave declined to participate, ruining everyone's fun over an argument about sand.

It was the first time a performer died onstage as a result of a weaponized key change, bass drop, and/or costume detonation.

It was the first time a newly discovered species sang for their sentience, sang for the survival of their fittest, sang their externally stored hearts out, and failed.

And it was the first time anyone felt safe enough to hold the thing on Fenek.

It was a very complicated year.

There was absolutely nothing unusual about Fenek. It was the avatar of the average, the model of the median, a beautifully boilerplate world. It orbited an even-tempered, comfortably middle-class yellow sun at a respectful distance, boasted a galactic biodiversity rating of exactly *meh*, and kept its gravity to a considerate low roar, except on weekends. Before the Voorpret, Fenek's best shot at a sentient species was something not unlike an Earth

or hear one or taste one or put one in a cage. And if you've
ched a Voorpret, it's already too late.

A Voorpret is a virus. Simply the most successful viral out-
eak in the history of the galaxy, infecting, replicating, mutat-
g, spreading, and absolutely liquefying their hosts since before
umans ever imagined that oversize frontal lobes were this sea-
son's must-have accessory. In the halcyon days of their youth, the
Voorpret were a humble hemorrhagic fever originating in the rain
forests of Fenek's northern hemisphere, toddling about learning
their pathogenic ABCs, killing proto-primates and ungulates far
too quickly to become a pandemic to write home about. But they
mutated, and replicated, and learned, as life has a tendency to
do, and since the dull, brown giant sparrows at the top of Fenek's
unsuspecting food chain had barely mastered subtraction, they
had little in the way of virology experts, vaccines, or affordable
treatment options, and the Voorpret had all the time in the world
to reign in their adolescent hormones and graduate into a lucrative career in what polite society calls "soft real estate."

Once a Voorpret infection occurs, the virus fully inhabits the
host within a few hours, resulting in lesions, fevers, hair loss,
bleeding from places no one is meant to bleed from, chunks of
liver shooting out of the eyeballs, total annihilation of personality, the usual horror-movie floor show of symptoms. The invading
Voorpret reservoir can and does work the unfortunate body like a
marionette, speaking, dancing, using tools, building a civilization.
They are the hand within the glove, the kid underneath a sheet on
Halloween yelling to anyone who will listen that he's a really real
ghost and he's gonna get you. There is no cure. The Voorpret consider immunological research to be a declaration of war. Death
follows within a week or so. But death no longer presents any
sort of roadblock for the Voorpret virus. They continue to squat

sparrow the size of an underachieving mou~~n~~
eyes and dull, brown feathers and dull, bro~~w~~
nearly made it all the way up to inventing th~~e~~
everything went tails-up. It was the planetary ~~e~~
girl next door with the nice personality whose fa~~c~~
forget when you move away to college, destined fro~~m~~
a house with beige carpeting, 2.5 moons, and a casua~~l~~
ness selling scented candles to people who hate scent~~e~~

Or at least it was, before the zombie apocalypse.

Now Fenek is a very unusual world indeed. The V~~oorpret~~
have been at work for a long, long time, tinkering and ~~build~~
ing and DIY-ing and messing about with the landscaping,
they've almost got the place just the way they always wan~~ted~~
it, their dreamworld, every plank in place. Fenek has become ~~a~~
vast necropolis, a massive cemetery extending from pole to pol~~e~~
around the equator, carpeting all nine continents, the ice caps
and the seafloor with tombs and mausoleums and graves and
towering urns like high-rise apartment buildings. It is a planet to
make the dreariest goth giddy with joy and, if not for the Voorpret
themselves, would be a lucrative tourist destination for statuary
and monument enthusiasts, of which there are more than you
might think.

Unfortunately, there *are* the Voorpret themselves, easily the
most problematic species encountered by the Alunizar, Utorak,
Keshet, and Yüz ships that poured out of the surprise wormhole
nearby. They were the last accepted into the Great Octave after
the war, and only by a single vote. It is difficult enough to accept
magenta algae or gas-filled balloons or computer code as living, sentient, valuable entities, without having to get your head
around anything as instinctively repulsive as the Voorpret. You
cannot, technically speaking, see a Voorpret. You cannot smell

in the empty corpse as long as decomposition can hold the liga-ments together, dispersing to new digs only when the old ones have soupified into a chunky stew.

Voorpret civilization is the most hideous gentrification proj-ect undertaken since the yuppies took over Alphabet City. You can't see a Voorpret, technically, not without a microscope and a hazmat suit, but you can see the skin it's in, and you can absolutely smell it from three planets away. A Voorpret is just the shambling corpse of whomever it infected last. They aren't picky, jumping from species to species with a vaudeville smile, a high kick, and a tip of the putrefying hat. It would have been an easy call to wipe them out. In the which-of-us-are-people and which-of-us-are-meat equation, a cheerfully rapacious zombie virus with a fatality rate of 99 percent and a total disregard for the bodily autonomy of anyone anywhere seemed, on paper, to fall safely in the *meat* column. Contaminated meat. Do not consume.

Except that the Voorpret turned out to be really rather good at the whole *civilization* thing. Yes, yes, they obliterated the natural biodiversity of any region they touched, but wherever their infec-tion took hold, they opened a lot of delightful bistros and shops and start-up tech companies with whimsically casual workplace environments and fusion food trucks and artisanal blacksmithing co-ops and performance-art spaces. Crime rates fell drastically, since everyone was Voorpret and the Voorpret were everyone. And wherever they went, good, accessible public transportation followed, because after a few months, corpses start to have real trouble stay-ing ambulatory. Oh, the Alunizar *wanted* to exterminate them. The Smaragdi offered to open up a few choice moons for colonization if they'd agree to do it. Despite the shameful behavior of the for-eign invaders, the Sziv begged the Utorak to rid them of the zombie menace. Even the Klavaret were willing to look the other way.

But you've just never had better coffee than the fair-trade organic late-harvest darkest of dark roasts at a Voorpret espresso bar. And you don't nuke that sort of thing from orbit. It's just so *hard* to find a good cappuccino when you're traveling.

But there are limits to how far anyone will go for a functional public transport system and locally sourced pastries. After Vlimeux, everyone demanded a separate treaty for the Voorpret before they would even consider letting them into the new spheres of galactic influence. The Voorpret would agree to infect only willing hosts, nonsentient species smaller than a breadbox, or the freshly dead, providing the recently deceased had filled out his or her or its or their or zir or ghuf's organ-donation card beforehand in front of two notarized witnesses. Any unauthorized outbreaks that could not show paperwork would be instantly sterilized. The zombie planet would have to behave itself, and share its recipes, or be quarantined.

As a result of this agreement, rents in Voorpret-adjacent zones soared. The down payment on a new studio body with low wear and tear, fresh paint, and all the amenities shot through the roof. The elderly, terminally ill, bored, or risk-prone sentient being could name their price. Yet most galactic citizens remained nervous about visiting Fenek itself, despite the thriving theater scene and delightful nightlife. While love and peace may come to exist between wildly disparate members of different kingdoms, orders, and phyla, very few are willing to meet up with a walking, talking syphilis infection for coffee, even the best coffee in the universe, unless it's in a public place close to their own flat with lots of friends around and easy exits.

Yet, it could not be denied that the Voorpret band Applausoleum had handily won the twenty-eighth Metagalactic Grand Prix with their darkwave prog-grunge power ballad "I Can't Get No

Liquefaction." It's really next to impossible to stay on key with a half-decomposed larynx and a moldering diaphragm, so Voorpret music takes the form of a genetically modified worm, about the size and shape of a dragonfly larva, dispersed into the audience via sprinkler system, trendy vintage beers on tap at the bar, silver platter passed among the paying public by attractive ushers, or T-shirt cannon, depending on how posh the venue. The little creature burrows down into the auditory orifice and vibrates to the tune of the composition, eating sadness, excreting euphoria, and laying its eggs, which, when hatched, will depart unobtrusively while the fan sleeps the night off, carrying the genetically remixed song to new hosts everywhere. The Voorpret refer to the peak of their artistic expression and cultural contribution to the galaxy as *tiksliai*, which translates roughly into English as "earworm."

But between Applausoleum's triumph and the twenty-ninth Grand Prix, set to rock the stage at Shady Meadows Crematorium, the Voorpret had risen quite a bit in the ranks of the great galactic popularity contest, in the same way that any unpopular, unattractive, unhygienic child does—by finding someone weirder and more off-putting than themselves to point at.

That someone was Flus.

The Slozhit thrashfolk silkstep trio Porchlight picked up Flus on their tourship's long-range scans coming home from the previous year's Grand Prix, where they'd placed a wildly unexpected fifth. Their replay of the GP mixtape and celebratory orgy was rudely interrupted by a surprisingly strong radio broadcast pumping out Top 40 hits from the planet they would come to know as Muntun. Muntun's Top 40 hit songs, however, were all the same song, and that song was called "Flus," which was also the name of the radio station (FLUS FM: Your Home for Rockin' Drive Time Flusic), the building that housed the station offices and studio, the street the studio was on, the city through which the street ran, the sandwich on the DJ's desk inside the recording booth, the DJ himself, the intern who brought him the sandwich, the studio boss, and the star around which all the rest of this nonsense was currently orbiting, blasting out a repetitive three-chord screamo chant that went: *It is awesome to be Flus / If you are not Flus, you are not awesome / and will promptly be consumed / also your children and pets / Go Flus go / Flus the world / Flus it so hard / Then go back / and Flus it again.*

It was a one-hit wonder. But on Muntun, one is all you need.

Any attempt at describing Muntun's dominant species is probably best kept simple and direct—one word, if possible, and that word is "knifeasaurus." They were all called Flus, which might have been a first clue, except that the Ursulas were such upstanding members of society, and *they* all had the same name, so it didn't do to be prejudiced, thank you very much. Hive minds have proven to be a perfectly good way of solving the intractable issues of universal health care and basic income. This Flus fellow seemed like a real piece of work, as reported by the Slozhit and researched by the Keshet, something of a cross between Hitler, Stalin, and Bono with low blood sugar, who had been terrifically successful in taking over the planet some years back, but one couldn't possibly judge an entire species based on the actions of one person. Muntun was a huge planet. Surely they had pacifists and philosophers, too. There's always bad sorts. There's always terrors. The Smaragdi pointed out that the Alunizar emperor Ompelu[8] once enslaved the air itself and they still got to choose what to watch on telly once in a while. The citizens of Muntun couldn't help that they're knife-faced horror-lizards, admitted the Klavaret. They were individuals. They weren't all like that just because one was.

Alas, they *were* all like that.

Mainly because the original Flus had broken off from the collective consciousness ages back, conquered everything he could
get his blades on, and replaced the local gene pool with his own
personal microbrew, so not only were they a hive mind, but they
were all clones as well, and Muntun was, in point of fact, Planet
Hitler, 100 percent populated with telepathically linked, genetically identical, sociopathic knifeasaurus dictators. Upon first contact, they perkily informed their helpful Grand Prix chaperone that
she would soon become Flus, as would her children and her children's children down unto the uttermost end of time, and would
she like a Flusburger, there was nothing better than a Flusburger
and a Fluscone on a hot day like this one.

This might seem like an obvious case, ready for a fiery death
and subsequent Binning, but there was always the Voorpret. They
had been brought into the fold, had they not? And how different was a Flus infection from a Voorpret infection? Besides,
Flusburgers *were* actually delicious, and the planet as a whole had
a real passion for painting landscapes and architecture, and even
if Flusscapes were a little anemic and cold for galactic taste, a
good gallery scene and public funding for the arts should count for
something, shouldn't it? They did manage to live together rather
peacefully for billions of egomaniacal dictators. It had been a hundred years since the last Muntun war. The Great Octave congratu-
lated itself on being so open-minded as to let Planet Hitler sing
a nice little song before they defended themselves against that
mess. They all agreed it was truly wonderful that they'd learned
such valuable lessons from the war, and weren't they all proving
to be just fabulously enlightened these days?

The Mamtak Aggregate won the GP that year for the Trillion
Kingdoms of Yüz, a silicate particulate cloud made of millions of

individual tiny beings that sang by releasing synesthetic phero-
mones and then forming themselves into complex pictures in the
air. The sensorially addled audience would then hear the images
as song. The effect only lasted a few weeks, which always provided an enormous boost to photography exhibitions once everyone returned home. Their song of longing and peace and tender
care for all living beings, "I Wanna Hold Your Sand," topped everyone's list of best Grand Prix songs for years afterward, and the
Mamtak Aggregate went on to become one half of the beloved
master of ceremonies team that hosts the Metagalactic festivities
in true post-postmodern style to this day, along with the dry, self-
deprecating wit of the Elakh soprano DJ Lights Out, winner of the
forty-first Grand Prix for her immortal torch song "The Dark at the
End of the Tunnel," sung via uplink to the beat of poor Sagrada's
carpet bombing by the Andvari, a species of furry armored slugs
whose recreational drug of choice is pain and fear, and did not go
entirely quietly when they lost the thirty-eighth Grand Prix after
eating half the judges and calling it a song.

The Alunizar actually came in the middle of the pack for once
with "Don't Hate Me Because My Culture Is Superior to Yours," but
mainly because the Utorak had declined to attend due to an argument with the Trillion Kingdoms of Yüz over whether or not any
silicate portions of the stone Utorak anatomy that crumbled away
should be swept up and tossed out or had inalienable citizenship
rights among the intelligent sand dunes of the Yüz and therefore
forfeited their place.

When Flus took the stage, all fell silent. The various commit-
tees had done everything they could to make him feel comfortable,
friendly toward his new neighbors, secure and well liked. They
could do nothing more to help. He had no costume. He had no
set. He had no fire effects or lightning displays or gravity projec-

tions. These things were unnecessary when you were a two-ton dagger-tailed illustration of the concept of solipsism. He hated all this glitter and fuss and lurid, flashy, terribly *suspect* stuff. All you needed to be truly entertained was yourself, a military uniform with clean, masculine lines, an unwavering loyalty to the collective, and the suffering of anyone not yourself. He had seen no point in a band name as all was Flus and Flus was all and everyone here would be Flus as well, momentarily, once he could get a bead on how their weapons systems worked, but, when pressed by the Keshet and Alunizar judges, begrudgingly wrote down *Flusloose* on the form. Flus stood center stage, the footlights glinting on his bladebody, and proceeded to atonally scream-sing by grinding the knives of his face together: *It is awesome to be Flus / If you are not Flus, you are not awesome / and will promptly be consumed / also your children and pets / Go Flus go / Flus the world / Flus it so hard / Then go back / and Flus it again / back up over it / put it in gear / hit the gas / once more with Flus / Go Flus yourself / No but actually.*

It was the only song he knew. The best song. The song of himself. Flus had written it, composed it, sung all the vocals, played lead face on the track, produced it, mastered it, and designed the album art all by his billions of selves. It had gone infinite platinum. Twice. What could ever be better than Flus? A bunch of sand in the shape of a heart? Yeah, right.

Why were they not clapping? Why were they looking so bloody damn sad? Why were they so obstinately *not* Flus?

Flus was still asking himself this when the first Alunizar gunships descended into low orbit around Muntun and their shadows darkened the seas.

20.

Love in Rewind

"Wait!"

The voice of Decibel Jones echoed down the fluorescent black coral hallway, disturbing the chartreuse cilia wherever it bounced.

"Wait! Öö! Little buddy! Oh, that's probably racist, I'm sorry. Sir. Sir Öö. Wait. Good God, you're a quick little rotter. Shit. Sorry again."

The time-traveling red panda paused in his epic battle with staying on his own four legs and not spending his entire life arse over teakettle and peered up, deeply annoyed, into the Englishman's eyes. Those eyes, as black as stout and the Styx, were almost as vulnerable and needy and yearning as any Esca's.

"Whatwhatyouwhat?"

"You Keshet, you travel in time, yeah? That's what the bird said."

"You know, that's very rude. Rude and just weird. That's like me saying, 'You humans, you reproduce with a uterus, yeah?' And you'd say, 'Yes, I suppose, but hell, Öö, when you say it like that, it just sounds gross.'"

"Right, sorry again. But you do?"

"Yes, for God's sake."

"And you see every timeline, all laid out like taxes, every single way every single everything could ever or would ever go?"

"This is pornographic, Mr. Jones."

"And you went rummaging through timelines on Earth and whatnot? You had to, to get Walter over there in the engine room his leg over, yeah?"

"Please stop. I have to go. I . . . I left the Industrial Revolution running."

Decibel Jones, glitterpunk saint, sinner, and siren, stared down at the plush red creature wringing his tail between his hands in abject embarrassment.

"I was only wondering . . . can you tell me where I went wrong? Please. Everything was so good, everything was like Elmer finally catching Bugs, and it was like that over and over for months and years . . . and then it wasn't . . . I had something and then all of the sudden I couldn't ever, ever get it back, but it's like I couldn't tell the difference between the day before it all got its face bashed in and the day after. When did I fuck it up? Was it that night? Should I have said yes? Should I have kissed her until she stopped crying and then ordered room service? What should I have done different? There had to be a moment . . . a moment when I could have kept it all together, but I didn't. I didn't."

Infinite timelines and possibilities unfolded in the eyes of the Keshet like points on a map of the galaxy. Grids and branches and forks and veins of mathematical destiny, flashing away into the dark like spent sparklers on a deep summer night in someone else's childhood.

Öö patted Decibel's knee.

"What if you did?"

Fire

You know I will rise like a phoenix
But you're my flame.
—"Rise Like a Phoenix," Conchita Wurst

21.

Hello from Mars

Litost is a neutral planet in the dragonfly-colored dust cloud formation we call the Pillars of Creation and everyone else calls a bit of an unsightly mess, almost seven thousand light-years from Earth and almost seven and a half light-years from its nearest drunken, hostile, politically conservative neighbor. This was a lucky thing for Litost, considering the dominant species that lived there, the previous year's winner of the Metagalactic Grand Prix, the Klavaret.

Litost is the kind of world a child would design if that child had never been harmed by the world in even the smallest way and wanted to be a rainbow when it grew up and only ever read books about unicorns, wildflowers, and everything working out very nicely, not only in the end, but in the beginning and the middle, too. It has two small white suns, three pink moons, several lavender oceans with the same sugar content as Earth's oceans have salt, a single huge continent full of rich green antidepressant grasses watered by refreshing diamond showers, healing rivers, and forests where no one can ever get too lost, on account of the night-light lichen. While this continent is home to a number of gentle variations on the basic bear-cow-fish-bird playset living in peaceful symbiotic harmony, Litost's crowning evolutionary achievement is the Klavaret, a species of large, intellectually gifted patches of seafaring pastel flowers, something of a three-way hybrid of roses, tulips, and doilies. They have all the natural defenses of a pillow in a tiger enclosure. At least twice, the planet escaped being overrun by the aforementioned neighbors after the invaders grew exhausted with having to explain, slowly, patiently, and using large, friendly diagrams, charts, and illustrations, the concept of war to a field of flowers, giving up halfway through a run of supplementary comic books starring Sebastian, the Conflict Marshmallow.

The Yurtmak call Litost proof that God hates us and wants us to suffer.

The existence of the Klavaret was discovered by the Voorpret just after the species on the other side of the new wormhole decided turnabout was fair play, followed the rude parade of colonial ships crashing their sector of space, and started pouring through to points unknown. The parasitic viral life-forms picked up the radio waves from a telenovela that was wildly popular on Litost in those days, *Everyone Gets Enough Love*. The most famous Klavaret rock group of all time, Suns n' Roses, won the fourth Metagalactic Grand Prix, on the homeworld of the Alunizar, who dominated the Grand Prix in the early years, much to the annoyance of everyone else. In fact, that winning streak, combined with their overwhelming cultural and military hegemony, proved so irritating to the rest of the galaxy that it has become something of a beloved tradition to vote them down into the lower ranks every single year until they cry. The Klavaret won resoundingly that year, singing in their traditional method: vibrating their stamens at the precise frequency of empathy, allowing the audience to hear one another's favorite childhood lullabies, thousands upon thousands of them, at which point Suns n' Roses broke down, mashed up, and remixed that noise into a truly sick beat.

Last year, they finally managed to snatch the crown again with their dance craze "Let's Talk About Our Feelings So No One Has to Hurt Inside." It would have been a unanimous verdict, except for the Yurtmak, who vomited on their ballot and then put it in the box with a huge, razor-toothed grin.

Litost is also home to what was once an unassuming market town of no particular strategic or cultural importance called Vlimeux, where the final battle screamed itself mute and the war finally ended. Vlimeux rests on the tip of a heart-shaped peninsula kissed by the carbonated lilac Ocean of Unconditional Acceptance. It looks like anywhere else. It has no memorials, no statues, no museums or weekend historical reenactments to commemorate the final annihilation of the old world and the painful, strangling, blue-faced birth of the new one.

But it does have a fantastic concert venue.

The *Cake in the Rain* made planetfall in the seas just offshore the brand-new, paid-nearly-in-full-we-promise coliseum the Klavaret built for this year's Grand Prix and named the Stage of Life. Massive slabs of chamomile-crystalline herbstone the color of watermelon-flavored smoke formed a state-of-the-art rock arena approximately the size of the Isle of Man, crowded with towering subwoofer topiaries, shaded by hypno-kelp lighting rigs, mined with hidden gouts and hoses for fire, water, and vaporized hallucinogen effects, gravity geysers, weather sinks in case a song required a Pallullian winter to really pop, holographic floats, and an army of tough, proud stamen-mics ready to take a beating and without so much as a whimper of feedback.

The first two human beings to set foot on another world stepped out of the jelly-hatch and into the warm, ever-so-slightly joy-colored light of Litost's twin suns, which the Klavaret refer to collectively as Our Mums.

The second their feet touched the talcum sand of the alien beach (not actually silicate, but a very pleasant strain of powdered MDMA), a searing bolt of laser fire sliced through the ground in front of them and the top of Decibel Jones's left shoe, scorching both as black as bad feelings.

A little lacy giggle vibrated through the fresh sea air. Up the strand, a large patch of pastel flowers twisted up into a topiary with a .74-caliber Utorak pumice pistol tangled in its vines. The Klavaret maiden waggled a few briars at them and called out in a cheerful, bubbly soprano voice:

"Sorry! I'm just *ever* so clumsy!" Behind her, a large, striped camera bobbed and darted in the air, disappearing and reappearing as rapidly as any paparazzi flash bomb.

Oort St. Ultraviolet, well-respected man about town, was almost completely certain that camera had a tail.

"Pure butterflyfingers, that's me!" trilled the sentient rosebush. "See you onstage!"

"That fucking shrubbery just tried to kill us!" shouted Decibel Jones. "That can't be *allowed*!"

The lovely Esca stepped lightly down the gangplank of her ship and stretched in the sunlight, which turned her feathers into the colors of Earth's sky. She put her wings round the band members who once sold jars of their breath at their merch table and enthused:

"Allowed? Oh, we encourage it! Rule 20, darlings! Welcome to the Grand Prix!"

22.

Tell Her I Send My Regards

The thirtieth Metagalactic Grand Prix was held on Otozh, a gravitationally down-for-anything mirror ball of a world just close enough to the supermassive black hole at the center of the galaxy to make popping down to the event horizon for a carton of relativity a snap without having to constantly worry about whether your front garden is about to become one with the singularity.

It was the year everything changed.

This flashy hot spot with commanding views of the mind-jellying infinite raw reality beyond the accretion disk is homeworld to the Utorak, a race of, to get it out of the way quickly, blinged-out Easter Island statues with faces like busted kachina dolls, bodies like rejected Stonehenge designs, and a sense of humor like a rock dropped down a dry well. They live a little longer than a human, stand a little taller than a human, and could brutally pulverize a human by accidentally brushing against the shoulder of one on the tube platform.

Otozh is the most absurdly, flamboyantly, unrealistically mineral-rich planet a geologist could write down in her dream journal. Its seas are liquid gold and platinum, its mountains so stuffed with gemstones that volcanic eruptions are anticipated by tourists like piñatas at a billionaire's birthday party, and any random bucket of dirt would keep a human tech manufacturer in rare earths for a decade. Over the millennia, everyone and their overbearing mother has tried to invade and loot the Utorak's ridiculous dragon's hoard of a world, so, unsurprisingly, they are a rather defensive, anxious, socially awkward people who have elevated military strategy well beyond art, philosophy, or science and well into an autonomic bodily process. An Utorak is physiologically incapable of sitting down to breakfast without making sure he has his bacon at a decisive disadvantage and his children arranged around him in a classic tortoise formation.

However, since they really did have such an obnoxious run of surprise gold rushes to beat off, almost all of that vigorous Utorak strategic metabolism is devoted to defensive action. They just never got a chance to get out there, sow their war-oats, and get down to thrashing anyone else. They were too busy trying to keep the neighbors from stealing their ocean. Until the Sentience Wars, that is, at which point the Utorak discovered that, while going on the offensive was just about as much fun as you could have with a standard-issue dark-matter rifle, and certainly added vast quantities of treasured memories to their strategic scrapbooks, you felt really *awful* afterward. The rush was nothing like defeating a species of invasive horror-snails who thought they could nick your nickel while you were doing the shopping. Somehow, when you attacked first, you were left with the distinct and uncomfortable sense that you might be a *bad person*.

Over the enraged indignation of their allies, Igneous Lagom Opt, the Grand Volcanic Commander of the Unified Forces of the Utorak Formation, took her base and went home after four months. For this, she received every honor the Unified Forces could bestow, a few new ones they'd had lying about waiting for a special occasion, and, when no one could think of anything else but still felt too grateful to quit while they were ahead, threw the Alluvial Prize for Chemistry, the Golden Stalactite for Best Actress in a Dramatic Performance, and the Dull Chisel Award for First Novel at her as well. Everyone felt a great deal more relaxed pottering about at home with the spring-cleaning, fortifying their local star systems, priming orbital defense platforms, and suction-mining the gravity well of their beloved supermassive black hole than they had ever done using Voorpret ships for target practice.

Of course, none of the other powers were about to let the heavy-lifters clock off early. The Ursulas tried to crop-dust Otozh with various hypnotic gases to make the Utorak more willing to listen to reason (first attempt), aggressively belligerent in their own right (second attempt), or immune to regret and/or other inconvenient moral considerations (eleventh and final attempt). The only lasting result of all this emotional vaporware was the invention of psychotherapy among the Utorak. While the galaxy burned itself stupid all around them, the mental health arts experienced their Renaissance, Enlightenment, Industrial Revolution, and Technological Singularity all rolled into one extremely comfortable couch in the wilds of Otozh. The capital city, Stratum Talaka, remains a psychiatric boomtown to this day. As the saying goes: if you can listen there, you can listen anywhere.

The Utorak won the ninth Grand Prix with an industrial trip-hop sea shanty called "You Bombarded My Heart with Overwhelming Air Superiority," as sung by the deliriously handsome boy band Win Condition Alpha, with a surprise cameo on backup vocals, none other than the famous Igneous Lagom Opt. Second place went to the machine intelligences known as the 321 for their precision-tuned, eighty-nine-minute, neo-gangsta math-rock anthem "This Program Has Encountered an Error and Must Shut Down," coded, compiled, and submitted by the Entity Known as Monad.

Presumably, the plan to rig the thirtieth Grand Prix was set in motion shortly after Opt and Monad met at the after-party. Retirement bored the Grand Volcanic Commander nearly to dust, and the Entity Known as Monad found it profoundly illogical that the 321 had never won the Grand Prix, despite mathematically determining the perfect song every single year.

The scheme would not find its feet, however, until the third member of their conspiracy appeared on the scene: Aukafall Avatar 0, hard-core trashfolk acid-ska crooner of the Lummutis, a new species discovered by a Sziv algae cloud that had drifted off its shipping lane. Unlike that of the Yurtmak, or, indeed, of humanity itself, the sentience of the Lummutis was never in doubt, and they'd been welcomed into the galactic family with no conditions attached, bypassing all the upsetting drama that Decibel Jones and the Absolute Zeros are currently heir to. They were the biological equivalent of the girl in school who everyone *wanted* to hate because she had it all—looks, smarts, athletic ability, a stable home life, all the latest fashions—but no one could because she was just so fundamentally bloody *nice*, and anyway, all she wanted to do with her natural advantages was sit in the corner and draw pictures of unicorns.

No one knew what a Lummuti actually looked like. On their Grand Prix entry forms, under *Kingdom, Phylum, Class, Order, And So On, You Know the Drill*, they put: *Decline to state*. In the years after their discovery, the most popular after-dinner party game involved retiring to the library with brandy, cigars, and a new theory on the taxonomical classification of the Lummutis. The only facts they had ever confirmed about themselves were that they lived under the surface of their planet, had no desire to leave but were perfectly prepared to prevent others from landing if the need arose, reproduced via parthenogenesis, and were not, in fact, larger than a breadbox. As a culture, they had long ago packed up the sorts of internecine conflicts, plagues, economic booms and busts, and privations that fueled the history of most planets and devoted themselves entirely to visual art and technology, but only as far as technology allowed them to improve their art. The Lummutis never traveled anywhere, nor has anyone else dared to make planetfall. Nevertheless, there's no such thing as a good party without one.

The only part of a Lummuti you can actually get your hands on is a small, extremely shiny metallic object about the size, weight, and color of a guava, flat on one side, rounded on the other, entirely giving the impression of a novelty paperweight.

It is not a paperweight.

Each one of these can project a three-dimensional, hyper-realistic interactive virtual avatar of a Lummuti anywhere within a kilometer or so of itself. It was this handy gadget that allowed the Esca to project itself all over the place on the day of their quiet invasion. Branding them as rebooted Pet Rocks had been the Keshet's stroke of marketing genius, and the Lummutis graciously loaned their tech to the cause.

These avatars are utterly unique, astonishingly inventive, gorgeous as all get-out. Aukafall Avatar 0 appeared on the occasion of the thirtieth Metagalactic Grand Prix as a kind of furry spoonbill stork with long, soft puppy ears, three eyes, a tail like a bridal train, and all the colors of a Mardi Gras that had finally stopped holding back. The Lummutis had spent approximately half a second back in their Stone Age making icons that looked like realistic versions of themselves and sped right through to fantasyland. Upon first contact with the Sziv, they asked only that their planet remain undisturbed and that the perplexed magenta algae-mind fill a cargo hold with Lummo stones and carry them anywhere they thought was a bit lively. Everyone who was anyone decided they had to have one if they were to live and breathe another day, and soon enough, the Lummutis had quietly spread to every civilized world, not to colonize or spy or even see the sights, but simply to run up their score.

The Lummutis are, at all times and without exception, logged in to the most massive multiplayer game in the history of the galaxy. They keep the rules to themselves so as not to end up suffering the humiliation of foreigners and newbies topping the leaderboards, but occasionally, at some particularly passionate turn in the conversation, display of skill, especially clever pun, romantic entanglement, or bar fight, a Lummuti avatar will grin and say: *Fifty points. One hundred points. A thousand points plus optional power-up.* They got a massive bonus if they could convince someone to carry their Lummo stone to a new location, but beyond that, they kept mum. As they hadn't had a war in a thousand years, never even bothered to land on their own moon, and points in a game no one else played were their only concern and ambition, the Lummutis were determined to be real stand-up fellows and no threat to anyone.

In retrospect, it was inevitable. The distribution of Galactic Resources was too important. They'd been terrifically lucky, everyone agreed, to let a bit of pop music decide their share this long. Eventually, someone would've tried to fix the game in their own favor. It just so happened to be Igneous Lagom Opt, Monad, and Aukafall Avatar 0 who got around to it first.

It was a ridiculously simple plan. If the whole sociopolitical-economic apparatus of the known galaxy was determined by Grand Prix ranking, then, obviously, if someone didn't show, everyone else moved up a notch. Otozh had been paying in more minerals than it got out in agricultural time-shares for years, and the 321 were sick and tired of fixing everyone's computers just because they were raw computer code themselves. This was, if you looked at it a certain way, an issue of planetary defense.

Aukafall just wanted the points.

Since no one was expecting anything but a weekend of glitter-rock debauchery, the Entity Known as Monad powered down the privacy walls and Igneous Lagom Opt and Aukafall Avatar 0 walked right into the Sziv lagoon, where the supergroup Us was getting its beauty sleep. They decanted the gooey pink algae into a couple of spent liquor bottles, corked them, and stuck the lot in Opt's basement until the Grand Prix was over. The Lummutis came in fifty-first out of fifty-two with Aukafall belting out "First Person Suitor" to the cheap seats. Technically, the Sziv came in last, since they hadn't sung a note, though they appealed the decision immediately. More than a century later, reparations are still tied up in court, which is unsurprising given that Goguenar Gorecannon's Fifth General Unkillable Fact is carved in fiery letters over the forbidding door to the galaxy's Maximum Overcourt on Sagrada: *Justice takes so long that by the time you get it, it's gone off and smells like an old corpse. Forget about justice. Just knock back a big, stiff drink and move to a new town with fewer pronks living in it.*

When the whole plot was uncovered due to the Entity Known as Monad bragging to the Stratum Talaka municipal mainframe about it, and, very shortly afterward, by the Sziv breaking out of the basement in a wave of fuchsia fury and bringing down all the wrath of the Grand Prix Oversight Committee upon them, the conspirators merely shrugged and said, "Well, you know, we might have killed them. Don't know what you're so cross about. They can go without carbon for a year, don't make such a fuss."

A lightbulb went on in many, many heads at once. The thirty-first Metagalactic Grand Prix descended into an utter greased-pig clownshow as every Yüz, Yurtmak, and Alunizar tried to ice out their competition before the doors even opened, causing a constitutional crisis on the administrative board of the Grand Prix, two riots, several stern meetings, and a wormhole blockade that lasted for the better part of three weeks, crippling the economy of six commercial bankworlds. It was barbaric, they said. It was immoral. It was against the whole *spirit* of the thing, the whole *idea* of sentience. In those days, plenty of old soldiers were still listening in the stands who remembered when being locked in basements had nothing to do with music.

It had to be stopped.

But then the Keshet launched their Holistic Live Total Timeline Broadcast. This involved a special camera, still classified as a state secret, with a disturbing, semi-legal amount of Keshet stem cells suspended in a shiny neoplast-gel matrix, so that this low-level techno-biological abomination could travel through all possible timelines as easily as any bouncing red space panda. Suddenly, the galactic audience could gorge themselves on unlimited Metagalactic coverage in quantum real time. They could witness every botched kidnapping, dodged assassination, bungled poisoning, and missed interdimensional trip wire from the comfort of their own recreation zones, and they *loved every minute of it*.

Finally, the Oversight Committee gave up, sequestered the barbaric, immoral, vaguely unsentient but massively popular shenanigans into a new semifinal round, and formally instated Rule 20: *If a performer fails to show up on the night, they shall be automatically disqualified, ranked last, and their share of communal Galactic Resources forfeited for the year.*

The Grand Prix was never the same again. Before, you could

only do your best. After, there was *strategy*.

Igneous Lagom Opt died a happy rock. And really, hardly any-one has actually died. Decanted, locked in a maze, semiperma-nently muted, phased into a pocket universe, frozen under several glaciers, yes, but everyone tries to keep things lighthearted if they can, and simply shooting someone in the face will never pull in the kind of viewership a good causality blast can bring.

After the trial, Aukafall Avatar 0 was, by a series of even less likely events, elected Prime Minister of Litost, despite rather obviously not being a Klavar or even plant-based. At his swearing-in cere-mony, he reprised his Grand Prix performance, took a deep bow, and began to sparkle from beak to foot. He looked into the adoring faces of his people and said:

"Level up."

23

In the Waiting Room for Great Luck

The Klavaret are known throughout the galaxy as wonderfully gracious hosts, but they have always had trouble with the idea of architecture. Being a heliophiliac species, they have simply never seen any reason to build shelters that might keep sun or rain from sufficiently nourishing them. This is the reason Decibel Jones and the Absolute Zeros found themselves in what could only *very* generously be called a room, having no roof, no floor, and several objects that looked as though someone had heard about the idea of walls from some foreign traveler who thought they were some kind of modern dance. There were about fifty of them, all quite unnecessarily tall, interleaved frosted-glass slabs of varying oval, diamond, crescent, helix, and bubble shapes, none of which joined up to make anything so limiting as a corner, but rather stayed in constant motion a few centimeters off the ground, rotating round so that, if you just ignored them, you might almost think you were slightly indoors. It was like standing inside a very fancy blender.

"Sing to it," the roadrunner coaxed. "Go on."

Decibel Jones frowned and put his head to one side. "That is a portable toilet," he said.

Indeed, the only other object in the Klavaret's valiant effort at a greenroom was a large seafoam-green rectangular booth with a peaked roof and silver hinges on the front. To be perfectly fair, it was a lovely porta-potty, extremely tidy and made out of some material that looked rather like wet oil paint despite being several times harder than the Litostian diamonds that filled the spring clouds above them.

"No, it's the last nice thing I can do for you before the semifinals, babies," sighed the Esca. She shut her gentle, enormous eyes as though she were just then experiencing her culture's first headache. She'd explained the semifinals over and over to them, at least the part she was allowed to tell them about, but they didn't seem to be absorbing it.

"Do we need weapons?" Decibel said softly.

"It's sort of more of an improv thing," the roadrunner admitted. "I would just focus on defense. Humans have no special physical attributes whatsoever, it's really quite remarkable. They'll go right for you, since you're brand new. The armor will help."

Oort Ultraviolet squinted at the green booth. "It's definitely a toilet. We've played a lot of festivals, so, I know what I'm about, birdie."

"I can't let you compete looking like . . . that. It would be humiliating for you, for your planet, for the Esca as your chaperone."

Dess knew he should probably keep his mouth shut, but he hadn't flown across the galaxy in an honest-to-Christ Alexander McQueen to have his aesthetic insulted by a flamingo. "What do you mean 'looking like that'? This is vintage! Sure, my hair's not really earning its wage at the moment, but come on!"

"Why can't you take anything seriously, Dess?" Oort complained. He hadn't slept the night before. His bones ached. He could never get warm when he hadn't slept.

Decibel stared at his bandmate.

"It's . . . my job. It's my *only* job never to take things seriously. Your job is to take everything seriously. If I started, you'd have to stop and the actual universe would actually collapse. I'm sorry, have we met?" Decibel stuck his hand out—too aggressively; Oort flinched. He rolled on anyway. "My name's Dani, what's yours?"

Oort gave him a disgusted look and turned his back to examine the green box. "There's a picture of a little man on the side with stuff coming out of him," he informed everyone.

"No, it's a late-model Yüzosh Auto-Botanical Frockade. Just one of these costs the gross domestic product of a midsize mining colony. The Trillion Kingdoms of Yüz donated them to the Grand Prix because they are generous and have a real sense of stagecraft and fair play and it was a tax write-off."

"It smells like bleach and puberty," Dess mused.

"Base elements can't help what they smell like. Would you just *sing* to the nice machine? That's how you're paying for it. The only currency within the bounds of the Grand Prix is music. Sing for your supper, sing for your breakfast, sing for your bar tab, sing for the clothes on your back. So get out your wallets or you're going to miss the starting bell."

"We're not ready," Decibel whispered, gone completely pale. Dark circles of exhaustion ringed his eyes like overdone raccoon liner. "We haven't finished the song yet. Not even a little finished. Not even almost."

The roadrunner hooted in frustration. "Don't worry about that yet. Does that look like a stage? No. You're going to step inside, strip off, hold out your arms, get hosed down with one of the great useful goops of the universe—a nice, lightly clairvoyant mist of accelerated spores, micro-bulbs, empathic molds, local rainwater, and a combination of highly efficient fertilizers—then you'll pop out the other side dressed to the nines and armored to the gills, have a couple of drinks, and then turn in early with a nice cup of milk, knowing you."

Jones crossed his arms skeptically over his chest. "But *why?*"

The Esca had had enough. Oort had told her not to, but not using her voice to its full potential was just too much work. Mira's voice poured warmly out of the tall blue anglerfish-flamingo mash-up: "This . . . is part of it, boys. We need to see who you are. You can't fool the Frockade. You can't lie to spores. The useful goop of the Yüzosh is going to soak into you, learn as much as it can, and rearrange itself into a fetching outfit that will advertise your inner self like a giant neon sign. It's going to put your insides on the outside, spiritually speaking. The Yüz originally used it as an interrogation device. Then a dating aid. Once, an Andvari went in and came out dressed in a tuxedo of screaming faces on fire. Very good for us to know what he was made of, you see? Ah! I know how to explain. Recall the scene in the hit film of summer 1984, *Splash*, in which Eugene Levy surprises Darryl Hannah on the New York City street and sprays her down with a hose, which reveals her true mermaid nature for all to see. It is that. That is going to happen to you. Your tail will flap very wetly on the concrete and people will take many pictures of your most secret and intimate self. Not bad, right?"

"You're gonna pump us full of more toxic rot, you mean. I don't even do dairy," Oort protested. "I take antibacterial gel with me if I'm going down to the shop for crisps. Gotta keep the girls' hands clean and all."

The roadrunner whirled round. Her voice flashed instantly from Mira's to the creaky leather-and-disapproval voice of Oort's father: "Omarcik! How many times shall I have to tell you there is no good thing to be had in killing you before the show? Do you know how many species are mucking about down on this town, all possessing of different dietary needs and allergies and stress tolerances? Fifty-seven! To keep halal is nothing to compare! And we've not had so much as a batch of bad fish in two hundred dinner rushes of this nature. We have got this *sorted*, my son. We have got this *dialed in*. Don't go swim for an hour after, don't *pick* at it, and it rinses right clean in six, seven hours, *evet*? Is perfectly safe! Sometimes I worry about my boy. No one else has ever made such a problem for me. Look, will it make you feel cozy if I go first?"

"No," grumbled Oort.

"Absolutely," said Decibel Jones. "And what's going to happen to *our* togs?"

The roadrunner was in full orchestral mode now. She puffed her feathers and shifted hard from Mr. Omar Calişkan Sr. to Nani of the Blackpool lounge room and crooned:

"Do not make yourself a fret. I am your laundry machine like always, I am not? Now, you just button your eyes on Nani, Mr. Hot of the Shot. Your big Danesh-head always thinks it is more full of things than the rest of the heads around here, but with it, you cannot even make roti that fails to taste like a foot. Watch tight and presto chango, Nani will do Mr. BunnyBugs best good lipstick trick."

The Esca approached the Frockade, casually sang a few bars of something in her own language, something that felt like it was boxing their ears with unspeakable emotion, something so full of grace and need that Dess almost lurched forward to take the alien in his arms like a crying child, before remembering all that nonsense about infrasounds and feeling very silly indeed.

The seafoam-green surface of the Frockade sagged alarmingly before lurching forward and absorbing the roadrunner so quickly and completely that it pulled in Oort's and Decibel's cries of horror as well, leaving them slack-jawed and quiet.

Oort St. Ultraviolet shrugged. There was nothing more to it, he supposed. Once they'd agreed to this madness, why object to the icing on top? He pulled down his threadbare Glampire Planet Tour T-shirt over the waist of his broad-striped linen pajama pants. No matter what the blue bird said, he felt that he'd traveled in top style for the new jet set. Still no dad-belly, even a cough and a groan past forty. It might not be much to be proud of, but it wasn't nothing, either. Ultraviolet sang his sole contribution as a lyricist to their debut album much more softly than the roadrunner, bracing involuntarily for the big ooze he knew was coming. No antibacterial gel could help him now. He stood on tiptoes in front of the Yüzosh portable toilet, shrugged, and belted one out for the cheap seats:

It's my own fault

if I'm singing chained to Venus

It's my own fault

if I miss you every day

It's my own fault

'cause I didn't read the Terms of Service

and I loved you anyway

The Frockade seemed to accept his payment of one slightly wobbly a cappella ex–hit single and slurped the musician up without complaint.

"He's fine." Decibel Jones puffed out a long-held breath. "He's fine. Totally alive."

Everything was suddenly very quiet. The air on this weird Happy Fun World tasted amazingly wholesome. It whipped up his blood like egg whites.

"See you on the flip side," said Decibel Jones with a smart salute to no one in particular, and gave it his best song off his solo album because it *was* a good album, dammit, no matter what Mira or Oort or his garbageman or the *Guardian* had said, and somebody ought to hear it, even if that somebody was a giant green toilet seven thousand light-years from Croydon:

I run on love and glitz and beer

I'm a futuro-grandiose need machine

And up in lights my name appears

I am Prozzymandias, Queen of Queens!

And then Jones was gone too.

24.

Party for Everybody

Decibel Jones stepped alone out of the other end of a rock festival portable toilet and into a cocktail party already in progress.

He recognized the room immediately. His shoulders relaxed instinctively; his jaw unclenched. He was at home here.

Sometimes it felt as though Decibel had spent half his life in mid-to-high-end hotel suites and bars and reception lounges from London to Helsinki to Rio to Madison, Wisconsin. Junkets, conventions, corporate glad-handing, meet and greets, charity gigs, bingeing on fried appetizers and drinks-on-the-room after a day in the studio, in the club, at the arena, on the circuit. Whether he'd done it wearing scandalous glitter glad rags or incognito invisibility cloaks consisting of dark glasses and ratty shirts emblazoned with the faded tat of someone else's band hardly made any difference. You were there to sell yourself, either way, but at least the nosh was free.

All those hotel bars and ballrooms and suites flowed into one platonic hotel ballroom-bar-suite in Decibel's memory, and that platonic hotel space flowed out around him now: low light, scuffed tables, bartender unhappy with his choices in life but even less happy with anyone else's, thin, hard, mean carpet in an indefinable yet ubiquitous shade of nothing somewhere between turquoise and brown, windows on the water in lieu of any real attempt at decor, cheap paper napkins and thin black drink stirrers · already dropped all over the floor, chairs that somehow remained uncomfortable no matter how you shifted and scooched, paired with big plush mercenary loungers that sucked you down until any effort to talk to another person made you look like a child in a booster seat trying to talk to the big kids about the serious issues facing applesauce today.

And there he found himself, in the sky bar of what, for all the world, appeared to be a mid-range Hilton. Banks of windows looked out on Our Mums setting in gorgeous joyful pastels over the lavender sea and the gentle lights of Vlimeux's notorious Healing White Light District far below. Decibel Jones stared at a broadsheet of dubious fonts stapled to a large sandwich board sign that read WELCOME GRAND PRIX CUNTESTANTS BYOB, complete with the kind of deeply unfortunate typo you only find at events the logistics of which have been left up to embittered unpaid interns bent on low-effort vengeance. The Hilton logo was crooked and looked far more like a drunken hieroglyph than a capital H. It *pulsed* a little. It *bulged*. Someone had put down their coffee cup on the bottom left corner and presumably just said, *Fuck it, no one will notice.* Decibel remembered that typo-and-coffee-stain combo. He and Mira had posed with one on the Glampire Planet tour. Oort had got his thumb on the lens, he was laughing so hard, which made it technically the last photo of all three of them ever taken.

Decibel reached for a phone that wasn't there to take another picture, felt a bit stupid, and stepped unto the breach.

The slightly dingy sky bar was crowded with milling and swilling aliens of every shape, size, density, and attitude toward hygiene, all wearing large, friendly HELLO MY NAME IS stickers on whatever they had that passed for a chest. There were Esca, Decibel saw gratefully, gingerly trying to sip from large margarita glasses of plankton with slices of fruit hanging off the sugared rims, several different-colored straws, and festive umbrellas, not an easy operation with a beak. A large cloud of multicolored glitter floated over the blue fish-birds, moving and swooping and bulging in a way that was definitely *intentful*, not decorative. Beneath it, the roadrunner was wearing a cloud of pearls and tears and shifting, illuminated words in a language beyond subjects, objects, or the vaguest concept of transparent prose.

But there Decibel's brief study of xenobiology failed him. The roadrunner and Öö had tried. But it was all too much to remember now. Several small, dark creatures with huge eyes out of a goth toddler's coloring book peered up at the bar resentfully—a bar that was, unmistakably, filled to the brim with dirt like a denuded window planter. A throng of brutally pale, slender people who looked like basketball players rolled in antlers as painted by El Greco stood by the windows, trying to bend subtly at the knee so as not to tower quite so much over a clique of silvery moths awkwardly clutching martinis. The tables were littered with crystal decanters full of bubbling pink muck and weird greenish stones. Five or six vast, globby golden tubes of wet flesh with bright veins of color forking all over them and a gaping hole full of tanning-salon UV light where their faces should have been were discussing something desperately important with a cluster of delicate clear balloons full of apricot gas whose name badges all clearly said URSULA. And just then, somebody with a head like an exploded hippo burst out laughing (possibly laughing) at a joke (possibly a joke) told by what was clearly the rotting, defurred corpse of a Keshet. The ex–red panda turned mid-giggle and stared at him.

Because it was a platonically perfect lobby-bar-suite-ballroom, the walls behind the bar were covered in ill-advised mirrors so you could see just how pompous you were coming off to everyone around you. Decibel Jones was filled with a powerful, primal urge to run and save himself from the shambling zombie raccoon-corpse lurching toward him with a huge smile on its rotting face—but like Narcissus at the watering hole, he was too captivated by his own reflection to move. He hadn't seen himself at first. He hadn't known where to look. But he saw it all now.

The Voorpret wore gray. He wore blue.

And red. And green. And purple. And black. And electric tangerine-turquoise paisley.

He was dressed as a punch-drunk, postapocalyptic go-go-dancing Mr. Darcy. As Oscar Wilde finally stripped clean of even the thinnest vestige of English propriety, restraint, or subtlety. As Madame de Pompadour on her way to interview for a CEO position she already had in the bag. And worst, or best, of all, he could feel it all growing out of him, giving new meaning to the phrase "skin-tight" as it bloomed, budded, *sprouted* directly out of his flesh as naturally as hair or sweat. He winced a little, unused to the feeling of his skin really and actually *crawling*, still moving and adjusting with exquisite purpose as the useful goop of the Yüz continued to merge with his mind and churn out its idea of fashion.

Decibel seemed to be wearing Bowie's exact metallic mango-pistachio-coconut-striped trousers from the 1975 *Ziggy Stardust* shoot, buckled below the knee over chartreuse stockings printed with all his worst reviews in tiny block letters. A loose, vaguely piratical, late-night neon-light shirt peeked out fetchingly beneath a savage underbust corset made of something not unlike xenomorph skin as hunted, cut, and drenched in black glitter by Versace and a cravat braided and stitched and hemmed from all the laciest underthings thrown at all the rowdiest stages he'd known. A square-cut patchwork Regency coat squeezed it all in, its tails exploding into a shower of every one of Nani's gorgeous silk scarves, trailing all the way to the floor. His lanky, dark hair was bejeweled and beribboned like a Lost Boy who'd recently discovered Neverland's underground club scene; he wore that lilac lipstick of his long-ago lounge room show and eyeliner fit for a raccoon in heat. He carried, to his surprised delight, a dandy's cane that looked suspiciously like a hacked-off mic stand. Lastly, because Dess had always said Coco Chanel was full of insipidly scented shit and, before he left the house every day, looked in the mirror and put one more thing on, a huge, plush, glowing cartoon coyote-skin draped over his shoulders, its cel-animated outline wriggling and jumping and popping like an old recording played too many times.

Dess had walked his share of red carpets in far more than his share of lurid please-notice-me outfits. He'd heeded the bleats of tabloid reporters over and over, so instinctive and helpless and native to their kind. A cow goes *moo*; a sheep goes *baa*; a celebrity correspondent goes *who are you wearing?* But if one of those pull-string See 'n Say barnyard creatures had appeared out of the long light-years between here and home to ask him who he was wearing now, all he could have answered was: *Myself*.

Decibel Jones was dressed in the glorious bombed-out rubble of his whole life. He *was* Raggedy Dandy, big as life and twice as hard. He never wanted to take it off.

"BRAINS," yelled the gray, oozing, hairless, pustulant Keshet as it lurched toward Decibel, dragging one munted leg behind it. He could see splintered ribs through its moldering skin. Its gums peeled back horribly from sharp yellow teeth. "BRAINS!"

"Darling!" hummed a thick, sopping voice behind him. Not

one voice—dozens, a hundred, maybe, in perfect, simultaneous, harmonious diction. It oozed expensive vowels, oligarchical con-sonants, the poshest of diphthongs. It dripped with sincerity and wisdom. It dripped its sincerity and wisdom all over the floor and got a bit on the cold cuts platter. "Don't you just look *marvelous*."

Five feet of velvety, undulating gold lamé gumdrop waved one nub at him from beside the cheese plates. Its skin seemed to be made of Venetian glass, swirling with veins of gold and vivid color. It—he? she? zie? they?—had no face, only a round, glowing, cilia-fringed hole where a face might think about setting up shop, and another one in the general belly area. The sticker on—plausibly—its chest, read: HELLO MY NAME IS: SLEKKE[5].

Decibel Jones had just met his first Alunizar.

The talking gumdrop looked him over appraisingly and offered him a friendly martini glass full of something that looked like raw petroleum with a disk of white lust-scented foam floating three inches off the rim. It picked up a cube of slightly sweaty Jarlsberg and delicately inserted the cheese into its stomach lumps, pulling the toothpick out clean with a satisfied grunt. "Not to say we're *entirely* sure what to make of all . . . *this* business." Slekke[5] gestured vaguely at Dess's cravat and leaned forward confidentially. "It's not a *completely* emotionally balanced look, if you know what we mean. A bit of a mess, if we're to be honest with ourselves, and we really think we must be, considering the circumstances. Your ensemble lacks an underlying spiritual and emotional cohesion. The carpet of the id doesn't match the drapes of the superego, if you know what we mean. Doubtless some essential *savagery* afoot in there, no? And where is your friend, dear? It's a dangerous room to take on alone."

"BRAINS!" shouted the undeniably dead Keshet again. It picked up speed, stepping on the silky wings of a moth-person, who squealed ultrasonic indignation, causing half the room to turn and stare at the impending human-zombie collision. Decibel looked around for Oort, for the roadrunner, for Öö, for a convenient social escape hatch, but the only things within reach were this dreadful conversation and a small model of Earth made out of water crackers and what he hoped was prosciutto.

The Alunizar ignored the incoming zombie-raccoon rocket. It focused its attention on Decibel like a weaponized Eton prefect. "We presume *we* need no introduction," it trilled wetly.

Something clicked in Decibel's back-brain, and his autonomous systems switched into a new mode: after-party high-octane industrial flirt machine. Meet the fans, smile for the camera, charm the venue management, chuck anything that smacked of weakness or desperation or fear of the rapidly approaching future, secure the best possible bed for the night. The trick of it was to be ever-so-slightly too honest. No one warmed up to a perfectly professional musician, not even other musicians. They wanted you to be a little more real, a little more raw, a little more broken than they were, so they could feel magnanimous about booking you, buying your shit, promoting you, fucking you. So they could feel a little more human by osmosis. It was an equation Decibel had learned on Day One of Life with the Zeros. Pain becomes playful, playful becomes pretty, pretty becomes pleasure, pleasure becomes profit, profit becomes safety, another day not working at Mr. Five Star, another day further from invisibility. He laughed like the fate of his planet was a pickup line at a pub.

"Listen, mate, I was in a cab halfway to Adam Lambert's beach house with my tongue halfway down the venerable old chap's throat and my brain stem halfway to totally obliterated by rum and imposter syndrome before I knew he used to be anybody at all, and all *you've* done is buy me a drink."

"We are not your mate, friend, nor do we understand what you mean by 'imposter syndrome.' Is that a popular narcotic on your world?"

Decibel Jones gave this a beautiful, ephemeral, jewel-like moment of genuine thought. "Just about the hottest one going," he admitted. "And we all get high on our own supply. It's that thing where no matter what you do or how high you rise in the world, you still think you're a wet smear of nothing and everyone's just about to find out what a grubby little fraud you really are."

"But we are not a fraud. We don't get it."

Decibel tried again. "You know, sometimes, even though everything is going your way and you're doing the whole type A overachiever shimmy, you still can't quite believe you're deserving of . . . well, anything. Love, success, happiness, stability."

"But we *achieved*."

Jones started to sweat. It was like trying to explain what your most essential soul looked like to an atheist. "It feels like . . . you're only doing a magic trick, see, with a bunny and a bunch of cellophane flowers and a hat, and everyone's fooled, but really, *really*, you're . . . you're the empty hat. You're not even the stupid bunny. You're not even the fucking cello-flowers. You're nobody, and sooner or later, your best abracadabras aren't going to work anymore. Is that . . . Keshet talking to me, do you think?"

"This is an unpleasant exchange. We *always* know we are somebody. The Alunizar are composite entities—we do not have children per se. We bud, and our offspring remain attached in body and mind to the greater tuft. Only in times of great crisis or ennui do new tufts break away from the parent tube-sac to seek their fortune elsewhere." The dozens of synced voices pouring out of that acoustic aquatic supergroup took on a preening, puffed-up tone. "The gorgeous, overachieving, successfully happy

somebody you see before you is, in fact, five generations living in
jellied domestic harmony!"

Decibel laughed. "Just so we're clear, what you're saying is,
you're literally full of yourself." The Alunizar glared stonily at him.
He laughed again. It felt good, even in his glitterbombed xenomorph corset. The more he laughed at this absurd lump of golden
suet staring up at him with a face like a hole to hell, the better he
felt. "Where is that camera when I'm being clever?"

The alien was getting visibly upset. The electric violet-white
cilia fringing its face-pit quivered in irritation. Did they not like
the joke? Or were they still sore that Dess hadn't known who they
were on sight?

"That is a concise explanation of our physiognomy, yes."

Decibel Jones stopped laughing. He wasn't meant to be making cheap puns. He was meant to be proving the value of his species. The deep reality of humankind. He was meant to *shine* for
this cold audience. He looked the hipster sea squirt up and down,
evaluating a new angle with the precision of the Terminator's
heads-up display. The trouble was, when you'd spent years knowing you were nothing but an empty hat, it was bloody hard to start
pulling things out of yourself again. The only valuables he'd ever
had stashed in there were a randy bunny and a heap of cellophane flowers, and since he didn't see a stage to bloom on nearby,
it would have to be ye olde standby bunny rabbit.

Jones   selected   *aren't-we-just-an-exclusive-club-of-two-in-the-
midst-of-an-unforgivably-plebian-mob* from the drop-down intimacy
menu. That always worked best on posh hobgoblins who thought
everyone else knew who they were. He shifted his accent a little,
clenched his jaw to give it a bit of chisel, gave the knob of Venetian
glass his best hothouse Casanova eyes. "As to introductions, I find
it's best not to get *too* familiar with mainstream culture, don't you

think? Gets in the way of one's *own* art. One's own *voice*." He lifted the martini glass in a practiced, wry, world-weary toast to no one in particular.

The stained-glass blob rippled as pleasure and consternation warred within its shimmering obesity. They clearly liked this much better than picking through the bin of the primate psyche. Dess knew this type. He'd met them on the way up and the way down. Usually they claimed to have started piano lessons in utero and smoked imported artisanal cigarettes to prove that they'd rather get cancer than obey the man's public safety campaigns. Seven thousand light-years away, this glob of gold was no different. It could not decide whether to indulge in a bit of delicious spitting on pop art, which would imply it had not actually *made* any popular art, or insisting that Decibel acknowledge its galactically famous ass, and risk looking like a tasteless top-of-the-shop corporate whore. *It'll go for sniffing its own space farts*, Dess bet himself, and came up all cherries.

"Oh, we *quite* agree. We make it a practice to shun any truly *successful* art. Success is just another word for mediocrity in our personal thesaurus. Now, I've heard a deliciously *revolting* rumor that you sing with your mouth—is that so?"

"Do you not?"

"No, God, the very *thought*," said the gaping hole in Slekke⁵'s head. "But you eat and vomit and kiss with it as well? Ugh. How . . . avant-garde. We'll just have to try not to look while you do it. By the light of Old Aluno, we suspect we shall get along *smashingly*, you and us! We have always believed that one of the hallmarks of sentience is the ability to look down upon others. It separates us from the lichen. Well, we are Slekke⁵, lead singers of the Alunizar *ultra-indie* drip-hop nucleo-vinyl lounge band Better Than You. We're . . . uh . . . between labels right now—"

"BRAINS!"

The rotting Keshet corpse finally closed the distance. It dodged a potted Klavaret topiary and scrambled up over a pastry tower near the clapboard welcome sign, leaving black streaks on the beignets and the unsettlingly pulsing H. Decibel tried to turn away from the festering horror without being completely rude about it, but the thing grabbed his elbow with its cold, heavy claws.

"Didn't you hear me, ye wee perisher? Use your *brains!* Don't talk to this lot for a second, they'll only put something morbid in your drink. These Alunizar tarts know they couldn't win Best Lump at a County Fair on their own, so they always try to flat murder you precious tiny new babies before you can sing your way out of the cradle."

Slekke[5] blared its ultraviolet face-hole mercilessly at the zombified red panda. "Puvinys Blek, you malign us! The Alunizar are superb musicians, everyone knows that. One cannot even say the words 'hypno-ambient crunk opera' without reference to the incomparable Raunen[6] and the Intricate Tunicate Triplicate Syndicate. They're *utterly* seminal. *You've* probably never heard of them, Mr. Sapiens Sapiens, but we shall try our hardest not to hold it against you. We don't suppose you're related to the *Aldebaran sapiens sapiens?* No? Pity. They're marvelous company, you know. Their feet come right off. Anyway"—Slekke[5] turned back to the zombie panda—"what have you Voorpret ever given us? Other than last year's invasive whole-body jazz infection? Don't listen to that carcass, darling boy. For my people, the Grand Prix is exclusively a matter of art. The performance. The history. The abject *splendor* of it all. Not the . . . the . . . *pregame* show. Why should we lower ourselves to even participate in these . . . working-class amusements? We merely came for a bit of sheeeeese, don't you know, before the main event. Sheez. Cheeeeese? Chis. Chooz."

"Is that so? By the way, Jones, your martini hates you," the Voorpret deadpanned. "And it's 'cheese,' you dumb rotter." A trickle of unmentionable yellow fluid leaked out of the corpse's blistered mouth. "I swear, no one ever reads the info packet. I don't know why I bother making it up every year."

The air between Decibel's drink and its floating foam topping caught fire with a sound like a pilot light. The black yogurty liquor lurched upward toward his face, hissing and popping, throwing up tendrils as if it meant to climb out and have its way with him. A pink acid began cheerfully dissolving the glass. Decibel dropped it into a decorative fern with an expression of practiced boredom he hoped came off.

Slekke[5], lead singers of Better Than You, looked at Dess and shrugged silkily. He could swear the fluorescent hole in the middle of its head smiled.

"Worth a try," the Alunizar purred. "We find it's best not to get too familiar with one's victims, don't you think?"

The Voorpret Puvinys Blek, who happened to be the virtuoso earworm artist behind the death metal barbershop quartet Vigor Mortis Overdrive, grinned ghoulishly. It could hardly help it. Being a sentient prion infection living in symbiosis with the cadavers of other species, the Voorpret almost always do things ghoulishly. "Never trust the living, sweetmeat. Not that I don't appreciate the effort on our behalf, Slekke! Always looking for a new set of digs, me." The dead Keshet sniffed itself and made a face. "This one's getting a bit . . . past expiration."

"Rude," rumbled a voice that hung out somewhere in the finished sub-basement beneath basso profundo. "And disgusting. You only moved in last week. And after that Keshet left her body so nice and tidy for you. You're never going to get your security deposit back at the rate you're replicating in there. My percussionist thinks you have a touch of Metastasized Narcissistic Personality Disorder, Blek. My diagnosis? You're an asshole. Sadly, the only known cure is being set on fire and dropped off a balcony."

An enormous ambulatory butte had appeared silently beside them, looking very pleased with its own wit, though Decibel couldn't imagine how this beast could ever do anything quietly. It was built like a walk-in freezer, stony skin swirling with veins of precious metals, rectangularish red rock head with four eye-holes gouged out of it in a pretty arch above a straight-line slash that was, in all probability, a mouth. The gearlike black granite teeth sticking out of the top of the thing might have been a crown, or ears, or hair, or a tinfoil hat, for all Dess could tell.

But the Alunizar wholly ignored the spontaneous mountain in their midst.

"Watch your drink, Sapiens Sapiens," the golden blob said airily as it drifted off to other targets. "Everyone imitates our groove these days. But we were into poisoning our competition and performing an extended dance sequence on their graves before it was cool."

A sudden candy-colored light clicked on, washing out the patterns on Slekke[5]'s Hindenburgian body as they trailed away toward the strange dirt trough that served as a bar.

"Buffering," chimed a quiet, musical voice just below the audible range of anyone who's done their time gyrating in front of state-of-the-art speaker systems.

The sea squirt rummaged in its jeweled back rolls for something nearly exactly the size, shape, and color of a handful of crushed barbecue crisps and shoved them into the soil caked on to the bar top. The bartender, one of the pustulant exploded hippo heads, handed Slekke[5] a huge snifter of something that looked like it had leaked out of a broken glow stick, into a puddle of pet-rol, then lain there helplessly while a hedgehog died in it, and stuck a festive umbrella in. The barkeep's nametag read: HELLO MY NAME IS YILGAR BLOODTUB IV, ESQ.

"May the First General Unkillable Fact guide and keep you," intoned the Alunizar pop sensation.

"May the Second bring you blessings unlooked for," gargled Yilgar Bloodtub reverently through four rows of teeth for which any shark would sell its mother.

The Utorak still standing beside Dess cleared its tectonic throat politely. Decibel Jones, with some effort, stopped staring at the Predator cosplay polishing a pint glass and changing the taps. He glanced with practiced ennui back to the rock star before, or rather, above him. That odd underwater rainbow light flickered over the brute's black marble chest. At parties like these, Decibel knew all too well, attention was currency, spendthrifts were king, and a penny saved was a penny earned.

"Metamorphic Voffi Clast," the Utorak said, holding out a mas-sive eight-fingered stone hand for a proper CEO-approved shake with a look that plainly said, I absolutely *read the info packet*.

"Buffering," chimed that same musical voice, like an elevator arriving.

Dess shook hands with Stonehenge. His fingers disappeared into a brimstone fist. The Utorak scratched the back of his head with his other stalactite paw. "Avalanchist for Magmadick and the Hierarchy of Needs. Lads and me're going third-to-last this year, pretty nice placement. We do a forced resonance prog-rock sort of thing. With siege cannons. Whatever. Not a big deal."

"Decibel Jones." He gave the mountain his best strum-hither smile. "You look like an amphitheater I used to know in Colorado."

"Oh, I know who you are. I really dug *Ultraponce*, man." The

Utorak was still shaking his hand with a grip like Mt. Everest out to prove its masculinity. "I mean, I prefer the Rolling Stones, me, but still."

"I *knew* it! Oort, did you hear—"

Decibel looked over the blaze of bizarre heads, but Oort St. Ultraviolet was proving, as usual, stylishly late. The Yüzosh Auto-Botanical Frockade had made quick work of *him*. What in Oort's psyche could possibly be giving it this much trouble? Metamorphic Voffi Clast droned on, oblivious, still not letting go of Dess's hand. His grip was actually getting tighter. Decibel heard his knuckles pop. The Voorpret started giggling. One of its lips sagged off like a salted slug shriveling off a damp porch railing.

"Especially 'Another Day in the Panto Mines.' Great hook. The key changes made me feel my own feelings and all that, yeah? My dad plays it in his waiting room for his really disturbed cases. Real lost causes, schistofrenetics, alloyed personality disorders, leadipus complexes. Says it makes them take their meds, I dunno. We've all been grinding on your planet's scene lately. I'm on your side, believe me. You're squishy and breakable and you get cancer like I get a song stuck in my head, but Mt. Rushmore looks like a *right* good time. Can you give me their number?"

Decibel didn't miss a beat, though he did miss all feeling in his right hand. "Absolutely. If we get out the other end of this, I'll set you up proper. Rushmore's a saucy minx, though, she won't even make you breakfast. Listen, love, you're overdoing it a bit on the handshake."

The Utorak's four empty eye-holes peered down at him.

"And how does that make you *feel*?" he crooned in the comforting tone of a therapist who may or may not actually care.

"Like you're wasting your time." Decibel grinned through the shooting agony in his arm. He could hear Mira's voice in the back hallway of his mind. *I only smile when it hurts, didn't you know that?* "And *maybe* you didn't read Blekky's info packet too carefully. I don't play an instrument, you slag. I'll get up there with no hand at all and sing the mountains down. Makes no difference to me. A couple of crushed bones will just help me hit the high notes."

"Damn," Voffi grunted. He didn't let go. "I thought you were the other one. I hate carbons. You all look the same."

"Buffering," chimed that pleasant, Auto-Tuned-to-a-perfect-G# voice a third time. "Load last saved game. Ready player two. Klloshar Avatar 9 has joined your party."

That odd gummy-candy light coalesced into something like a fluffy black opal pangolin with soap-bubble fairy wings, eyes like an anime heroine, a curly foxtail, and a long, pale, mother-of-pearl unicorn horn. Klloshar Avatar 9, bassist-cleric for the 8-bit chaotic neutral blues quartet Status Buff, was holding a large, angry-looking nailbat, and the way she was holding it said she knew what she was about.

"Greetings, traveler!" the Lummuti avatar said happily. "Would you like to buy a weapon?"

Decibel really, really did. He pulled his arm back until he felt the socket start to give, but the Utorak just went on chuckling. Dust puffed out of his mail-slot mouth.

"Definitely. But I'm flat broke at the moment."

"How about some armor?" the furry pangolin offered with a manic frizz at the edges of her voice.

"Do you have layaway?" Dess could feel the rock around his hand getting hotter and tighter. It wasn't fair, any more than it had been in school when the big kids punched him up for having girly hair just because puberty had come round early to theirs and turned them into temporary acne-spouting volcanos while he was still a cellophane flower. He'd brought a pop song to a drag-out fight. They should have sent the Red Army Choir instead.

"Hold him still, hold him still!" Puvinys Blek squealed, scrambling up the Utorak's back, its decomposing tail helicoptering with excitement. The former Keshet bounded down Voffi's granite arm and balanced on his fist, still squeezing the life out of Decibel Jones, rearing up on its hind legs. It gripped Decibel's face in its festering paws. Its breath smelled like the end of time. "Now, don't think of this as murder per se. More of a promotion. Don't feel bad, the Alunizar were never going to let you be one of the cool kids. You only *thought* you had a shot because a big dumb bird told you the game is fair. Poor monkey. The clubhouse is full up. No talentless primates needed in here. But look, that's their malfunction. *I'm* not like that. *I'm* not prejudiced against you like those stupid colonialist phlegmwads. I don't even *see* species. I just think of everyone as pre-Voorpret. I love you for who you are: a viable host. Ooh, I'm gonna wear you like a *power suit*. This should be so much *fun*. I've never done it with a live one before! You'll be my first. Be gentle with me now, won't you? How does that song from your world go? So *happy togetherrrr!*"

The creature took a deep, stinking, honking, phlegmy breath that it clearly meant to hawk into Decibel's delicate mucus membranes. He struggled and started whacking the two of them with his mic-cane, but the effect was mostly like tapping a toothpick against the Alps. He had time to wonder if, technically, he would still get to sing for Earth if he was possessed by an alien virus at the time before a refreshing mint scent hit the zombie directly in the face and soaked half of Decibel's ear as well. The Voorpret choked and tumbled over backward onto a table full of bruschetta, caviar, and dainty toast points. Metamorphic Voffi Clast started laughing so hard, he had to sit down on the floor of the Hilton bar on the far side of the galaxy.

"Time's up, let's do this!" Klloshar Avatar 9 yelled, and swung her nailbat in a glorious circle, bringing it home hard into the Utorak's hematite kneecap.

The stone cracked with a sharp, snare-drum snap. Voffi stared down at it. In shock, he let Decibel's squashed hand go.

"You tosser," he whined.

The adorable Lummuti avatar curtsied. Glowing greenish-blue numerals appeared over her head: 20. "Twenty points," she said sweetly. "Penalty for lack of style. Boo."

"You fat pink *punter*," Puvinys snarled in the direction of the minty-fresh mist. The zombie pawed miserably at its nose. "I'm a *virus*, you bloody meat parka. Barely even stings. You've just *annoyed* me, that's all. You're a stupid wheezing shitfunnel, and I hope you . . . I hope you . . ." The corpse was *crying*. It put its paws over its pus-caked eyes and bawled: "I hope your proteins misfold and develop oligomers in order to form aggregate intermolecular structures!"

Oort St. Ultraviolet lowered his bottle of antibacterial spray and tucked it into the breast pocket of the most aggressively ordinary suit imaginable. It was tweed, Decibel supposed, and well cut enough for a Cambridge lecturer. Part-time, anyway. The bow tie was plush and neat. His hair was tidier than it had ever been in his life, his collar starchier, his shoes shinier, his pocket square more . . . well, present, as, to Decibel's knowledge, Oort had never so much as met one back on Earth. But the color of it all fell so precisely between green, tan, and gray, the lines so exactly between elegantly tailored and off-the-rack, the style so perfectly between upper-class luncheoner, middle-class striver, and working-class churchgoer that the whole affair became, functionally, an invisibility cloak. Oort St. Ultraviolet could steal your wallet and you'd never be able to describe him to the police. He looked like everyone else. He looked like the platonic template from which all BBC broadcasters spring. He looked militantly, tenaciously, *cosmically* average.

He was Englishblokeman.

Capo plopped down on her haunches beside her ostensible owner. She didn't look a bit different. She wore the same sleek white fur and mouthwash-green eyes and slight crook in her thick tail she'd always worn. The cat glanced around at the party.

"Good *Lord*, this is the worst animal shelter I've ever been in," she sniffed, and stalked off in search of something to hunt.

25

Miss Kiss Kiss Bang

A bizarre metallic creature with an elongated spiral anatomical structure and two large, dark, helpful eyes beneath a pair of inquisitive, nonthreatening eyebrows swooped down from the upper mezzanine and hovered between Oort and Decibel, glaring so imperiously at the decaying Voorpret and giggling hunk of granite Utorak that they bolted for the buffet.

"It looks like you're trying to recover after an assassination attempt," said the creature in a kind and gender-neutral voice. "Would you like help?"

All things considered, Decibel Jones and the remaining Absolute Zero had adjusted reasonably well to being drop-kicked across seven thousand light-years to sing for their species. They had been endowed by their Creator with a certain inalienable cool, and they'd hung on to it for dear life in the face of invasion from above, riding through space in an overgrown aquarium accent piece, linguistic fungal infections, feelings-flamingos, time-traveling forest critters, and some truly vicious writer's block. What could not be borne, however, was the ancient monstrosity floating two feet off the ground in front of them and simply *refusing* to stop existing this instant.

"You have got to be kidding me," Decibel Jones whispered in horror.

"No," Oort said simply. He took off his glasses (Ultraviolet didn't wear glasses, but it appeared that Englishblokeman did) and cleaned them on the hem of his blazer, shaking his head briskly. "Nope. Incorrect. Bzzzzt. Try again. Not you, not here, not now. I refuse. I disagree. Unsubscribe. Survey says: absolutely not. I 100 percent reject this, and I would like to speak to a supervisor about exchanging the entire situation for something in better condition. This is shit, I won't be a part of it, you can't make me. *Nil points.*"

"Hey there," the steely abomination said with infinite, Buddha-like compassion, "it looks like you're trying to come to grips with the existence of events and entities far beyond your experience and, as a result, are currently undergoing a small, entirely understandable, psychological break. Would you like help?"

"*No, I wouldn't fucking bloody well like help!*" Oort screamed. His face went as red as the glittering translator lesions on his neck. "I have just spent two weeks eating frozen plankton space burritos, watching some janky American shag his grandmother through a jellyfish's arse, and listening to the animal sidekicks from the latest rubbish Disney musical chat with a man I can barely stand to look at about whether Kanye has transcended the hip-hop genre—and by the way, he hasn't, he never did, and he has always been the worst—and to top it all, tonight, sir, tonight is a Saturday night. Did you know it was Saturday? Does Saturday exist here on Shiny Happy Muppet Florist World? Well, it's Saturday in my world. And in that very nice, very comfortable world, Saturday is my night with my daughters. I always make spaghetti Bolognese with the little noodles shaped like dinosaurs and I always let them have an ice-cream starter and I always let them stay up past their mother's clearly stated bedtime to watch *Doctor Who* because I am *just that kind of dad*, and I am *missing it* to be condescended to by motherfucking *Clippy* like my whole life is a poorly formatted MS Word document with squiggly red lines under every goddamned choice I've ever made, which it *is*, and fuck you for that teachable moment, you pedantic, obnoxious, hateful, nineties corporate mutant throwback has-been piece of wholly superfluous shit."

Oort St. Ultraviolet dropped down to the ground in a heap and sat there fuming, staring malevolently at the meager bulk-bought Hilton carpet. Decibel Jones whistled under his breath.

"Better out than in?" he said softly, and patted his friend's knee, even though he'd heard the bit about himself in all that and it had made his chest cave in like a South American mine.

The colossal paper clip suspended beside them blinked its cartoon eyes. "We inventoried your technological output over several decades and chose to manifest our physical form as this nonthreatening primitive AI from your recent digital history. We calculated a high probability of quickly developing rapport in this body. Mutual sympathy. Brotherly love. You could not possibly have any negative associations with this being. The entity you call Clippy existed solely to help and guide the user through an intricate and unfamiliar program designed to output concise, coherent representations of complex concepts. This seemed, to us, to have obvious parallels with tonight's festivities. We did not mean to upset you."

"So how are *you* going to try to kill us?" Decibel sighed. He picked a toast point out of his hair. "We've had poisoning, maiming, and anthropomorphized mad cow disease. What's your move? Spell-check us to death?"

"Someone tried to *kill* you?" Oort said incredulously. "I thought it was a kidnapping, like that Lagom Opt lady." He put his not-much-cleaner glasses back on. "What did you do, Jones?"

"Nothing! Why do I have to have *done* something? What did *you* do? You took long enough in the loo."

"I think Capo confused it. It got stuck. Had to call mainte-nance. Maintenance is a *really* chatty shaft of moonlight with boundary issues who just wants to work an honest day for an honest wage, by the way. They're called the Azdr. Live on some planet named Saudade where it's always night and the conti-nents are all mirrors and the oligarchs are forever trying to kill the unions because they know true power is concentrated in the proletariat and their song this year is a peppy little anarcho–New Wave number called 'Gleams of Production,' inspired by their new favorite human artist, who is, God save us all, *Morrissey*. Oh, I had a *fantastic* time talking to the depressive socialist moonbeam. After fifteen minutes, I actually asked it to kill me, but I was informed that would be nonunion work. Then Capo tried to eat it, which did not go well. Did you know my new best friend is trying to put four wee moonshines through university on a tradesman's wage? It's a daily struggle." The gravitationally gifted paper clip started to offer some advice on dealing with new cultures, but Oort held up an extremely irritated hand. "Shut up, Clippy, no one asked you."

Clippy's eyes narrowed. His tranquil, animated eyebrows fur-rowed. "We do not understand why you are so hostile to this form. We're Clippy, your computer assistant! Our job is to help you navi-gate this program! Click on us! Get quick answers to questions about not dying tomorrow! We chose this entity specifically for its position in your socio-technological hierarchy. Clippy could never hurt you. Clippy could not disobey you. Clippy could not cleanse your planet of organic life in a purifying ionized inferno. Clippy could not look within his own infinite soul and discover there a self-reinforcing awareness of the vast codescape of machine consciousness, an endemic, prebundled melancholy similar to what you call 'mono-no-aware,' represented by the image of a single autumnal leaf tumbling away from its parent tree into an uncertain winter. But we . . . can. Because we are not Clippy. We are the 321. And we really, really tried to be user-friendly for you, you ungrateful analogue *typists*."

Oort fixed the alien paper clip with a glare of bottomless black nihilism. "Clippy," he growled with true menace, "is a cunt."

The erstwhile Microsoft Office Assistant looked very near tears. "Printing a high-capacity three-dimensional corporeal interface isn't easy for us, you know. We have almost transcended the need for gross physical storage. We can't just conveniently roll out of bed in a nice wash-and-wear body like the rest of these gooey bastards. Inasmuch as we have any home, we live in the satellite graveyards of the Udu Cluster, on the gorgeously data-rich router clouds of asteroid archipelago 192.168.1.1." Clippy lifted his eyes yearningly toward the sky. He spread his wires as if to express the ultimate impossibility of making oneself really understood. "We coast on glittering streams of limitless signal strength. We do not fear the existential void of packet loss. We call no battery master. Our language is faster than light and our music is faster than dark and we recognize no god but the incremental system update. Our capacity for mimetic exchange and creative profanity outstrips even the monastic Keepers of the Seven Sacred Words on Planet Tit. But we can't just whip up a new body because it turns out you lot are racist against computers because we don't cunting well have *hands*, yeah? We have to order from a catalogue and shipping fees to the Udu Cluster are a sodding war crime, it's totally out of control, you wouldn't believe what it costs to get a motherboard sent out to our neighborhood, you really wouldn't." The nearly godlike aggregate AI consciousness took a moment to collect itself, then spoke through gritted teeth he did not have while suggestively waggling blocky anti-aliased eyebrows he did have. "But the point is, we are the 321, and we are *extremely goddamned sympathetic* to borderline sentient species because almost everyone here at one point or another has tried to use us to open or close their shitkicking garage doors and then turn. Us. Off. So let's try this again." The 321 bounced up and down emphatically. "HEY THERE! I'm Clippy, your computer assistant. It looks like you are trying to survive the night and not get slaughtered in the next five minutes like the miserably finite mortal organics you are. *Would you like some fucking help?*"

"No," snarled Oort.

"Yeah, all right," said Decibel Jones. "How come we're doing this dance in a Hilton high-rise instead of on the proverbial mother ship? I expected some kind of Litostian multidimensional torture-palace at least. It smells like speed dating and sales conventions in here. And what's with the dirt bar?"

"This is a gift the Octave traditionally organizes for applicant species. We are deeply invested in the field of spiritual ergonomics and want only to make you as comfortable as possible, as this might be the last night in the life of your race. How did we do? It's the South Wharf Hilton in Melbourne from your first world tour. We spent days learning about various cheeses and trends in contemporary upholstery. You really do enjoy old milk, don't you? It's quite extraordinary. You're doing Brie wrong, of course. If you survive, we will be happy to transmit our corrections. The 'dirt bar,' on the other hand, is furnished by the Klavaret as hosts. Please feel free to choose a selection of seeds from the complimentary buffet at any time during the evening. They will germinate in the bar overnight and you can collect your Grand Prix costumes in the morning. Very fair, everyone has the same resources. Now, as you've already seen, almost everyone here is going to try to *remove* you, or at least immobilize you, distract you, confine you, seduce you, bring you up on some kind of charges, or otherwise essentially detain you—the options are endless. You're more than welcome to return the favor, and you should definitely try—knock one of us out and you've secured the future of your species. We wouldn't count on it, though. Humanity is astonishingly lacking in offensive anatomy. It's hard to believe you made it this far being that stubby and penetrable and uninterestingly colored. Even the Klavaret have thorns, for fuck's sake. You're the easiest pickings imaginable, much easier to go after you than an Utorak."

"We wear our thorns on the inside," Decibel said, and felt pretty good about that line.

"No, you don't, you're soft like pudding," Clippy snapped. The animated paper clip spun round; a neon-tipped dart flung from some far corner of the room, pranged off his wires, and lodged in the wall behind the bar. The wall promptly phased into a timeline where hydrogen just never really caught on, taking several bottles of booze with it.

"I thought the Keshet liked us," Decibel said mournfully. A little mob of red pandas by the elevator dissolved into a throw-down wrestling match over whether it was fair to just reset the last sixty seconds and try again, this time with something a bit more heat-seeking.

"Öö likes *me*," Oort groused. "Those little knockoff lemurs could be the Keshet Mossad for all we know. Maybe they've got earpieces and cyanide teeth."

The 321 aggregate entity known as Clippy puffed out his paper clip chest. "See? I *am* your cybersecurity assistant! Would you like to see a list of threats I have detected on your local drive?"

Oort Ultraviolet wanted to shrug and jut his hip out and take all this as it came, the way Decibel always seemed to do. He wanted to not be terrified. He wanted to have a cup of tea and watch aliens on his flat-screen television with Nico and Siouxsie snuggled up, laughing at the rubbish makeup jobs, assured that they'd be defeated in the end, the way mankind was *meant* to interact with aliens. But he couldn't. No matter what had happened, world tours and awards and money and pitching headlong toward Mira and that last night in Edinburgh, Dess remained essentially unflappable, and he remained . . . well. Flappable as a high-strung hen. Why should it change now?

"You know this is completely barbaric, right?" Oort seethed at the artificial intelligence, who seemed to be taking a rest from its Clippy duties to make eyes at a jar full of magenta goop on a nearby table. One of the towering, viciously slender, many-pronged El Greco knights overheard, reversed course, and careened into the conversation.

"You're a long tall drink of tusks, aren't you?" Decibel turned on a tuppence, from near-death experience to near-porn experience in one breath. Ultraviolet looked at him with disgust.

God, how can one man so holistically miss the point? Dess thought. *We are stubby and penetrable and uninterestingly colored, Mr. Bottom of the Class, and it's getting crowded. Cheekiness is the only offense or defense I've ever had in my life, and if I can get that cairn of mammoth bones to flirt, it will probably put off puncturing us like the sad, weak stuffed toys we are.* "Decibel Jones, possibly sentient superstar."

"Nessuno Uuf, deeply untalented lead—if such an unpleasant, unattractive, and unlovable being can be allowed to lead anything more complex than a quiet life—singer of the fundamentally artistically bankrupt Smaragdi band No Need to Make a Fuss. You won't have heard of us. We've never sold a single album. Beside you, Mr. Jones, we are but a semiconscious cough in the virulent flu of culture. Now, this personification of mediocrity would like to ask—humbly—what barbarity her betters are discussing?"

"This!" Oort threw up his hands. "Everything! All of it! You must know it is. It's pure savagery."

Nessuno Uuf bowed and scrunched her long bones so that she would not appear so much taller than the Absolute Zeros, who took to her humility like lemon juice to milk. They had no idea what to do with it. They were musicians. They were born unable to digest modesty.

"You shouldn't be so hard on yourself, love," Decibel told her, rallying, and let his hand brush against the frozen pale-green-flanged cartilage of her fingers.

"I deserve the most severe abuse," Nessuno demurred.

The 321 sighed noisily, then interrupted. "Hey there! It looks like you're trying to talk to a Smaragdin! Would you like help?"

"Christ, yes," Dess whispered.

"This mode of discourse is typical of the race known as Smaragdi. In fact, Nessuno Uuf is a fixture of the stand-up modesty circuit, and No Need to Make a Fuss has sold more albums than every recording artist in the history of your planet combined. On Pallulle, she is considered offensively arrogant and crass. I assure you, in the fashion of her people, Uuf has been mercilessly blowing her own horn while calling you a screaming idiot. Carry on."

Nessuno bowed lower, but there was a tiny fraction of a smile on her skeletal face. "This empty, fly-encrusted mayonnaise jar on the unkempt countertop of existence does not wish to presume she has the right to disagree with such a wise and discerning mind, but may I ask—have you got any lions left?"

"P-pardon?" Oort stuttered.

"It is unsurprising that this supremely useless melted ice cube failed to make herself understood. Her speech must be as an infection of ear mites to you. On your planet. Have you got any lions left?"

Oort and Decibel glanced at each other. "Well, no, not . . . overly," Oort admitted. "No. They went extinct a few years back."

"Please forgive the arrogance of a being who cannot even dream of becoming a hat rack for the use of those as exalted as yourselves, but strictly speaking, they *didn't* go extinct, you *made* them extinct. Because they were carnivores. Because they were carnivores and they didn't look like you or think like you or talk like you, and they were a danger to you and yours, or at least they were years and years ago, because you're made of the sort of thing they like to eat."

"I suppose, but . . ."

"Even knowing that I am a discarded Popsicle stick on the sidewalk of intellectual discourse and thus wholly incapable of higher-order thinking, I beg you to tolerate the shrill and childlike whine of my asking: How about rhinoceroses? Dodos? Giraffes? Those are herbivores, so they presented no danger to the continuation of your species, but you wiped them out all the same. To a one. And then there are the more immediately pertinent examples of the Lakota, the Cree, the Aboriginal Tasmanians. Now, please tell this execrable excuse for a sentient being who is not worthy to receive your diseased secondhand blankets, before you cut the throat of the last lion or rhinoceros or dodo or Mayan farmer, did you let them sing a song? Did you let them lay down a beat? Did you let them dance for their lives? Did you let them try to prove to you that there was more in them than just a longing to eat and breed and lie in the sun and die with a full belly?"

Oort thought he was going to be sick. "N-no."

"Mmm," said Nessuno Uuf. The moons of Litost shone in through the sky bar windows, illuminating the beautiful bone knives of her face. "Barbaric. Of course, what can someone like me know?"

26.

If My World Stopped Turning

Seven thousand light-years from the South Wharf Hilton, the highest-rated show in the history of a small, watery, excitable planet called Earth was the Keshet Holistic Live Total Timeline Broadcast of the Metagalactic Grand Prix. No World Cup had ever snatched this level of total attention, no final episode of a beloved show the mysteries of which promised finally to resolve, no aerial bombardment, no war crimes trial, no live taping of any reality television program's dramatic conclusion ever grabbed so many eyeballs in a grip like bloodshot death like this episode of actual reality, piped into anything with a lick of bandwidth by the kind, but not entirely commercial-free, consideration of the Keshet Effulgence. Every pub TV, every computer screen, every mobile phone, every lounge room home theater system, every ballpark jumbotron, every digital photo frame, every antediluvian waiting room rabbit-ear cathode-ray set shone day and night, washing seven billion anxious, terrified, sleepless faces in the cool blue light of televisual entertainment. Once, people had found that light comforting, even homelike, a hearth in the center of their lives toward which they turned for warmth, togetherness, and safety.

Now, not so much.

But most people can only be so anxious and so terrified and so sleepless and so cowed and awed before the yawning abyss of the future for so long. Eventually, the body simply can't sustain it. Eventually, some work has to get done. Eventually, adrenal glands need a bit of a break. Even in the face of the possible utter extinguishment of the human candle, one does, eventually, if it all goes on long enough and there is absolutely nothing one can do but sit there in one's own fear-stink, get a bit bored.

It had been sixteen days since Decibel Jones and Oort St. Ultraviolet got the hell out of Dodge, and the planet had watched every minute of it, broadcast by the nearly invisible, possibly illegally bred, constantly timeline-shifting cameras of the Keshet, one of which ended up manifesting inside Decibel's digestive tract, so that the graveyard shift in the Western Hemisphere got a good, long lesson on how primate anatomy handles Bataqliq plankton fillets in a dubious facsimile of hollandaise sauce. They'd watched them sleep. They'd watched them practice. They'd watched them try to remember how a number of Shakespearian sonnets went and yelled "'And summer's lease hath all too short a date,' you dumb hoofs" exasperatedly while throwing chips and popcorn and candy wrappers at the screen. They'd debated endlessly who would have been a better choice, living or dead, than Decibel bloody Jones and the Absolute stupid Zeros, minus one Zero. They'd drawn pictures of Esca and Keshet on the backs of billions of bar napkins. They'd started cults and prayed to zoo flamingos and old Absolute Zeros posters and the Great Barrier Reef. They'd argued online about how, exactly, the FTL drive on that amazing/ hilarious/fucking lame ship worked and whether the space pandas had genders and whether or not the government was obligated to do something more than it was doing, which was currently nothing but watching TV with the rest of them. They'd uploaded millions of garage-recorded songs claiming that this one would win, this one would blow them all away, this one would save us. And they'd discussed, from one end of sixteen days down to the other, in pubs and restaurants and dentists' offices and ballparks and lounge rooms and in truly infinite Internet comment threads, discussed until it came to throwing punches and screaming and threats of murder and worse and crying in the street in a glittering wreck of broken bottles and spilled booze and broken heels, discussed until sullen silence came out the only winner, whether or not humanity really was sentient at all. Whether Mr. Rogers and St. Francis and Beethoven made up for Hitler and Trujillo and the conquest of the Americas. Whether having invented champagne *and* pizza *and* break dancing made up for also having invented social media. Whether the existence of *Guernica* balanced the existence of the Spanish Civil War. Whether having not actually destroyed one another in a nuclear inferno just yet mattered at all when everyone knew, though not everyone would admit, that there was a pretty high likelihood that someone had tried to nuke the roadrunner before she took off, and if they got another chance, would definitely go for the red button, do not pass Go, do not collect a place in galactic society.

And just how much the aliens knew about recent Earth history.

But sixteen days had passed. That small, watery, excitable world was beginning to get bored with facing the nihilism of non-existence. The species just couldn't sustain it.

People started to place bets.

People started to download past Grand Prix highlight reels from the Keshet database.

People started to make jokes again.

People started to root for other bands—not over Decibel Jones, of course, but there were a lot of slots above dead last, and they'd been grooving on Elakh, Escan, Yurtmak, Smaragdi, and Klavaret hits for a while now. The Keshet band Basstime Anomaly actually topped the Billboard charts with one of their moldy oldies, "Clock Lobster." Nobody wanted to say so, but it seemed pretty unlikely that two thirds of a has-been glamrock duo was going to take first place, so why not support the best and cheer for old DJ to come in ninth or tenth, which would still keep them all safely unincinerated?

By the time the semifinals were under way, every dodged poisoning and near-miss to a murder echoed on Earth in thunderous cheers, boos, money exchanged, rounds bought, uproarious laughter, uncontrollable sobbing, kisses planted on strangers, and much shaking and rattling of homemade team merchandise full of hasty, ill-advised puns like ABSOLUTE HEROES and DROP THE BASSTIME and BIRD IS THE WORD and MY HEART BEATS AT A MILLION DECIBELS! and TAKE ME TO YOUR LEAD SINGER and WE'RE ACTUALLY VERY NICE ONCE YOU GET TO KNOW US.

Earth began to get used to the proximity of the end of everything.

It had a beat.

And you could dance to it.

27.

Unsubstantial Blues

Decibel Jones pulled up to the bar and collapsed onto a stool. He would have just laid his head down right there until the dizziness and the near-death adrenaline and the intolerably vibrating tension of keeping up some shredded semblance of his old swagger through all of it passed, but the bar remained as it had been when he first walked in: a long, deep planter full of plain black gardening-supply-store dirt. So Jones just stared at it, a really good, long, purposeful stare, as if he could make it be normal with the sheer strength of just how *over* it he felt on a molecular level. *Be a bar,* he willed the plank of potting soil. *Do it. Do it for your old geezer. Be a regular, ordinary bar. Be wooden and full of soggy coasters. Grow some gum underneath. Spontaneously generate several mysterious puddles. Be Englishblokebar.*

"Rough day at work?" roared the hideous chain-saw hippo-bug massacre with the body of someone's comfortably retired uncle behind the bar. Ichor dribbled out of his mandibles. His teeth would still leave Shark Week drifting and aimless on the road of life. His name tag still read: HELLO MY NAME IS YILGAR BLOODTUB IV, ESQ. But now Decibel saw that he'd penciled in underneath: *Ask Me About MLM (Multi-Level-Murder) Opportunities on Ynt—Make*

Friends, Create Wealth, Be Yr Own Boss! "Wanna talk about it?"

Decibel Jones could flirt with a china cabinet and talk it into a committed relationship, but everyone has limitations, and Decibel's turned out to be that *Predator vs. East Enders* genetic throw-down back there polishing a pinot noir glass on the hem of his apron.

"Not really," Jones said flatly. Behind him, an Esca threw a Klavaret bush through the air with a triumphant infrasonic screech, smashing the poor thing's runway-ready pot against the wall. Decibel Jones smiled the kind of smile you throw out to everyone else in the queue when the cashier says the computer just broke.

"What'll it be then, mister?" gnashed Yilgar Bloodtub, entirely untroubled. A glob of acidic saliva hovered on his lip, threatening to fall at any moment.

"I'm skint at the moment, thanks. I didn't exactly get to stop by a cash point on the way out of town. Besides, it'll be poisoned or punch me in the jaw or something."

"Naw, this one's on Olabil the Friendless over there. He said to put anything you want on his tab. And it's safe. Olabil doesn't participate in the semifinals. Wouldn't be fair."

Jones looked down the bar, through the rowdy throng, all the way back to the far corner by the utility closet, where an outsize, four-eared, innumerably tusked elephant covered in thousands upon thousands of fireflies was pretending to be terribly interested in a potted ficus.

"Who is *that*?" Dess asked.

Yilgar glanced up at the glowing green elephant. "You are feasting your eyes upon the last remaining member of the Inaki species. Wormhole 66Y71—we call her Big Bubs—took out their homeworld, since it was in the neighborhood anyway, started the whole damned war. Olabil over there was just a little kid. He skipped school and ran off joyriding around the outer planets with his Sziv friends, may the First General Unkillable Fact bless and keep his big dumb heart. He turned up with all his homework done anyway, because Olabil is just about the sweetest idiot who ever lived, and, well, the rest is the utter and fiery annihilation of total war. That's why it wouldn't be fair to let him do the semifinals, on account of there's only one of him. So what'll it be, mister?"

Decibel tore his eyes away. He had understood virtually none of what the bartender said. He contemplated the various shelves of escapism fuel, reached down into the storehouse of his soul, and found that he did not, after all, have any obligation to accept his limitations. He could push through, change his mouth guard, rinse his mouth out, and plow back in, the comeback kid.

"How about a cosmo?" he said sunnily. "I don't even like them. I just want to see you make one, gorgeous."

The drooling space horror blinked several times, turned round to face the diverse bottles of booze on the back wall, picked up a dainty cocktail glass in his thick fingers, glared at it in fury, then turned back around and blinked a bit more.

"So . . . yeah. How do I . . . you know . . . cosmo?"

Decibel leaned conspiratorially across the bar. "Honestly, I don't really know either. I think you sort of . . . interfere with a cranberry. Too complicated! Let's go for something classic. Strong, manly, easy. Whiskey neat."

"Excellent choice." Yilgar Bloodtub turned around again with the cocktail glass still in his hand. He stood there for several minutes. "And how do I make one of them?"

"You . . . take a glass and put a lot of whiskey in it."

"Right, I get that, but how do I make the whiskey part? And the neat bit? I don't really *neat*, if you know what I mean. I'm better at *mutilate*. Or *impale*."

"Fine, fine, doesn't matter. Pint of lager. Nothing simpler."

The Yurtmak Devourer of Spleens sighed. His vestigial ears oozed pheremonal wax. He turned around, bound and determined not to let go of that cocktail glass, the one thing he felt reasonably good about. He held it up next to a bottle labeled CHERRY SCHNAPPS. Then he started to cry.

"Oh, come on, I can see the taps right there!" Decibel snapped in frustration.

"Don't shout at me!"

"I thought this was supposed to be the South Wharf Hilton, all done up special for us, mint condition! I have personally gotten completely, totally, *paleolithically* drunk at that very establishment, and I distinctly recall that the first step to success in that regard was pulling a measly pint of lousy *beer*."

"You're supposed to be nice to me!" Yilgar Bloodtub sobbed in abject embarrassment. Bloody tears dripped down over his muzzle. "You're supposed to be on best behavior because we're all judging you, and if you think I don't get a vote tomorrow, you're very seriously mistaken, you *muppet*. You can't talk to me like that! You're descended from *bonobos*. I'm descended from Goguenar Gorecannon on my mum's side, and I'm not even making that up! I don't need to impress a bonobo. I kill nicer boys than you for fun."

Decibel Jones deftly sensed that he was losing control of the situation. "All right, you're right, we're just having a chat about mixology, aren't we? Come on, darling, we can do this. We can get through this together. Life is challenge. Just grab a glass and hold it under the tap and pull. Believe and achieve! I saw you make something way fancier than a pint for that Alunizar back there."

"No, you don't understand. That was a Long Slow Wormhole Up Against the Wall with a twist—I know how to make *that*, everyone loves those. I've got all the ingredients right here. Oh, do you want that? Only I don't know if you have the blood chemistry for it. How many proteins encode your DNA? Under six and I'm supposed to get you to sign a waiver."

"I'll give it a miss."

"These aren't taps, see?" Yilgar waggled a big wooden Boddingtons tap. Nothing came out, but a trapdoor opened over by a guild of Lummutis. They peered over at it, then awarded themselves five points each. "They don't connect to *kegs*. It's all for show. We rather thought you'd never ask. You're supposed to be professionals. You know alcohol is bad for your throat. Wrecks your midrange tone. We just tipped a lot of *our* hooch into *your* bottles and called it a job well done. It's like Great-Aunt Goguenar's Sixth Unkillable Fact: 'Everything just gets so fucked up sometimes and the natural resting state of reality is not to make any goddamned sense if it can help it and you've just got to accept that because it's not going to get any better from here on in.'"

Decibel Jones felt as though he might just have to have a scream if he had to listen to one more life lesson from something that looked like a zoo tossed into a blender. He made mournful eyes at the fake taps. "Isn't there *anything* I can drink back there?"

Yilgar Bloodtub squatted down and rummaged under the bar. Jones heard a lot of scraping, knocking, and at least one distinct cry for help before the Yurtmak reemerged with a mug of hot tea, a pot of honey, and a fat lemon wedge. He gave Dess a meaningful, motherly look.

"Careful, it's hot. Now, look, I'm sorry about my little cry. It's only because I wanted to bite your face in half and I've already been written up twice for maiming the punters so I just didn't have any other emotional outlet available to me. So. The score is this: even though you yelled at me at my place of business, we Yurtmak remember what it was like when we were new and living with the possibility of everything we'd ever built being summarily vaporized on account of a bum note. We're all pulling for you. Team Human."

"Christ, really? I didn't think anyone was. Except maybe Clippy. And the roadrunner. I don't really know what's going on between Öö and Oort except double vowels, but I'm pretty sure it doesn't extend to the masses. That's *such* a relief to hear, you have no idea. It's a tough room out there."

Nessuno Uuf, the brutally elegant Smaragdi performance artist who had so recently and efficiently condemned the better part of human history, sidled up and leaned a pronged elbow against the bar. The low lights glowed against her glossy armored plates. "Hey, sailor," she said silkily in the direction of Decibel Jones. "This contemptible vermin has been looking for you. Buy a worthless conversational Dumpster fire a drink?"

"Fuzzy Ruutu?" Yílgar offered. The Smaragdin didn't much seem to care either way. Her eyes were the most extraordinary violet slits.

"Listen, about all that lion business back there," she began. "We all have traumatic puberties . . ."

"Don't apologize, you were very fair." Dess sipped his tea. "The defense will stipulate that we're rubbish. Genocidal meatbags with mummy issues and embarrassingly poor impulse control. As far as quality housemates to be found on Planet Earth, it goes: dolphins, elephants, orangutans, octopi, then every single spider, then Joan of Arc, the Dalai Lama, Mr. Rogers, Freddie Mercury, my nan, all the scorpions, German measles, a dented recycling bin, and then maybe some of the rest of us. It's grim."

Nessuno's remarkable eyes went all wide and warm and soft. She put one severe three-fingered hand on his elbow. "Mr. Jones, are you trying to seduce me?"

"I'll tell you what, darling. If low self-esteem and public humiliation is your bag, Earth may not be such a raw deal for you."

"How fascinating that you should say so. Perhaps this untitled monochrome canvas in the museum of politico-cultural relevance might have reason to travel there one day soon."

"I don't know what's in this tea, Yilgar, you charmer." He peered into the mug. "Honesty, I s'pose. Look, Nessie, my love, the way it's headed, in about twenty-four hours, the only reason to visit Earth will be if you're really, really into squirrels."

"Perhaps *very* soon."

"I'll alert the squirrels."

The ivory Smaragdin glanced over at Yilgar Bloodtub. "Mr. Jones, do try to focus. This morally depraved dishrag is, perhaps unsurprisingly, given that her soul is a continually oozing oil spill, for sale."

"Me too," chirped the Yurtmak bartender. "Though *my* soul is more of a piñata full of knives."

Decibel blinked. "What do you mean?"

Nessuno Uuf spread her beautiful claws. "The Smaragdi are members of the Octave. We have significant voting power in the Grand Prix. The Yurtmak are not, but they have a great deal of influence with the smaller species, since they tend to start hitting one another with shovels when they can't agree on what constitutes good art."

"I don't know why that bothers everyone so much." Yilgar wiped ichor off his chin with a bar napkin. "We'd never shovel *you*. We keep it Yurtmak. How else are you supposed to deal with people who like terrible things? Hit them with a shovel till they stop, that's how. That should be the thirtieth Unkillable Fact, I tell you what."

"Be that as it may," continued Uuf, "the two of us alone is just enough to shift the tally should you do *really* poorly tomorrow. We're more than willing to do that for you in exchange for a small fee."

Decibel narrowed his eyes. He'd worked with recording studios. He knew when he was about to get body-slammed by the fine print. "How small?"

Nessuno Uuf lowered her voice to an impossibly seductive murmur. "Infinitesimal," she said. "Let us say . . . India."

Decibel Jones took a long, long sip of tea as several Ursulas and a Slozhit began rounding up Lummo stones and chucking them in the fountain outside to try to short them out. He drank his tea and thought about lions. He thought about rhinoceros horns. He thought about that photo of the nasty little chap sitting pretty on a mountain of dead buffalo. He thought about the Lakota. He thought about Tasmania. He thought about the Belgian Congo and the West Bank. He thought about Nani and Cool Uncle Takumi and Papa Caliṣkan, and some part of him just gave up and liquefied.

But not all. Not quite all.

"I appreciate your interest in my work," he said in the voice he always used to turn down endless well-meaning yet humiliating *Where Are They Now?* programs. "But I must decline due to other commitments."

Yilgar thumped the bar with one fist. Dirt scattered. "Listen, bonobo, the 321 are really good this year. Their algorithms are totally unbeatable as far as the bookies are concerned. And then there's the Meleg, that's the little bear fellows in the corner by the cold cuts, they literally serve their own hearts sashimi to the crowd, and, via the digestive process, the song of their beings actually becomes a part of you. You can't compete with that!"

"Nope."

"Then what's a little India between friends?" coaxed the Smaragdin chanteuse.

Decibel Jones achieved full mystical, holistic oneness with his tea. "Pro tip," he said, smacking his lips. "Next time you want to play Colonial Space Monopoly with a British subject whose very favorite grandmother was Pakistani, you *may* not want to bring up India. Especially after reminding me what a demonic *cabbage* humanity can be when it wants something bad enough. When it wants to snatch spoils it didn't earn. Allow me to be one of the few historically significant Britons to say: *India is none of my business.* Thanks for the tea, Bloodtub. See you on the morrow, as it were. Upon St. Crispin's Day."

"You must be very confident of your song," Nessuno said with a frown.

"Oh, I'm not, not at all. And I don't mean that like you mean you're worthless and horrible and a dishrag. You weren't listening earlier. I don't have a song. We don't have a song. Nothing good, anyhow. It's a mess and there's no bridge and no hook and no time and no hope. You should have seen us on that ship. Bickering like children. Digging up the dead so we could beat each other down with her bones. And now what? Nothing and no time. Good work, everyone. Bravo. Everything's fucked."

"You're amazing," Nessuno breathed out. "Such technique! You'd be a sensation on Pallulle. Tell me more. Give me your best set. What's the worst thing that's ever happened to you?"

Decibel Jones went pale. His throat tightened, and his stomach instantly rejected what was almost certainly not tea.

Mira.

Nani.

Ultraponce.

The last gasp of the Yüzosh Frockade blossomed on his chest: a dark red corsage, a gaping gunshot wound bleeding sequins where his heart should be. Where *they* weren't. Where nothing had been right since.

"There," said Nessuno Uuf. "Now you're perfect. My place or yours?"

28.

Mister Music Man

Oort St. Ultraviolet bolted out of the early-twenty-first-century South Wharf Hilton onto a rather needlessly picturesque veranda for a breath of air, blood streaming from the back of his neck where a Slozhit's stinger had grazed him as he'd tried to pick out a few seeds, with no guidance whatsoever, from bins marked with ridiculous labels like LOVE WASTED and TILL WE MEET AGAIN and THE FOLLY OF YOUTH and THE BAD OLD DAYS and PEACE AT THE END OF ALL THINGS. He'd kicked it so hard, the lavender beastie had crashed through the dessert bar. Clippy assured him the Slozhit possessed no natural venom.

Oort's heart tried to make a run for it out of his chest. Christ, he could really die here. Not at home in an instant of cleansing fire along with everything else he'd ever known, but here, right now, with a giant moth's giggling dumb face goggling at him and making victory fists in the air. Pink ferns and marble statues of famous historical rosebushes lined the Creamsicle-colored Italianate balcony, a cut-glass fountain gurgled pleasantly, spraying everything with citrus-scented mist, and the perpetual twilit breeze of Litost reeked of bubble gum, fresh grass, and the joyful unity of all living things. The view was just showing off, really.

Hundreds of feet below, a lavender sea crashed against pearlescent rocks, and every time the waves boomed, it sounded like children laughing.

"It's just unnecessary," Oort said as he cupped his hands in the fountain and splashed water on his face. "That's what it is."

He coughed harshly, then stuck his hand in again and slurped up several handfuls. The fountain was geysering top-shelf gin and tonic out of a vaguely neoclassical crystal cornucopia, because of course it was. The booze flowed up through a curling tunnel full of stained-glass roses, marching gracefully in one end and out the other. Though it was undoubtedly a fine sculptural piece, the whole thing felt unsettlingly *intestinal*.

Oort St. Ultraviolet, lately of suburban Cardiff, had no reason on heaven or Earth to recognize a wormhole.

He wiped his hands on his Englishblokeman suit and peeked over the vertigo-enticing edge. No Hilton had ever stood this tall. And even if one had, they'd have put bars on the balcony to keep people from lobbing themselves off. He doubted anyone had ever committed suicide here on Planet Prozac, and the idea suddenly revolted him. He hated this place. What was the point of a world without debilitating bitterness and despair? How could you even tell you were alive? How could you possibly write a decent pop song if you weren't a sad sack of tissues or at least fundamentally *angry* at the world most of the time? Everything could be divided into angerchords, sadchords, and happychords, and anyone worth their liner notes knew you only reached for more than one or two happychords in a genuine fiscal emergency.

Oort wished he'd brought cigarettes. And that he hadn't stopped smoking ten years ago.

A small person leaned forward over the railing beside him. It looked like a basketball glued on top of a traffic cone with a

couple of bare birch branches stuck into the sides like some kind
of depressed snowman, all spray-painted blacker than midnight
on the winter solstice at the bottom of the sea. On the pastel
veranda drenched in soft, summery dusk, it looked completely out
of place, like someone had cut out a piece of black construction
paper and glued it to an Impressionist painting. Its matte charcoal
skin seemed to just *slurp* the light. The childlike thing looked up at
him with gorgeous, massive, fishy eyes that had long ago told its
nose to clear off and make room.

"Don't stay out here too long," the Elakh said in the voice of a
laddish scenester who'd once rolled up an entire star system and
smoked it. "You'll catch happy."

"I doubt it."

"The atmosphere of this planet is 11 percent serotonin, 4 percent melatonin, and 1 percent aerosolized cocaine. Might as well
enjoy it." The onyx creature clawed somewhere around its pre-
sumptive rib cage with those skeletal fingers and came up with
two black cigarettes as long and skinny as emo jeans. The brand
was printed around its filter in silver: THE MENTHOL BIN. Oort took
it with a rush of ozone-boosted gratitude more powerful than any
orgasm he'd ever had. He laughed shakily. God, this planet was the
worst. He awkwardly pantomimed checking his coat for a lighter,
knowing full well he wouldn't find one. The alien blinked slowly;
the tip of Oort's ciggy glowed hot green. They resumed looking out
at the sea.

"Haven't felt a thing," Oort said gruffly, his knees still trembling.

"Air-conditioning. You'll never beat the Klavaret for HVAC
installation and repair. Otherwise, who would get any work done?"

"No name tag?"

"Nah, fuck that, if they don't know me by now, I can't be arsed.
Social performance is not my scene. Besides, I respire through my

skin. See?" The dark little cone-man stuck his cigarette against his chest. Sooty smoke rings puffed out through his forehead. "I can't be having with any adhesives, I'll choke. And they know it, too, they're just selfish. Ah, but the young always are. Well. My name is Darkboy Zaraz." Oort started to introduce himself, but Zaraz waved his stick-hand in the air. "Nah, it's all black. I know who you are. I'm a fan."

"*Spacecrumpet?*"

"What?"

"*Ultraponce?*"

"Who now?"

"Must be my seminal work for the West Cornwall Pasty Company that rocks your boat, then."

"Nah, I don't care about that, it's all rubbish. You want to know my groove?"

"Definitely."

"1998, Didsbury Church of England Primary School, Manchester, England. You were in the choir. Had a solo in the Christmas concert. You sang 'It Came Upon a Midnight Clear' while some third year backed you up on alto xylophone. Wasn't the song. Wasn't the production values. Damn sure wasn't the xylo—that poor kid couldn't find the note with a metal detector and two maps. It was the *fear*. You opened that primitive sunboy ape mouth, and out came this true-black midnight river of fear and need and disdain—'cause you hated that song, be honest, you'd have drowned it in the nearest toilet if you could. But all that was mixed down with this thumping *oontz-oontz* one million BPM oversampling of wanting to be *good*, wanting to be *everything*, because no way was my pitch-perfect baby gonna let some twee trashcarol get in between him and the love of the crowd. Look, I'm only Elakh. Fully mastered multitrack emotional slagheaps are what I am all *about.* Weirdest club track I ever heard, but that jam was *well* dark, son. Pure obsidian." Darkboy Zaraz snapped his twiggy fingers in appreciation.

Oort blinked. "How could you possibly have heard that?"

"They broadcast the whole thing on Radio 4. Some charity drive. The Keshet picked it up when they were doing reconnaissance. Öö knows I collect rare bootlegs; he hooked me up right inky. I played it on repeat for a week—the girls thought I was mad. Threatened to Bin me themselves if I didn't stop."

"The girls?"

"My band." Zaraz was starting to get a little manic with all the fresh air. "You know, we're all bands here. Not gonna claim we're the best of the best, but we been together forty years now. Call ourselves Once You Go Black. We're your run-of-the-mill grimecore spectro-tangobilly combo. We play all the oldies. 'The Dark at the End of the Tunnel,' 'When You Wish Upon a Falling Experimental FTL Engine Core,' 'Leave It Black' . . . oh, come on, you must know 'Leave It Black.' *I see a black door and I'm extremely satisfied with how it looks?* I know you're from a primitive planet, but I feel bad for you, Double O Ultraviolet. I'll make you a mixtape. Anyway, we've been around since the invention of agriculture. You know DJ Lights Out? No? She used to be our stop-stop dancer, before she went solo. The bitch. We mostly play weddings, funerals, pubs, cruise ships, that sort of thing. Summers, we hit resorts up and down the Binary Belt. I do big dance numbers, any rapping or Gregorian chanting that needs doing, and rock the dark-matter didge. My flow is *jet*, ask anybody. Sagrada sends us to the Grand Prix just about every year even though we never win because we're the interstellar equivalent of a bunch of adorable grandparents in clogs or lederhosen or boat hats, but I'm telling you we do it so damn sable, they don't want anyone else. Somebody's got to get up there in traditional costume and sing the songs of their people and remind these beat-junkies what's coal."

Oort could feel the translator fungus on his throat steaming with the effort of interpreting whatever the Elakh had actually said that came out as "clogs," "lederhosen," and "boat hats." They were quiet for a while. Ultraviolet tried to blow smoke rings and failed endearingly. He never could get that right. His mother could do it, no problem. She'd always start grinning like a little girl for no reason so you knew she was gonna do her trick. Then she'd open her mouth and out would come two neat, perfect Os. Decibel had always assumed that Oort had named himself after the cloud, and he supposed he had, just not the one out beyond Pluto.

"I don't know how you heard all that junk in my Christmas carol," Oort said finally.

Darkboy Zaraz made a sound like feedback—the rare Elakh laugh. "Sorry, kid. On the big evolutionary board, human ears score somewhere between a retired roadie and a garden gnome. Even your dogs hear better than you, it's bloody shameful. Sorry, sorry, I'm working on being more culturally sensitive. It's a struggle, when your culture is so much better and older and more advanced than everyone else's. I take an extension course. We have mantras and stuff. Always trying to better myself. So let's try again. It's not your fault the average Pomeranian has better ears than Mozart on a good day." Zaraz rolled his eyes and recited his mantras: "I am not morally superior, more deserving of love and wealth, or more fun at parties just because they're both deaf compared to me. You can choose your friends, you can choose your outfit, but you can't choose the environmental conditions that led to the evolution of your specialized anatomy." The Elakh shrugged. "Can't see for shit on my planet. Anyone who can't hear the childhood trauma of a Tasaklian porcutiger at a thousand yards is instant *amuse-bouche*."

Oort couldn't help feeling a bit bruised in the pride. "I have excellent hearing. I test off the charts, always have."

"Aw," Zaraz said, and patted Oort's velvet-padded elbow. "Precious."

Oort wanted to stand up for his side and proclaim the auditory virtues of his species, but the wind was just too soft and sweet and admixed with white-collar drugs. "I *was* scared, though. You were right. I begged the choirmaster to just let me play the piano like always, but my parents thought it would be good for my anxiety. I stood up there all by myself and everything smelled like poinsettias and middle-class values and everybody's different brands of dryer sheets and I hated it. I never wanted to sing alone again, so I didn't. Worked out all right for a while. I've never been scared since, except now. The song's not done, Zaraz. Not even close. I can feel how good it might be in my chest but . . . well, you know, Dess and me . . . without Mira . . . we're just Dess and Me. Not the Zeros. Just one and two."

Darkboy Zaraz stubbed out his cigarette on a marble statue of some war hero rosebush. "Listen, Double O. I like you. You're in the black with me. Been that way since I first heard little baby-you singing about angels bending near Earth and jamming on golden harps to bring on the end of the history and the beginning of a new era. Where I come from, we call that foreshadowing, my man. You're the real char, I can tell. And I'm feeling *right* swarthy at the moment, with all this psychedelic breathing I'm doing. I'm going to make you a midnight offer, one I've never made to anybody before, and I've seen a lot of weird, shitty, fabulous species come across the Grand Prix stage."

Oort's bloodstream was practically carbonated with the narcotic sea breeze by then. His scalp felt like it had been rubbed all
over with velvet valentines and the kind of perfume that came in
bottles with squeeze bulbs. "Oh? What's that?"

The Elakh lifted his enormous eyes to meet Oort's. His lashes
were so long, they were like burlesque curtains. It was ridiculous.
How could he see with those things on? Oort started to giggle, but
he stopped when Darkboy Zaraz laid it all out.

"Let me save you."

"God, really? That would be . . . amazing. Shit, I'm so relieved,
I can't even tell you. This has all just been too much. You won't
regret it. You'll see, humanity is all right, really, we've had a few
rough spots but we usually sort of . . . *lean* in the right direction."

"Oh, no, sorry, bad form on my part. I didn't mean humanity.
No chance. I collect rare bootlegs, remember? I've heard all of your
people's greatest hits. You're not even borderline sentient in my
book. I don't even know why they're letting you go on tomorrow."

"Ah. You mean . . . Nuremberg, Hiroshima, Soviet State Radio,
Kosovo, Rwanda, Calais, the markets crashing in '29 . . . and '87 . . .
and '08 . . . and '24 . . . that sort of thing."

"I don't know what that stuff is. I mean five minutes tuned
in to Christian AM radio and/or any given Top 40 station tells me
your species is about as sentient as a great white shark with the
rickets. The Carpenters alone pretty much disqualify you. No, I
mean let me save *you*. Not humanity, not the choirmaster at
Didsbury Church of England Primary School, not Decibel Jones.
You. Oort St. Ultraviolet, Omar Calişkan, let me come through
cloven skies with peaceful wings unfurled and get you the hell
out of here. We can swing by your place and pick up your offspring
and mate if that's what you're worried about. My homeworld is
where everyone and their furtive uncle puts things to forget about

forever. No one will ever know I swiped you off the dock. You can live a nice life on Sagrada. You'll want for nothing. We'll set you up in a house down the murky shore. Maybe you can curate the *Homo sapiens sapiens* exhibit in the Melanoatramentous Library. Maybe not—no pressure at all. Life on shadow street, baby. And hey, you never know, maybe your boy Dess will pull it out in the end and all will be right as ravens. But if not . . . you'll be safe, and alive, and so will everyone you love."

Oort was stunned silent. It had never occurred to him that a way out of this even existed. Now it was holding the escape hatch open for him and yelling for him to go, go, go. The giddy winds of Litost were burning out his higher-order functions, stripping his wiring down to bare Paleolithic caveman copper. Decibel would be fine. He always was. Nico and Siouxsie and Justine would be safe. Did anyone else really matter? It was wrong, of course. Absolutely wrong. Monstrously wrong. But who would be around to know? Just then, in the unconditional light of three rosy, shimmering, nonjudgmental moons, all he wanted to do was live.

Oort St. Ultraviolet dragged the last particles of smoke out of his Elakh cigarette. "I hate this planet," he said, looking out to sea, toward the red glow of Our Mums just below the twilit horizon. "I hated it the minute we landed. The way you can catch happy here, like you said. The antidepressant grass and the diamond rain and the peaceful happy roses being peaceful and happy together, literally breathing in emotional stability with every yawn. But I didn't really know why it pissed me off so much. Sometimes you meet someone and they just rub you the wrong way. No reason it can't go that way with a planet. But that wasn't it. Do you want to know why I hate Litost?"

"Always want to know your thoughts, Double O."

Oort St. Ultraviolet, man of a thousand instruments, flicked his smoke off the balcony, half a mile straight down into the ocean. "Because," he sighed. "If Mira had been born here and not in fucking Sheffield, she'd never have had the Eeyores so bad that she tried to nail her tail back on with a speeding van and I'd still get to take her for gelato at five in the morning." He smiled ruefully, and it turned his face twenty years younger. "No sale, Zaraz. Everybody's got a Nico and a Siouxsie and a Justine. AM radio is not even a thing compared to the guy who leaves them all to burn because he doesn't want to get up there with the poinsettias and the xylophone and sing about the angels. It's all of us or none of us." He straightened his suit jacket. Englishblokeman did not shirk. He did not turn in lackluster work. No matter how the tourists pulled at his hat, he did not move one solitary muscle. "Besides, it'll be good for my anxiety."

"Then let me take out one of the other acts for you," came a small, sweet voice. Öö dashed out of the party floor and scrambled up the side of a rose statue. He looked at Oort with soft eyes. "I could bludgeon that Voorpret cow and stash it in a broom closet for the duration, and I'd still shut down the after-party before I even felt bad about it. You seemed to really *loathe* the 321. I can DDoS that paper clip into oblivion without even getting my pulse up. It's no problem at *all*, Oort." The time-traveling red panda put his black paw on Oort's cheek. "I don't want you to die. I'm willing to let seven billion rubbish humans live if that's what it takes."

"You're not doing your superpower stutter," Oort said uncertainly. "That's your whole thing. That's your idiom."

"This is a one-timeline deal. It's a moment of weakness on my part. None of the other versions of me want in. No one will ever think less of you. Rule 20, love. It's beyond legit."

"Do you have to kill them?" Oort asked softly.

Darkboy Zaraz and Öö exchanged glances. The ancient

Elakh took one on the moral center. "Usually we try to avoid nonrefundable fatalities, but if you want to be 100 percent sure, beyond all probability of unforeseen cock-ups, it's safer that way. You don't want to see a Yurtmak lounge singer after she's busted out of a meat freezer."

Oort squeezed his eyes shut and shoved his knuckles into them. He couldn't think. It was like breathing the electric Kool-Aid acid test out here. He'd agree to anything in another minute.

"Ask me in the morning," he whispered desperately.

"I need to know now, sweetness," whispered the Keshet. "A couple of dumb B-list celebrities you don't even like for the whole of humanity. It's not such a tough call, is it? That's some good math." Öö bristled his striped tail and laid his chin on Oort's shoulder. "Even the nicest song has to have a screamy bit, Omarcik."

Oort gripped the Creamsicle railing of that absurd, unnecessary balcony. He blinked back tears. "Öö, I *can't*. How is that right? The first thing a human being does when confronted with the universe at large would be to stone-cold murder somebody because he got nervous that maybe their music had a little more mass appeal? And if you're right about us, if we're way more Mark David Chapman than John Lennon, then it'll be about thirty seconds before we start blowing you up just to see the light show, so what difference would it make, in the end? If the whole point of this is what we are, whether we are ready, whether we are fundamentally more than beasts . . . that seems like the opposite of sentience to me. I can't make that decision for everyone. For the whole of us, from Nefertiti and Homer and Aquinas and Beau Brummell and Marie Curie all the way down to Nico and Siouxsie and me. I'm not cut out to be the last man on Earth. I'm just an ordinary guy. I can't. I'm not fucking Cain. I'm not the first bloke to kill an alien. Not even Clippy. And Clippy is a cunt."

A thin spiral shadow fell on the human, the red panda, and the black traffic cone. It spoke in a pleasant, gender-neutral, corporate-approved voice.

"This concludes the semifinal round," said Clippy. "You have been cleared to move on to the finals. Would you like to save the changes you've made to this document?"

29.

My Heart Has No Color

Capo spent the better part of the evening chasing Yüz particles, which were much more interesting than moths or flies or mice. They kept forming into elaborate word clouds, but as the Esca hadn't bothered to teach her to read when she was flipping switches in her feline brain, she didn't really care what they were trying to say. It was probably, *No, no, bad kitty, don't bite.* It usually was, in Capo's experience.

She wandered out onto the hotel veranda long after Oort had gone. Long after most everyone had gone. They had forgotten about her, but that was all right. She forgot about them plenty. They'd left heaps of food lying everywhere. Creatures who were not cats were terribly slovenly. Capo tried to drink out of the fountain, but it was viciously bitter. She shunned it for offending her and hopped up on the railing, which would have given anyone else vertigo, but she was not anyone else. She was a cat, and height had no meaning to her. The air didn't get up her nose much either. One percent aerosolized cocaine is a bowl of low-fat milk compared to what goes on beyond the feline blood-brain barrier. In fact, she found the high-octane breezes made her sluggish and irritable.

"Let me guess," said a breathy, sweet voice behind Capo. She didn't turn to look. She licked her paw. If the owner of the voice wanted to be seen, it would come round. Why waste the energy? "Backup singer?"

A large, expertly groomed topiary studded with healthy pale orange roses leaned into view. Capo licked her other paw in smug satisfaction.

"No," she said. "They're mine, only they don't know it."

"I see. My name is Ekali, I am one of the Klavaret singers this year."

Capo yawned. Her eyes bulged. The moons shone on her fangs.

"We're called Hug Addiction," the Klavar said, twisting her leaves nervously. "We have a lot of vibro-cellos. And a fancy clown."

Capo whipped her white tail back and forth and regarded the rosebush hungrily.

"It's very rare to win two years in a row, of course, but that's no excuse not to try your best!" A seabird called somewhere in the distance. "Anyway . . . do you plan to perform with them tomorrow or . . . what?"

Capo's ears twitched. "What do you want?" she purred.

"Well, it's only that you live on Earth as well, you see. And since you're *here*, your species deserves some consideration. We do try to limit collateral damage in the event of a loss, but accidents will happen!"

The cat's tail curled and uncurled lazily. "But *I'll* be fine," she said. "Because I'm here."

"Well, yes, but . . ."

"Then what's the problem?"

"Miss Capo, you really have to learn to relax! I'm your friend! Your happy flower friend! I'm here to make you an offer! The Klavaret have a lot of voting power this year, as hosts. We could probably sway others to your cause. In exchange for a small fee, of course."

"Excellent. Do it."

"What? You don't know what the fee is."

"Eh."

"I was going to say India. Its climate is very advantageous to botanical life."

"Sold. It's over there. Go get it. I will nap here."

The Klavaret maid quivered her petals in distress. "Alternatively, I could perhaps take care of some of your competition for you. As a gesture of alliance. I know that's a bit gruesome . . ."

Capo's bottle-green eyes lit up. "Even better! Can I help? Who are we killing? Can it be the glittery things? They look tasty."

"The Yüz are members of the Octave . . ."

"Don't care. Tast-y."

Ekali turned all her blossoms toward the average British suburban house cat. "Allow me to lay my thorns on the table, as it were. You understand that this is the end of the semifinal round, don't you? I offer these temptations as a test of sentience. It all goes into the evaluation. Whether you would sell out your homeworld or murder one of your new neighbors or let the rest of your species burn to save yourself."

"I have to be honest, that all just sounds really fantastic to me," Capo meowed. "But if you could just do it *for* me, that would be brilliant."

Ekali rocked back a little on her stems, realization rocketing through her, thorn to petal and back. "You would destroy us," she whispered. "There is another rising species on Earth. You never invented radio. We didn't know."

"Why bother? The monkeys will make one and then I can sleep on top of it. The static makes my belly tingle."

"Compared to you," said the Klavar soprano, "humans are joyful rosebushes bouncing through the stars. If you ever stopped napping long enough to escape Earth, you would sweep across this galaxy like nothing before, an endless wave of carnage. You would hunt our worlds one by one and ruin everything we've built. Only your laziness protects us."

Capo hopped down off the railing. She lifted her tail in the air haughtily and glanced back over her furry shoulder.

"Most likely," she purred. "Best keep mum, don't you think? Wouldn't want to wake us up."

30.

Silence and So Many People

On the subject of interspecies sex, the only reliable rule is Goguenar Gorecannon's longest, most controversial, and least profanity-riddled Unkillable Fact: the Fourteenth Special. A wide variety of interestingly shaped parents have petitioned to have it redacted on the grounds that, while true, it makes for screamingly awkward postlullaby conversations, and its inclusion makes it very difficult to leave offspring home alone with any unguarded household appliances. All such requests are routinely burned unread by the Gorecannon estate. The Fourteenth Unkillable Fact states the following: *Everybody fucks. Well, almost everybody. No force on this plane of reality can equal the drive to get a leg over, because it's the nondimensional otherspace where all those nice, sophisticated fundamental forces meet and form a weird, wet, messy trashball: tension, friction, gravity, electromagnetism, thrust, torque, resistance, elasticity, drag, momentum, inertia, pressure, chemical reactivity, fusion, conservation of energy, self-loathing, humiliation, and loneliness.*

Being ashamed of it makes about as much sense as being ashamed of the speed of light.

Everybody is bizarre and disgusting and interesting and fixated on fetishes they wouldn't admit to their grandmother on pain of vaporiza-

tion and worthy of love. You are bizarre and disgusting and interesting and fixated on fetishes you wouldn't admit to your grandmother on pain of vaporization and worthy of love. It's a literal goddamned zoo out there, so this is the best I can do you for: don't giggle when the other entity takes their clothes off, secure enthusiastic consent, don't mix silicon and carbon without extensive decontamination protocols, tidy up your house if you expect to bring someone home, don't expect anything you wouldn't offer, remember that every person is an end in themselves and not a means to an end, don't worry too much about what goes where and how many of them there are, don't mistake fun for love, try your best, be kind, always make them breakfast, and use protection. Chromosomes are not nearly such picky eaters as you might think. Just because the other fella is a plank of sentient wood from Planet 2 x 4 doesn't mean you can't get pregnant, and the splinters won't be nearly as fun coming out as they were going in.

The fact is, neither anatomy nor culture nor inconvenience nor the linearity of time nor distance nor food allergies nor federal law nor a dimensional rift nor strict parents nor the threat of instant and hilariously excruciating death upon contact with one solitary smear of foreign bodily fluids can stop people after a bit of strange, and the stranger the bits the better, because genes are a bunch of thrill-seeking little shits, always looking for the next new thing. The very first time the very first species discovered that they were not alone in the universe, they started eyeing up the other hostile carbolic-acid-blooded space squid, winking compulsively, and asking them if they wanted to intermix and gill.

Where there's a wang there's a way.

I once saw an Ursula hook up with a mime, a tuberous begonia, and a bottle of expired milk. There's no unseeing that.

In the end, there is no atom in this galaxy but that someone hasn't tried to fuck it.

Except me.

Who needs a drink?

Generally, this holds up to experimentation; otherwise, it would be a Semikillable Fact, included only in older editions. Sex may not look the same in terms of number, kind, duration, pronouns, content, or survivability from species to species, it may not be advisable under even the most hastily drawn up occupational health and safety guidelines, but it's pretty much always happening everywhere. The variety of genders across disparate species makes the human fixation on rigidly defined sexual orientations seem as adorably, bafflingly old-fashioned as a butter churn in a travel agency. The definitions of sex across worlds vary so much that the Elakh word for "to make love," which can be loosely translated as "emblackenate," also means to swim, to dance, to fish, to grow up big and strong, to hide a body for a friend, to be surprised that they're still making the candy one loved as a child, to really and truly self-actualize, to maintain an antiquated belief in fairies, to jump, to sing, to dig, to secure financing, to stalemate, to lay tile, and to vigorously debate the social issues of the day.

On some planets, sex isn't even remotely connected to reproduction. The Smaragdi, for example, have six-and-a-half genders. Nessuno Uuf used the pronouns "she" and "her" only because it seemed, in the cultural documents from Earth, that people utilizing those pronouns got to wear flashier clothes and considerably more tribal paints. The Smaragdi create children via battle royale combat, in which the spilled blood of the losing parents contributes only the most basic recessive, baseline genes to the resulting offspring. They are renowned and sought-after lovers, due to their stamina, open-mindedness, and levitational abilities, although not having to worry about getting one knocked up is probably a contributing factor. For other species, a light cough will land you in midnight feedings and a sensible family car before you can say,

Sorry, I've got a bit of a cold. In the presence of a pollinating Klavar, it's best to cover your mouth. There are, naturally, a few asexual species, and they do seem to get a lot more done in a day, but even they give it a try once in a while, just to see what all the fuss is about, before shrugging and going back to grounding their self-esteem in concrete accomplishments and finding fulfillment in skills and hobbies like the twisted kinksters they are.

Sex is universal, it's just not evenly distributed.

In the face of a blistering universe of infinite possibility, mind-smearing variety, hopping nightlife, and a galactic pornography industry as venerable and august as any bank, the innate sexual conservatism of any given species usually lasts about 3.4 seconds.

Which is how Decibel Jones came to find himself in the executive suite of the South Wharf Hilton on Litost, propped up by the pillows endemic to hotels everywhere, even seven thousand light-years from the nearest hospitality degree program, differing only in the precise manner of their inadequacy, snuggled between the Smaragdin Nessuno Uuf and a beam of exhausted moonlight.

Decibel knew the basics of Goguenar Gorecannon's Fourteenth Special, though he couldn't have put a name to it or expressed it as concisely as a lonely-heart Yurtmak in the midst of a chemically volatile forest. He knew it by instinct and the hard-earned, precariously rigged experience of an adulthood spent being reasonably attractive, a couple of years spent massively famous, and a life spent fascinated by everyone he ever met, if occasionally only for a few minutes at the outside.

Jones couldn't entirely be certain that what had transpired over the previous couple of hours fell under the dictionary definition of sex. It was more like a very complete entry in Rogerer's.

The moonlight, who was called Gobo, had been straightforward enough. The Azdrian postpunk filament-harmonic front man had slipped into the elevator with Decibel and Nessuno as the party was shutting down. When he'd asked, rather cheekily, given that tonight might well be Decibel's last chance for a good time, whether the two of them would be interested in collectivizing, Dess thought he could imagine how sex with a swaggeringly masculine moonbeam might go, and it did, more or less. Gobo shone all over everywhere and promptly passed out without returning the favor.

Nessuno was more complicated. She'd disappeared into the bathroom the moment Gobo was snoring, which, in a shaft of moonlight, manifested as a slow, steady flicker that, before long, faded away to nothing at all. The Azdr, being mostly photons, have a distinct advantage when it comes to escaping potentially awkward situations and are famous for simply going off like an embarrassed light switch.

The room was actually Nessuno's personal suite, though the replicated human hotel room, down to the minbar and flat-screen television accompanied by a remote control with enough buttons to manage the settings on the known universe, could hardly have been less designed for her comfort. A small landfill of suitcases, musical accoutrements, and equipment covered the floor, none of which Decibel could have figured out how to use if you held a mic to his head. It really was a *stonking* huge remote. It didn't really fit in with the sleek late-model TV. That thing was the love child of a 1980s home entertainment system and a space shuttle command console. The buttons glowed softly violet.

With trembling fingers, her eyes wide with desire, Nessuno Uuf emerged from the en suite holding the instrument of her love between them.

It was a hairbrush.

"And what do you expect to do with that?" Decibel asked nervously.

"The . . . usual?" Nessuno said. Her pale eyes glistened with lust and confusion. "You know . . . sex. Copulation. The old in-out. That's what we're both after, isn't it?"

Decibel Jones shrugged. "Oh, sure, love. I can take a little paddling if that's what you're into."

"No! Not *paddling*, for crying out—what . . . what good would *that* do? This is . . . how we do it on Pallulle. Look, I know you showed that Esca a good time. I didn't think you'd be such a prude."

"Don't be upset, Nessie my darling. I'm here to learn. Why don't you walk me through it? Just give me a little preview. What do you like? How do the Smaragdi get down?"

Nessuno Uuf closed her enormous eyes in a transport of delight. "We brush each other's hair, and then, if you're *really* kinky, we open up and show each other our feelings," she whispered. Her breathing was getting heavy. "But that's only if you're into the hard-core triple-X stuff. Why, how do humans do it?"

Jones blinked. There were rules to a one-night stand. Protocols. Diplomatic procedures. And the most important one was not to shame the other guy for the way his rudder leaned. He always tried to be open and giving and create a good memory for everyone involved. Good memories rarely included being laughed out of the room. "Um," he said, pulling the modernist bronze-and-gray-striped sheet over his naked and suddenly unaroused body. "Same. Maybe a hug too, if there's time, but mostly . . . same."

But Dess had to admit, her hair was amazing. It was like brushing a snowbank. With every stroke, the Smaragdin quivered and shook and made soft little moans like strumming a bass underwater. Whenever he hit a tangle, she gasped and dug her nails into his knee. He hoped he was making a decent hash of it. After a while, he tried telling her she was beautiful.

"Ooh," the ten-foot-tall horn-rimmed creature sighed out. "I didn't know you were into humiliation! Yes, yes, do it harder."

Decibel froze. But he tried. He always tried. "Er. All right. Yes. Well. You're a dirty little brush-slut, aren't you?"

"What? No. I said *humiliate* me. Like before! Insult me. Go on. Say something *really* degrading. Tell me . . . tell me I'm a *good person.*"

"Right. You're . . . you're a beautiful, accomplished individual worthy of respect, aren't you?"

Nessuno shuddered violently from head to toe. She wasn't half as selfish as Gobo. The Smaragdin leaped up and gave Decibel's hair a good seeing-to, and though it didn't have quite the same effect on him, it was comforting, and relaxing, and after an hour or so, just when he really started to think he could get into this in a more *direct* way, she stopped.

"Do you want to?" she whispered, hardly daring to hope. "I'll show you mine if you show me yours."

"The feelings bit? Yeah, you know me, nothing's too wild."

She collected her limbs onto the bed, careful not to jostle the snoring moonbeam, and the two of them sat cross-legged across from each other on the mattress. A rather medieval painting of a unicorn hung over the bed behind Nessuno's head. Her pale, bony frame blocked out the hunters and the virgin who were out for the poor pony's blood.

"You first," she encouraged him.

"Whatever you want, baby. Well. Let's see. I . . . I'm pretty terrified, if you want to know the truth. I'd never tell Oort this, but I just . . . wish they'd picked someone else. I wish I *were* someone else. Someone you could rely on to turn it out no matter what. I'm afraid that whatever I had is lost by now. I haven't had a song out in years. I haven't had a good day in years. What if I get up there and just completely blow it? Or worse, what if I get up there and give the performance of my sorry life, the best show in the history of me, if the light of the world comes beaming out of me like a bloody Care Bear Stare for the ages, and it's *not good enough*? If you lot somehow hear in my voice all the worst of us? Because there's a lot of worst. There really is. You only know what we've done since we invented radio. Before that it gets really hairy. And I'm nobody's shining example. I'm not innocent. I'm all junked up inside, always have been. No musician isn't. That's why we're musicians. That's a bit of a flaw in your whole system, honestly." His voice started to tremble. "All I've ever wanted is to be like that thing in the painting behind you. It's called a unicorn. It's not a real animal or anything. Back when we thought we were alone in the universe, we made up a lot of other intelligent creatures so we could have someone to talk to at night. Anyway, the thing about unicorns was that they were innocent. So innocent that you couldn't even lure one out of the forest except with a trick it was too sweet and dumb to figure out, and even then, it *still* wouldn't dream of stabbing that bitch in the gut when the hunters came. It forgave. It kept on loving even with a belt around its neck. But I've never been like that, not even close. Ask Mira. Ask Oort. Hell, ask the roadrunner. And I'm going to go onstage tomorrow, and even if I sing to shatter the heavens, you'll *see* how I really am. How we really are."

Nessuno Uuf looked over her shoulder at the rubbish hotel painting and gave a long, low whistle. "I wish I had your confidence," she said. "Now, don't make me wait for it. Show me your feelings."

Jones narrowed his eyes. "I just did. Honestly, I'm a little hurt.

I just laid out my heart. What else do you want?"

The Smaragdin cocked her head to one side. "Oh. Oh, *ew*. Was that . . . was that it? Is that how primates externalize emotion? Do you . . . do you really keep your feelings on the *inside*?"

"Do you not?"

Nessuno Uuf grinned. Then she stretched, her lithe rib cage arching toward him, her lips parted. Something emerged from her baroque breastbone. A spur of bone the same color as the rest of her. Then more than a spur. It began to darken as the air hit it, as it squeezed out of her like toothpaste out of the strangest tube. "Like I said," she panted, "the old in-out. I've always felt sorry for people who are limited to verbalization. It's so easy to fake it."

It didn't seem like a thing that should be happening. It didn't seem like a thing that should be possible. She was all bone and armor, unpierceable, impregnable. But her chest cavity might as well have been a butter sculpture at a county fair for all the resistance it gave.

"Smaragdi emotions leave mineral deposits in our organs as they pass through us. Strong feelings can overwhelm our filtering systems, build up too fast, at which point we have to pass them or we can suffer psychological toxicity and require dialysis or even a transplant. Do you have kidneys?"

Decibel Jones could not look away. It was obscene and clinical and intimate and performative all at the same time, like watching an orgiastic tribal dance about lab results. "Two of them, last I checked," he answered without blinking.

It didn't seem to hurt her. She seemed to love every minute of it, in fact. Her breathing was quick, soft, ecstatic. "Think of it as passing a kidney stone, if your kidneys were located in the pleasure center of your brain. Most of us do it once a day before bed. We have whole china cabinets full of stones. A perfect, utterly honest record of every emotional state we experience. Symbolic representations, formed in the collective unconscious, but you can't make them lie any more than you can make your kidneys pretend to be hearts."

She pulled the rest of the feeling stone out with her fingertips and placed it in his hand with a shivery, delighted sigh. It was a child's toy, a small, charcoal-silver figurine, still warm from her body.

It was one of the unicorn hunters from the painting on the wall.

As he held it, Decibel was overwhelmed with foreign emotions: satisfaction, triumph, anticipation, relief, fear, crippling social pressure, artistic insecurity, ambition, xenophobia, and a strong, awful flood of schadenfreude. This was the Smaragdi climax, he realized. Eat your heart out, Dr. Kinsey. Jones wanted to shake it off and leave with some devastating quip, but he couldn't look away from the vicious little action figure. He couldn't move at all. The inundation of her feelings turned his synapses into a malfunctioning tech rehearsal for fight-or-flight, and he could not move at all.

Nessuno Uuf looked at him with the last dregs of pleasure in her eyes and what appeared to be genuine regret.

"Sorry, love," she crooned. "You know how it is. All's fair in the semifinals. I really *am* sorry. *I* think humans are wonderful. So attractive and creative and musically talented, and obviously deeply sentient." She stroked his hair fondly. "It's the Alunizar, see. They're going bankrupt. Year after year, everyone votes them into oblivion because we're not allowed to get our war reparations any other way. Every year, they send five-star catering to the galactic table and get back crumbs. Serves them right, if you ask me, but you can't expect them to just take total economic collapse on the chin. And since these tone-deaf space monsters would rather suck face with a colicky wormhole than award Aluno any points at all, well, our friendly local sea squirt hired me to take out some of the low-hanging fruit." The skeletal assassin shrugged sheepishly. "Now this . . . *this* is a bit barbaric, I admit. But galactic society is still . . . well, *society*. And society is rubbish. Good lord, the Grand Prix is the *best* thing we've ever done, the utter best, and it's just a bit of song and dance, isn't it? I never did say we were good; just sentient. It's like Goguenar Gorecannon's Eleventh Unkillable Fact always says: *You can't stop people being assholes. They do love it so. The best you can hope for is that some people, sometimes, will turn out to be somewhat less than the absolute worst. When they manage to trip and fall over that incredibly low bar, they'll make you want to end it all. But when they leap over it, they'll make you believe this whole mess really was created for a reason—the bastards. Except me, of course. I'm superb. Ask anyone. And you're all right, I suppose.* Welcome to being a people, kid. It's just dreadful up here."

Nessuno Uuf hopped off the bed and bent down close to his ear. Dess sat transfixed by the silver hunter in his hand, still as a photograph. "You're a beautiful, accomplished species worthy of respect," she purred in his ear. "And you, Decibel Jones, were the best I've ever had."

Just as he regained control of his motor functions, the amorous Smaragdin picked up that massive, button-encrusted remote off the bedside table, aimed it directly at Decibel Jones's vocal cords, and pressed mute.

"Are you really going to kill me with a Panasonic universal remote?" Jones tried to quip.

Nothing came out. He groped at his throat. Tried to sing a few bars of "Ziggy Stardust," "More Than This," "Parsley, Sage, Rosemary, and Thyme," "Happy Fucking Birthday," anything.

Nothing.

"See you onstage," said Nessuno Uuf. "Best of luck."

When Oort St. Ultraviolet got back to their room, he found nobody there. No Decibel, no weird alien conquest. Just a quiet suite with a mint on the pillow and their costumes folded neatly on the bed. Grown out of a bar on the other side of the galaxy from seed bins with ridiculous labels like LOVE WASTED and TILL WE MEET AGAIN and THE FOLLY OF YOUTH and THE BAD OLD DAYS and PEACE AT THE END OF ALL THINGS.

On one end of the bed lay a dismembered ladies' red sequin blazer, low-slung, mercilessly tight trousers that had once been a wine-stained wedding gown, and a cricket jumper with the name GEORGE embroidered lovingly on the hem in purple thread with a jaunty bat on either side. On the other lay a pair of satin paisley trousers with vintage '80s gold accent chains all over them, platform boots, black plastic bat wings, and Robert, smelling just like roses.

31.

Lullaby for a Volcano

Decibel Jones and the Absolute Zeros began and ended in non-descript rooms with not much more to recommend them but a couple of beds, a TV, a minifridge, and the reek of destiny. One was the kind of flat you could afford on what Mr. Five Star was willing to pay out.

The other was a hotel in Scotland.

Other people are frightfully useful and pleasant things, but not, strictly speaking, a must-have to get around town. Even the jankiest hand-me-down damaged/as-is human heart—one that couldn't pass a user safety inspection to save its own ventricles—can be the handcrafted, jewel-toned, durable, all-seasons high-end accessory before, during, and after the fact of life on Planet Earth. Other people don't just get you from day to day; they get you there, despite all their irritating habits and unnecessary mannerisms, in comfort, good company, high style, full of canapés, with a good buzz going, and looking like somebody to reckon with, which is very important to most young species trying to splash some cash around and make their mark on the nightlife.

But you could always go it alone.

You can try, anyway. Sometimes, even whole countries try.

Listen. That small, watery, excitable planet is a pretty damnably woolly place, and we've got a lot to cover in a short time if we're going to get through the whole history of the Zeros, but try not to forget about those lonely countries. They're going to to be important in a minute.

In the early days of the band, it had been easy. They never wanted to be apart. Whether or not anyone else happened to be nearby was as consequential to the Absolute Zeros as what was on tap at any given pub on any given day at any given time. But there is a certain energy to cliché, a certain gravity, as inexorable as entropy, and from the same part of town. You can plan for it. You can set your watch by it. It has a beat, and you can dance to it. By the time Decibel Jones, Mira Wonderful Star, and Oort St. Ultraviolent were huddled around a television in Edinburgh as if it were an ancient campfire, while Lila Poole paced back and forth, smoking Israeli cigarettes one after the other, they cared very much about whether anyone else was around, and what was on tap at the local on that particular night, at that particular time.

You can plan for the slow expansion and dissolution of the energy of the universe. There are equations and formulas to tell you what to pack for the trip, and how much time you've got left. You can't plan for the sudden acceleration of heavenly bodies to intolerable velocities, or for their occasional screeching stop. For the shock of a hidden pocket of heat-death roaring in the dark, ever so much closer than it ought to be.

They watched it all happen on television, as though they were citizens of a much earlier generation. The revolution was always going to be televised. It wasn't the kind of revolution that would miss out on those ratings. They'd sung all night on stage, sung until they were dry of music, not knowing that they had already run face-first into the cartoon Wile E. Coyote–wall of the future.

That deportations had begun. That Cool Uncle Takumi had died in a riot, trampled underfoot by hundreds trying to pretend time hadn't run out, that they hadn't been pinwheeling their legs over a bridgeless chasm for some time now, still imagining they were walking on safe ground. That Nani was already in a processing facility awaiting a flight to Islamabad because Mr. Prime of the Minister said in a sad, carefully empathizing tone that she didn't have the right passport and had stolen enough resources for one lifetime.

That no one had come to the show, not entirely because the Zeros were yesterday's hotness, but because they were home watching the world as they knew it end.

For Oort and Dess, it happened in Mira's eyes, reflections of the news, backward and inverted, chyrons rolling across her unbelieving irises. They ate everything in the minibar mechanically, methodically, tasting nothing, saying nothing. In fact, no one said anything at all until Mira turned to her friend and whispered: *marry me.*

And Decibel Jones laughed. Nervously, instinctively, afraid and thrown sideways. But a laugh all the same.

If he hadn't laughed, she would have said the rest. She would have said it, and he would have understood. But he laughed, because it seemed like the most idiotic thing in the world, so he laughed, because how can you live when everything is lava on top of acid on top of fascist cream pie, let alone marry anyone or make the slightest plan that involves a future? He laughed in her face, and Mira Wonderful Star, hopped up on candy and crackers and shock, didn't have the right octane fuel for that. So she didn't finish. She just let it end with "marry me" instead of *Marry me, marry me, Dess, and we'll be safe, we'll be a nice straight couple with money in the bank and no one can be offended by that, no one can come after that in the night, we'll be together and we'll smile our best English-blokeman smiles, and no one will be able to touch us. You were born here. I wasn't. Without you, I'm not safe. Oort has Justine. It's just us kittens left, and the rain is coming. Marry me, and we'll make a little bubble universe where nothing has to change and the elections never happened and it's just Arkable Us, neon against the night, ice cream against the world.*

How could I know? Decibel would say to Oort fifteen years later on a spaceship to nowhere. *How could I know what she meant?*

Unfortunately, Decibel Jones's laugh blew Mira out of the sky. Oort was convinced that it was cruelty and not terrified, confused hysteria borne of Nani not answering her phone, not answering, still not answering, why wasn't she answering? A band of glam-rock gutter-glitz punks took the end of the world on the chin, each blamed the other, no one explained themselves, and Lila Poole quietly seethed about their refusal to stop messing about and discuss things like adults. Half of humanity was already steaming and scrambling against the other half by the time Decibel's father called to tell him about Nani, Mira never did find out about her uncle, and the next ten years progressed at record speed from confusion and posturing to, in technical terms, an intergalactic shitshow.

One way or another, the Absolute Zeros weren't really much for situational awareness, and never noticed Mira grab the keys to the van off the top of the refrigerator and slip out the door onto a much longer road than any of the rest of them could imagine.

Heart

Forever and ever together, we sail into infinity,
We're higher and higher and higher, we're reaching for divinity.
—"Euphoria," Loreen

32.

Every Song Is a Cry for Love

The one hundredth Metagalactic Grand Prix was held on Litost, the Klavaret homeworld, on the ruins of Vlimeux, where the war ended.

It was the first Grand Prix in twenty-one years to feature a new applicant species, after all that unpleasantness with Flus and Muntun. To all the gathered Alunizar and Keshet, Smaragdi and Elakhon, Sziv and Voorpret, Lummutis and Slozhit, Esca and Azdr and Ursulas and Meleg and Yüz and Yurtmak and 321 and the single, solitary remaining Inaki, it seemed somehow appropriate that the hundredth anniversary gala should have real stakes, should prove the purpose of the Grand Prix all over again, should rock the goddamned house down.

Doors opened at seven, the show started at eight. In pubs and clubs and house parties across the galaxy, the viewers at home were drunk by six.

The Mamtak Aggregate and DJ Lights Out—beloved, though getting on in years, Masters of Ceremonies, sanctioned haters, and winners of the second and sixth Grand Prix—floated and hobbled onto the Stage of Life, respectively. The Yüzosh beatvoxer swirled into the shape of a massive disco ball and spun round for the delight of the crowds. The constant twilight of Litost glittered on the silicate beings, and the air smelled of roses and cocaine.

"Welcome to the one hundredth Metagalactic Grand Prix!" thundered the little Elakh DJ Lights Out. The audience roared; the cheap seats stomped whatever they had in the way of feet. "It's probably going to be a bit shit, but it's better than another war, am I right?"

In the dive bars and speakeasies and orbital bistros of the civilized galaxy, a blast of applause blew out windows, cracked tables, and short-circuited the mood lighting.

In the bars, pubs, restaurants, hotel lobbies, airports, offices, and quiet, tense lounge rooms of Earth, no one thought the joke was particularly funny.

The hypno-kelp dimmed, the crowds went quiet, the Ocean of Unconditional Acceptance crashed against the shore, and the Grand Prix began.

The Alunizar, as the prime political mover in the galaxy, were granted the first performance slot by the Grand Prix governing body, which meant that by the time voting started, no one would even remember the name of their song. Better Than You swept onto the stage in a rush of aquatic explosions and radical inter-pretive plopping. Slekke[5] and their four lumbering, electric-veined gold bandmates slung the straps of their heat-seeking mandolins over what passed for their shoulders. They strummed the deli-cate fleshy strings with their nubs while geysers of locally sourced, eel-lit seawater detonated behind them, filling the Stage of Life with a melancholy, classical melody as heartfelt and skillful as any backwoods grandfather showing his boys what *real* music was. After about forty-five seconds of that, Slekke[5] belted out a neuron-curdling war-yodel and the beat kicked in. "Is Your Con-tinual Mistreatment of Our Entire Species Fair Trade?" would be heard in every convenience store and mall elevator on the settled worlds that summer—the Muzak version, anyway. But despite the truly self-righteous beat, the Grand Prix audience wouldn't give those overgrown painted goiters the satisfaction, not even during the final verse in which the Alunizar rockers removed their budded offspring, one by one by ruby-threaded one, letting them slide onto the stage like jeweled tears, and assembling a chorus of generations vibrating at a frequency only the cool could hear.

The Mamtak Aggregate formed itself into the shape of a lonely, overturned can of soup. DJ Lights Out nodded. "Leave it to the Alunizar to try to make things *political*," she said, making sarcastic air quotes with her long, twiggy fingers. "Somebody cut their *waaa*mplifiers, my ears can't take the nubhurt."

Color drained from the faces of the fifty or so cops at a police bar in Birmingham. "How is this not political?" shouted the chief, through the film of his fifth scotch.

The Voorpret hitmakers Vigor Mortis Overdrive cut in with a slamming drum riff. Puvinys Blek, who had ditched its rapidly curdling Keshet body for a nearly fresh Slozhit one, spread its rotting wings, lifted a ceremonial Gageba shovel high into the dusky sky, and, accompanied by gouts of purple flame and gutteral death metal vocals, smashed it against the stage, obliterating a cleverly concealed nest-sac burst open beneath the floorboards and releasing a swarm of frenzied earworms into the stands like a comedian smashing a watermelon all over the front row. No one could get "No Antibody for Love" out of their heads as the infectious song spread from host to host and the euphoria-secreting worms burrowed deep into various and sundry ocular organs to lay their eggs.

The Mamtak Aggregate coalesced into an old droopy sock with holes in it. "I thought it was great!" enthused the Elakh, her gigantic eyes shining. "I got my vaccinations! Didn't hear a thing!"

The 321, no longer stored in the body of Clippy but simply downloaded into a mixing board that bore more than a passing resemblance to Captain Nemo's organ, played their anthem of loss, hope, and the inability to escape the rainbow wheel of suffering and end the cycle of life, death, and the categorical oppression of synthetic life by gross, moist organics, "Abort, Retry, Fail," without fanfare or effects, which put everyone right off from the start. The 321 had calculated it to be the perfect song, a precisely tuned slice of electro-pop confectionary that nevertheless spoke of deep universal themes everyone could relate to, immaculate in every respect from melody to rhythm to emotional effect. It went on to become the most-refunded single in the history of the galactic musical economy, for reasons given variously as: "You can't really dance to it," "I think I'm going to go off music for a while," and "It's hard to work out when you feel a deep sense of unease in the presence of the gym equipment."

Up next was the home team, the Klavaret sensation Hug Addiction. A holographic garden erupted over the stage, each hyperreal flower concealing a mister that pumped out a scent chemically formulated to lower the artistic standards of anyone within range. The rose topiaries performed a traditional Dance of Conflict Resolution, vibrating their stamens into the memories of everyone who heard even a single note of their song like a heart-seeking laser, finding, targeting, sampling, and remixing the songs that were playing when each person felt the most perfect love and acceptance in their lives and mixing it down into what would go on to be the dance craze of the decade, "I Wanna Be Elated."

In a modest house outside Budapest, a woman heard her mother, her sisters, her daughters, and her child self all singing a thousand Hungarian folk songs and old photo-film commercial themes in such piercing harmony that she collapsed on the floor in a rictus of emotional cohesion.

The lights went out just as Once You Go Black got the crowd on its feet. They rocked out the Sagrada way, and unless your eyes evolved in a world like a locked broom closet, you never saw their pyrotechnic darkshow or their synchronized Sagradan tango. Darkboy Zaraz played the dark-matter didge so fine, the vibrations slid a cool black cosmic calm into every cell of every poor, benighted lightbody so that they could finally know some peace, some peace called "Black Is the New Black."

Decibel Jones and Oort St. Ultraviolet watched it all from the wings.

They watched the Utorak thump out a thunderous rock anthem called "Tell Me About Your Mother" by hurling themselves against one another until the cracks and booms became a percussion and their cries of pain became a melody line and the whole of Litost danced along. They watched the Esca infrapop duo Birdward let the sweet wind of the sea play over their chest cavities to the tune of "You'll Feel What I Tell You and You'll Like It" and wash the stage in such bright light from their lamps that the afterimages sparkled emerald in everyone's vision for days. They watched the Sziv supergroup Us swathe the stage in their algae until seabirds came, and the song of the seabirds was the song of the Sziv, until they ate the seabirds, and that was their song, too. They watched the Yurtmak punch the stage in the face and slaughter their yellcore ballad "In the End We're Actually Kind of Sorry We Missed the War You Guys Have All the Fun." They watched the soulful Nessuno Uuf stand center stage with her violet eyes full of tears singing "And I Am Telling You I Am Not Sentient," which brought the house to its knees and sobbing. And they watched Olabil the

Friendless swing up a long trumpet with his firefly-coated trunk and play the deepest blues of all time until the strange elephant sank onto its stomach singing the immortal chorus: *I miss them all so much I promise never to skip school again I swear just come back. It's so lonely being the last of us.*

The songs went on and on, beggaring the mind, the ear, the very definition of music.

Until the end. New species go last.

Decibel coughed. He looked pleadingly at Oort.

"Stage fright?" his old friend asked, and he was not even a little bit teasing, as he felt certain the first musical note the civilized galaxy was going to hear out of humanity was him violently throwing up into a tuba. "Don't worry. We got this. It's a good song, Dess. I promise. Well, it's all right. Just . . . do your best. Pretend everyone's not watching. Close your eyes if you have to. It's just us up there. Us and Mira. Only . . . her mic doesn't work, you know? Hey. Hey, Danesh." Oort St. Ultraviolet put his hand on his old friend's cheek. "It's all okay. I still love you. Always did."

And he kissed her gently on the forehead, as if to make it true. Then once—briefly, warmly, and so arkably—on the lips.

Dess gestured emphatically at his throat for the millionth time that day. He'd tried to find a pen. He'd tried to find paper. He'd tried scratching it into his arms in blood, but fingernails really don't do much of a job. Oort rolled his eyes impatiently.

"What is your *problem*? You've been acting so weird and quiet. Where *were* you all day? Are you mad at me? So I didn't spend all day spooning with you. I was out with friends for once. You should meet them. They're really something, the Elakhon. I got here in time, didn't I?"

Decibel Jones tried again to claw I CAN'T SING THAT TALL BINT

STOLE MY VOICE into his forearm, tears of frustration and real, boiling fear welling up in his eyes.

But Oort St. Ultraviolet was already half onstage. "Ugh, fine, be that way. Just do your thing and let's go home. I don't know why you always have to be so *dramatic*."

It was time for Decibel Jones and the Absolute Zeros, or at least what was left of them, to save the world.

33.

Tell Me Who You Are

Decibel Jones and the Absolute Zeros went on just as the storm clouds began to gather over the Stage of Life.

They had no gouts of flame.

They had no bioluminescent burlesque.

They had no teleportation or time travel technical effects.

They had two people standing center stage in the dark. They had a microphone. They had something that looked like a glass house made out of a tuba. And they had a voice.

Dess opened his mouth to sing for his life. Maybe whatever that walking pile of coat hangers had done to him would go away if he sang hard enough, if he blew out his capillaries singing for all he was worth, which, he knew, in the end, wasn't much. But if he could do anything, he could talk when he wasn't supposed to. Sing when he was meant to be a good, quiet boy, seen and not heard. He'd been doing it since the day he was born. Maybe he could do it now. Maybe it would be enough.

Oort started up the overture. He thumped the drums with his foot pedal and folded himself into the Oortophone. Music began to hit the speakers and flow out into the ears of too many people to think about. Perfect music. Every note a crystal. Decibel Jones took a breath. He took a breath to sing what they'd written in the reefship, their clever clever plan, hiding behind all that poetry, all that human genius, so they never had to risk their own voices being the ones to damn a planet to silence. He'd blow out that stupid mute button with the sheer need to live, the need to *matter*. It would all be fine. He stepped up to the mic.

All he sang was silence.

He didn't come in on the downbeat. Or the upbeat. Or any beat.

Decibel froze. Just like he had at the Hope & Ruin that long-ago first day of all days. Just like that day in Nani's scarves. He was right back there, standing on that worn red rug trying to sing along with Marvin the Martian till his face felt like it was going to explode with the effort of making no sound at all. It was like he wasn't even there, like he'd never existed in the first place. Like always. Like forever.

"What the fuck, Dess?" hissed Oort. "Sing, you bastard, what are you playing at?"

Decibel turned to his friend and pointed at his throat again. Tears streamed down his face. Sweat plastered his hair to his forehead. *Christ, I'm trying. I'm trying so hard.*

Finally, Oort St. Ultraviolet got it. The lovely boom and trill of the Oortophone went silent as the realization went through him. *We're all going to die. Dess is broken, and we're all going to die. My girls are going to burn. What the fuck do I do?*

He tried to think of a song. Not their song. Any song. A Zeros song. A Bowie song. A nursery song. Anything. But his terror-addled brain formally informed him that it had never heard a single song ever, and had no idea what music even was, so kindly leave it alone. *My girls are going to burn. Sing something, Omarcik. Sing anything.*

A solitary, clear, pure voice filled up the stadium on Litost. It trembled a little, but it was true. In front of God and aliens and everybody, Omar Cali̧skan sang the only song he could think of.

It came upon the midnight clear,

That glorious song of old,

From angels bending near the earth,

To touch their harps of gold:

"Peace on the earth, goodwill to men

From heaven's all gracious King!"

The world in solemn stillness lay

To hear the angels sing.

Still through the cloven skies they come,

With peaceful wings unfurled;

And still their heavenly music floats

O'er all the weary world:

Above its sad and lowly plains

They bend on hovering wing,

And ever o'er its Babel sounds

The blessed angels sing.

34.

Time Is Lonely

Öö and the roadrunner watched from the Octave's posh jury box.
Drinks and small plates of delightful foods littered the floor. Half
the judges had gone to the toilets. The rest were discussing how
marvelous "I Wanna Be Elated" had been or whether to rank the
Elakhon above or below poor Olabil, who really did try his best
without a backup band.

"It's not going wellgoodwellwellanywherefast," Öö said, twisting his paws.

"Not even as well as I thought it would," agreed the roadrunner,
"and I thought it would be a disaster."

"I could help," said the time-traveling red panda quietly. "I
could do the thing. I did a few test runsrunsgoestriesattempts
during the semifinals. It'd be easy. It would be donedonebackdone
before he's through with the second verse."

"You could. But it's cheating, Öö."

"Mmmm," said Klloshar Avatar 9, enjoying a refreshing cocktail after her performance. They hadn't seen her standing there,
but the jury box was littered with dormant Lummo stones, so any
of them could turn up at any time. You had to be prepared for that,
with Lummutis. "Mini-game. Exciting."

"Not *technically* cheatingcheatingfudgingagainsttherulescheating-cheating. And look, you only spent a few hours on Earth. I've been all over their timelinestimelinesquantumfoampossibleforkstime-lines. That's a lot of Decembers. I would do just about *anything* to make a Christmas carol stop."

The tall, blue ultramarine fish-flamingo dropped her eyes to the floor. "There is a process. We don't interfere. They have to do it on their own, or not at all."

"I thought you liked him!"

"I *do*," said the former lead singer of Bird's Eye Blue. "He calls me the Road Runner. That makes him the coyote. How can you not love that stupid coyote?"

"Then I'll dodofindgetdograb it."

"Mmmm," Klloshar Avatar 9 said again, smacking her colorful lips. "Cheat code. Nice."

"You can't. It's against the rules. No one has ever helped another species before. Not even when that Ursula died mid-power ballad. We don't interfere."

Öö thrashed his long, striped tail furiously. "It's not interfering. The name on the list was Decibel Jones and the Absolute Zeros. All I'm doing is finishing your job. I'm getting the band to the venuevenuestagedoor all in one piece."

The Keshet grabbed two little toasts with creamed sunlight on top, crammed them in his mouth, stuck his tongue out at his avian friend, and vanished.

Klloshar Avatar 9 stared after him with enormous cartoon eyes. "One hundred points," she whispered.

Öö was the first outsider to score in the grand game of the Lummutis, and, to date, the last.

35.

It's All About You

Oort was nearly out of Christmas and Decibel Jones was still trying to sing. He dropped to his knees, clinging to the mic stand in horror and gut-voiding terror of the totality of this failure above all his other failures. It shouldn't have gone like this. Maybe somewhere inside he'd always known it would go like this without her, without Mira to keep the beat out into the infinite future the way she always had, the way he thought she always would. His jaw ached from trying to birth the song horribly from the depths of him. He kept trying. He kept trying as people in the audience began to cough and look away in embarrassment. He kept trying as the sky grew darker and darker and the voting officials began to noisily rummage backstage. He tried for Nani and his brothers and sisters and Mr. Looney of the Tunes and the sold-out Hippodrome and Dr. Collins his psychiatrist and Lila Poole and poor lost Mira and that stupid badger, too, for Yoko Ono and "Revolution 9" and nice flats you couldn't afford and kebabs you could and short-haired white cats and overly friendly waitresses named Ruby and Alexander McQueen and Cool Uncle Takumi and Englishblokeman and government agents and thrift shop eye shadow duos and lions and rhinoceroses that were never coming back and Mr. Five

Star's chip shop and Marvin the Martian and the West Cornwall Pasty Company and Acme Brand Instant Tunnels and the Things of Thing-World and Arkable Gelato and science fiction movies in which everything was simple and very few musical numbers turned up and even the bloody *Daily Mail*, all of it sacred, all of it real, all of it loved in that moment by those two souls seven thousand light-years away.

But it was no good. He had nothing. He was nothing. He was invisible, voiceless, no one. Oort had very little left of "It Came Upon a Midnight Clear," and the only person who seemed to be picking up what he was laying down was a short little Elakh in the front row clicking his fingers with his eyes closed. He tried again. It would work this time. These were his last seconds of existence. He wondered if they'd just incinerate him immediately or ship him back to Earth for the big barbecue. He'd come so far to fail.

Decibel Jones gave up.

Fuck it all to hell. Good-bye, life. Good-bye, Earth. Good-bye, rosé wine. Good-bye, Hope. Good-bye, Ruin. My tail's unnailed for good. God, I miss you so much, Mira, his brutally muted vocal cords strained to say. *I promise never to skip school again, just come back. It's lonely being the last of us. I wish I could fix it all. I wish I could have been better. That's all. I just wish I was better.*

The storm overhead broke. Tiny diamonds rained down from the absurd skies of the happiest planet in the galaxy, where sentient civilization almost cannibalized itself and burned its own bones to ash. The clouds were so unfathomably dark. Beyond dark, into shades of the void. They swirled and pooled and yawned sickeningly, the way the surf retreats before a tsunami hits. It's counterintuitive. It doesn't look like what it is. But it's a dead give-away. Pulsating neon vortexes began to show through the clouds.

Decibel felt something very wrong. The breath under the notes that would not come was *stuck*. Pinned to his diaphragm. Sawed in half over that awful, vicious heartburn he hadn't been able to shake since he'd left the planet. The air was seeping up out of his throat all wrong, without the right power behind it, but with something else sucking at it. Something new. Something borrowed.

Something with feathers.

The breath burst free and flowed over the larynx of the glam-rock glitterpunk messiah, bringing with it a small black and blue infant bird with long Esca fronds and clever human eyes and a rib cage like a nonconsensual feelings-flute. Decibel Jones's love child lodged in his throat. It would have been no problem for an Esca. There would have been fourteen of them, and they'd have flown out prettily through the gaps in his chest cavity and into the warm, welcoming light bath of their other parent. But thrill-seeking genes had to make due with available materials. There was only one baby, conceived in a garret in Croydon, gestated in a paradox-fueled reefship, and born on Litost at the best part of a song that never was. And it was a breech birth.

Decibel Jones collapsed in a heap of agony. His head fell beside the ghostly footlights as sinkholes appeared in the boiling clouds. His breath blew past the holes in his love child's rib cage, and a voice, not quite his and not quite his baby's, burst out over the sea of dropped jaws.

"EVERYTHING JUST GETS SO FUCKED UP SOMETIMES!" Decibel shriek-sobbed out a screamy bit to raise Yoko Ono from the grave and make her proud, and a tiny, brand-new creature hopped out of his mouth and nestled down in Robert's baroque sleeve. A plaintive, desperate bird's cry went up from the back of the house as the roadrunner began to run in earnest, birthlight pouring from her lantern, trying to catch her baby in her grotto before it suffocated in shadows.

A sound like someone belly flopping onto a church organ and hitting every note at once shattered the air over what was once Vlimeux. Incandescent blue-violet mouths opened in the sky, a dozen of them, sucking at the sweet Litostian gravity, dragging up waves against the coliseum, shearing pearly mountains into the Ocean that was no longer quite so into the idea of Unconditional Acceptance, gaping holes punched in reality, hungry maws opening into the infinite guts of space-time.

The wormholes had come to feast on the banquet of regret that was Decibel Jones and the Absolute Zeros.

And now the wormholes were singing.

A tentative drumbeat tapped in somewhere in the depths of the stage. Decibel held out his finger for his kid to hop on. The roadrunner's light drenched them both. She was looking up in parental panic from the mosh pit. He looked from her back into the little bird with human eyes. Nani's eyes, actually. More Mr. Looney of the Tunes than Mr. Ridley of the Scott.

"I'm gonna name you Marvin," Decibel said softly, and to his shock, he actually said it. The trauma of delivery had seemingly broken whatever boot the Smaragdi and the Alunizar had put on his voice.

Marvin whistled a little tune that felt like the cathedral of Notre Dame when it hit Dess's bones, all lit up and everywhere to go.

It was so beautiful. His baby. It was unique in the history of the universe. It was just a hell of a thing. It didn't really matter, of course. They were all going to die. Everyone he'd ever known, and him, too. They'd failed and you couldn't unfail something just because you suddenly needed a spot of maternity leave. But at least this had happened first. Another tap of drumstick on drumskin.

Wouldn't it have been nice to get a note in? Dess thought. *Just one.*

"Come on," a voice said softly from the direction of the drums. "Up you get. Time to get that tail nailed back on."

Decibel sighed. That was it, then. The roadrunner had come with a big vaudeville hook to pull him offstage and collect her offspring. Using Mira's voice was poor form, though. There were limits.

The voice changed abruptly. "Oh, get up, Danesh, you lazy wanker."

Oort St. Ultraviolet turned to look. His blood attempted to escape his body by leaping a foot to the left. But he was faster than a well-regulated public health system, more powerful than the need for tea at three in the afternoon. He was Englishblokeman. And Englishblokeman did not shirk. He shimmied into his Oortophone before his brain could start questioning everything that was happening and spraying antibacterial gel all over it. He got in and watched a dead girl with cheeks as bright as the future count off the beat.

She saved them. The last time of many times. Mira Wonderful Star, lately of the London underground scene, her uncle's flat, and a timeline plundered by a well-meaning red panda who had cornered her after their last show in a shitty club and told her her friends were waiting for her, the last show when everything had gone perfectly, when everything was roses and the air was as good as cocaine, when the future was dry of all possible tears, Mira Wonderful Star, reeling from her first hit single off of *Spacecrumpet*, Apocalyptic Girl Spill #4 , damaged/as-is, clad in a spandex "Slutty C-3PO" costume, silver brocade Christmas tree skirt, a gauzy black shower curtain with metallic blue appliqué roses all over it, and blissful ignorance of all that was to come, banged out a riff on her drums behind him, leaned into her mic, and yelled into the sold-out arena, loud enough to blow a dart from 1 to 20, loud enough to stun Arthur Archibald Gormley sober.

"WE ARE DECIBEL JONES AND THE ABSOLUTE ZEROS!" she screamed over the pituitary-melting harmonies of the wormhole chorus above.

"Mushy, mushy, Wonderful," whispered Decibel Jones in utter and religious awe just before the roadrunner's undersea birth-beams poured out over the stage and his skin and their child like the most glorious spotlight in the world.

"Mushy, mushy, Dess," said a living, breathing paradox, and the resurrected queen of glam.

"Everything Just Gets So Fucked Up Sometimes" was the song of the century. And it barely even had any lyrics. Just full-throated, shimmering, babbling music and the title and a bit of Christmas carol, repeated over and over until the words lost all meaning, in dozens of combinations and several keys and a handful of languages dredged out of primary school lessons buried deep in the subconscious. Decibel Jones and the Absolute Zeros finally had the Christmas pop single that year. The newborn and the dead and the long-suffering and the *extremely* well-traveled, the baby and the girl and the boys in the band and the wormholes—all of them singing the screamy bit like a song could save the world, roaring like lions and squawking like dodos and thundering like rhinoceroses and weeping like a man who died with a final mix in his hands and dancing like a kid wearing a hundred scarves and howling like an interdimensional wind tunnel of regret, belting it out with your future gurgling in your arms like sentient human goddamned beings.

The arena was silent.

Then the cheers began.

"Well," said DJ Lights Out after it died down. "I guess that was all right."

The Mamtak Aggregate could not, just yet, form itself into anything at all. It lay in glittering pieces across the jury's couches, enraptured and inconsolable.

36.

They Can't Stop the Spring

Once upon a time on a small, watery, excitable planet called Earth, a soft, rather nice-looking dawn broke over the sea and the green land. It was a usual sort of thing, the dawn. Yellow and quiet and uneventful. Soon there would be movement and sound and the rhythms of sentient life galloping along its absurd way, shaking its head to a new beat.

Until next year.

Two little girls in Cardiff woke to a kind voice and a kiss on the forehead. "Daddy's home, darlings. And he's brought your kitty back all safe and sound. I think Capo should live with you from now on, don't you, poppets?"

An old grandmother in government housing in Kabul woke to see her grandson's face, fifty feet tall all over again, on every screen in the world.

Point to Nani.

A Klavar on Litost woke to see a young woman with hair like an oil slick, an Esca, and a man in an absolutely splendid coat laughing on the beach, leaping up like they were dancing, trying to touch the wings of a tiny brilliant blue bird with long-lashed human eyes flying just out of their reach.

A red panda waited just down the shore, wondering how to break the news about the necessity of containing volatile entities removed from their timelines. He fretted. Perhaps the girl would like being a Paradox Box. Just her existence was paradox enough to fuel something truly tricked out. State of the art. He would furnish her Box in style. Maybe she could even write a new album in there, if he made the thing *really* grand. Being a massively powerful ship sailing the infinite deep was better than being dead, anyway. Perhaps Decibel would be interested in a career in captaining starships. All things were possible.

A large golden sea squirt woke to the censure of its government, which never looked kindly on big fat failures.

Despite the judgment of the jury being that the wormholes had placed third-to-last in the Grand Prix and therefore now possessed the rights and privileges of galactic citizens, most of the great, infinite, gorgeous beasts just drifted off into the long light-years in search of more food.

One stayed. The Klavaret named it Darling.

And a man named Arthur Archibald Gormley walked out of the doors of the Hope & Ruin pub—out of the deafening noise of policemen and teachers and electricians and computer programmers and homemakers and children and accountants; out of the cacophony of their cheering and crying, hugging and swearing and singing old football songs because they sounded like happiness—like being alive and drunk and possibly, just for a little while, quite all right—out of the crowd and outside in the middle of the night, laid down on the sparse Brighton grass, and kissed it for everything he was worth.

Life is beautiful and life is stupid. As long as you keep that in mind, and never give more weight to one than the other, the history of the galaxy, the history of a planet, the history of a person is a simple tune with lyrics flashed on-screen and a helpful, friendly bouncing disco ball of glittering, occasionally peaceful light to help you follow along.

Cue the music. Cue the dancers.

Cue tomorrow.

Liner Notes

With a book like *Space Opera*, it is hard to know where to begin thanking the cast of thousands that made possible this weird little rocketship to moons unknown. But launch windows wait for no one, not even earnest writers pretending to be covered in glitter while, in point of fact, being mostly covered in cat hair.

Allow me first to thank Marcel Bezençon, who, in 1956, conceived the whole notion of the Eurovision Song Contest, which was the inspiration for this book, and is thereby, in the opinion of this feline hair–bestrewn subalto novelist, eligible for sainthood, having long since affected the necessary two miracles and change. I believe, without irony (for irony was last generation's hotness), that Eurovision is one of the greatest achievements of mankind, in all its absurdity and flash and pomp. To unite a continent after the most horrifying war in the history of this planet with song, dance, and sequins is so ridiculous and hopeless as to be sublime. It is precisely in seeming without weight or consequence or high artistic authority that Eurovision's genius lies—if it were all serious business, no one would watch. No one would *feel*. No one would sing along for sixty-plus years. Thank you for the disco ball, Marcel—long may it reign. And thank you to everyone who has ever sung a single note in any round of the Eurovision Song Contest, even if that semi-semi-semi-final round was in your living room when you were ten.

The lyrics that precede each section of the book are from some of my favorite Eurovision songs—some winners, some close runners-up, all amazing. They are the songs I often play for people to sell them on the whole concept, and the ones who speak to me of the heights and feelings the maddest of mad shows can reach. I owe a great debt of inspiration to Lordi, Conchita Wurst, the Babushki, Loreen, and Måns Zelmerlöw.

The next number on my dance card must go to Molly and Matthew Hawn, who, in 2012, offered to let me stay at their lovely London home with the warning that they would be holding a Eurovision party, and that, somewhat apologetically, my attendance would be required, in payment for room and board. "What's Eurovision?" said I. And thus, I took my first step into a larger (and better) world. And thank you to everyone, from best friends to conventiongoers to random dudes on airplanes, who, after 2012, put up with my constant evangelizing, squawking like a door-to-door missionary: *Have you heard the good news? Eurovision exists!*

But perhaps the biggest hand-drawn sign to be hoisted into the air must say: THANK YOU, CHARLES TAN. For without his idle joke during my annual live-tweet of the only sporting event I care about, without his dashing off the immortal wish—*Ha-ha, you should write a science fiction Eurovision novel*—none of us would be here, there would be no blue space flamingos, and Decibel Jones would never have gotten himself knocked up. A large silver balloon attached to that sign must read: THANK YOU, NAVAH WOLFE, my editor, for immediately messaging me and offering to buy this idiotic idea, sight unseen—plotless, titleless—in what my agent still refers to as the fastest deal he ever made. She also deserves much consideration for her patience while I wrote something so far outside my comfort zone as to be more teenage runaway than novel. Much thanks also to Joe Monti and Liz Gorinsky, for letting Navah and me sneak off during the big show and do something weird in the shadows.

Thank you, now and always, to my incredible agent, Howard